DANGER IN JERUSALEM

JONAH AGUS

ISBN 979 8 9919327 1 4

This book goes out to the ones I love.

PROLOGUE

A westerly wind rattled the corrugated tin roof of a warehouse in the Israeli West Bank settlement of Har Kesem. Inside the warehouse, the bright florescent lights flickered and the concrete floor assaulted the feet. A person standing there stood in agony, and felt as if days had passed, even if it was only a couple of hours waiting for the exchange.

Yossi had released the safety on his gun. Seeing the small army of criminals arrayed in front of him grated against his sense of pride. Yossi's mind slipped away, wondering *how have I, after dutifully performing my army service, been reduced to this?* Yamina told him work like this was a bad idea, but she, like him, also wanted to leave Israel, hating the way so many others looked at her Ethiopian skin. Yossi and Yamina dreamed of leaving together. They thought Yamina might be able to use her nursing certification to get a visa. *She really needed to finish her qualifications,* the unemployed Yossi thought. Or perhaps Yossi could get German citizenship. After all, it was a great uncle whose house in Lübeck had been stolen. Yossi had spoken with a lawyer who explained the types of relatives who would qualify to emigrate and the documentation that would be required; and he realized that their dream was a struggle with reality. Yet here he was, thinking about the paycheck that would help them afford their future lives.

Strange to think that a Jew would choose to go to Germany to escape racism. Yossi thought the observation clever, and that brought a slight smile to the corner of his mouth.

Ahmad saw the Israeli criminal smirk. He had heard about deals going bad, leaving behind nothing but bodies. Ahmad knew that those betrayals could only be the result of an inside job. The Israelis denied it, of course, but Ahmad swore he would not be the victim of such underhandedness. If only he could be back at the beach, and back in time before the Oslo Accords severed the West Bank from Israel, taking with it access to the Tel Aviv beaches. *What a disaster*, Ahmad thought. Instead of sun and surf, there he was, with a gun in a warehouse full of Israelis, just so he could buy his favorite nephew, Mehmet, a new backpack for the start of the school year. *But*, Ahmad considered, *I don't even want to get Mehmet a backpack*. He wanted to take Mehmet swimming in the sea, to learn how to play paddleball on the beach and enjoy late night sweets in Jaffa. With resigned determination, Ahmad narrowed his eyes trying to discern the intentions of the armed Israeli opposite him.

Yossi saw the tightening of the Palestinian's eyes. *That terrorist is checking out my gun; he is planning his attack.* Yossi swore beneath his breath, remembering stories of shootouts from hotheaded Arabs, and again wishing he had taken an alternative path. The terrorist's eyes darted quickly to the right, and Yossi, unconsciously, darted his eyes to the left.

•

Ronit Margolis kept on her reflective aviator sunglasses as she slipped out of her muddied white Ford F-250 pickup truck with its gleaming yellow Israeli plates, and into the warehouse in Har Kesem. A blue van driven by a burly leather-clad Israeli, Ronit's enforcer Dan, pulled up into the warehouse behind her. Opposite Ronit, a priest, Monsignor Jerome, exited a beat-up red Toyota Corolla station wagon that had green Palestinian plates.

After a tentative and unwanted clasp of the hand, Monsignor Jerome leaned close and whispered, "This is some plan you have cooked up, Ronit; some may even consider it callous."

"Monsignor, it is rich of you to be discussing callousness. Does not your entire religion place sin onto every innocent?"

"I admit that the good news is tough news to receive."

"And, of course, people who worry about sin is an effective message for religious recruitment."

"As you say. Still, the plan is not without risk."

"I made the plan and you agreed. We have done things like this before."

"You've arranged things with the Har Kesem security guard?"

"Yes, Monsignor, it has all been prepared. Who is this lamb you have brought to the slaughter, my shepherd?"

"Don't toy with me, Ronit; I have my limits. His name is Ahmad, and he will do nicely. Who is the simpleton gripping his gun like it might run away?"

"That is Yossi, my sister's husband's brother."

"You brought family?"

"Hardly. Besides, he is trying to leave our little region, so he might as well be useful before his departure."

"Alright then, let's get moving, Ronit; I want to be away from here and in bed long before those calls to prayer wake me."

"The plan is simple enough. I brought the weapons as requested."

"And I have the goods for payment here. Do we really need to use Ahmad and Yossi?"

"It must be. Weapons from military armories cannot just disappear. Small bits here and there, okay. But the types of large-scale exchanges we are making…no, it must be this way."

"As always, Ronit, you have made your calculations and argued them effectively."

Monsignor Jerome's bodyguard, Abdullah, slid the suitcase over to Dan. The contents were examined and confirmed by Ronit's diamond expert, Omer. Ronit called for Dan, Omer, and Yossi to get into her pickup truck while she tossed the keys to the van to Abdullah. The monsignor knew not to question Ronit's trustworthiness, so he decided he would wait until the van was in a secure location before he examined its contents: guns, a mix of Jericho 941 and Glock 19 pistols and a few modified M4 carbines and CAR-15 rifles. Instead of checking the gun cases, Monsignor Jerome signaled Abdullah and Ahmad to get into the blue van. The monsignor then rushed back to his red station wagon.

Meanwhile, Ronit's truck sped toward the front gate of the Har Kesem settlement. "Shit," Ronit shouted. "The tire light just came on. We can't risk a breakdown. You two go check the tire," she yelled as she pulled over.

The two men exited the four-door pickup to investigate. After examining the rear tires, they moved to the front. From the passenger side Dan thought he saw something and called Yossi over to take a better look.

"Yossi, you'd better see this."

As Yossi leaned in, Dan shot two silent rounds into Yossi's head. Dan jumped back into the truck, and they drove to and through the main gate.

At the same time, and as agreed, the blue van full of weapons made for the settlement's rear gate, just as Monsignor Jerome had explained to Abdullah before they left for Har Kesem. It was unmanned and unlocked, just as Ronit had promised the monsignor.

"Ahmad, go and open the gate for us," the monsignor hollered from the station wagon. Ahmad stepped out of the van and opened the gate. The monsignor drove through. As Ahmad went to close the gate, Abdullah closed the van's door and raced away, following the station wagon, and leaving Ahmad disoriented. As he stood there wondering what had just happened, a settlement security guard appeared from behind the guard box, aimed his rifle, and ended the life of little Mehmet's uncle.

•

"This is Channel 13 reporting on the scene. A terror-ist, identified as Ahmad Naser, was shot and killed by settlement security after gaining access to the settlement and murdering Yossi Seigler of Bat Yam. Mr. Seigler was visiting the West Bank to look for a new house. According to neighbors, Mr. Seigler had been looking to move out of the Tel Aviv suburbs. He leaves behind a wife, Yamina Seigler, whose parents moved from Ethiopia to Israel as a part of Operation Solomon in May of 1991 when the State of Israel heroically rescued 140,000 Ethiopian Jews from—"

"This is Arutz Sheva, here at the site of the terror attack. The perpetrator, 'Ahmad Naser,' was neutral-ized by settlement security but not before murdering an innocent Israeli who was merely considering embracing our God-given homeland in Judea and Samaria. The terrorist's house will be destroyed, leaving his moth-er homeless, in support of the policy of deterrence. The nearby houses of his close family members are also being dismantled. The army has declared an emergency and has been deployed around the region looking for those who aided the terrorist."

CHAPTER 1

Here I am, late again. Walking through the London rain. Again. The shopkeeper in New York swore my jacket was perfect for rainy environments, but never said anything about this type of humidity. Downpours, drizzles, gusts, gales, sideways rain, and mist so thick that I could drink the air, as long as I wouldn't mind a mouthful of exhaust. Remy Ripken pulled his jacket tighter until he could hardly move, yet even that failed to keep out the chill, and so he yearned for a warming cup of tea.

Remy dodged a taxi and leapt over a puddle to arrive at the imposing university building that housed the School of Journalism. Martin, the ever-friendly security guard, called a greeting.

"Headed to see the boss?"

"Hiya, Martin. Yes indeed."

"What time was your meeting, Remy?"

"Thirty-five minutes ago. You ever relied on the bus?"

"Only every day of my life."

Remy hustled up three flights of steps and down endless corridors to finally reach the office of Professor Roy Vandermere.

"Is that you, Remy? *It better fucking be you. God dammit, Remy,* do you know I have a life of my own?"

"Yes, professor, and how is Gloria by the way?"

"*None of your damn business.* But since you asked, we saw a jazz fusion band over at Club Fusion in Shoreditch. Ever heard of the place?"

"Yes, professor, I'm the one who told you about it."

"Oh, that's right...and it's because we enjoyed the show that I'm still talking to you now."

"Yes, professor. Sorry professor."

"Knock off this *yes professor* business and tell me where you're at in your project. Doctorates in Journalism don't write themselves."

"Well, to be honest, Roy, I am struggling to select a topic. There are just too many interesting things going on."

"Well, to be honest, Remy, you just need to pick one and run with it. Do something simple. Say, what did you eat yesterday?"

"I had a pita filled with grilled halloumi, roasted vegetables, and hummus."

"Hummus, great, that's an interesting substance. A mix of chickpeas and tahini. Which country is it from?"

"I don't know, The Levant? Egypt, Syria, Lebanon, Israel."

"Recently there was a journalism student doing research in Egypt who disappeared. Egypt is out. Syria is, of course, fucked, and Lebanon who knows. How is your French?"

"Not great."

"And your Arabic?"

"Could be better."

"Great, then it is decided, you will go to Jerusalem where you can get by with English. Go do an in-depth story on hummus."

"Are you serious?"

"That is your assignment."

"Ridiculous."

"So is the weather here in London. And Remy, you are starting to look rather pale. Some sun and adventure will rekindle your creative spirit. Do you know the departmental secretary Mrs. Harfroid?"

"Yes, she rejected my request for funding to attend a conference."

"Good for her. Most conferences are a waste of time, which is what I told her about your request. For this little research trip, I'll arrange for an approval, and away you'll-go. Don't forget to bring back a gift for Mrs. Harfroid and Gloria, as well as a fascinating dissertation on a topic that has, most likely, already been covered."

●

"Sami, I am sorry for the loss of your brother Ahmad. You know my son, Basul, is in the same class as your boy, Mehmet. If there is anything I can do to help…."

"There is. You are a police detective, Marwan. This situation does not seem right."

"It is true, my neighbor, why should you lose your homes due to the actions of another?"

"No, Marwan, what I meant is there is no way that Ahmad was a terrorist, or a freedom fighter, or any other man of violence. He adored our mother and my Mehmet. Besides, why would he have slipped into an industrial settlement to kill a single man on foot? It just doesn't seem right."

"The times in which we live are not right. One really can never know the mind of another, no matter how close they seem, Sami. Still, if you'd like, I can make some inquiries to see if anything out of the ordinary is happening around that settlement."

"Thank you, Marwan, thank you."

●

"Yamina, I'm so sorry for your loss. Why didn't you tell me you were thinking of moving east to the settlements?"

"We weren't, Becca. We only thought of moving west to Europe, to Germany. We would never move to a settlement."

"Then why was Yossi there?"

"I have no idea. It makes no sense to me, and I'll never get to ask."

"Well, Yamina, if you think there was foul play you can always go down the hall and ask Shachar to investigate."

"Becca, everyone knows Shachar has never been the same since he got back from the service."

"If it's crazy ideas you want, then maybe a crazy man is who you need."

"I know you never thought I was good enough to be with your brother. But can you now at least admit I made him happy?"

"Yamina, my former sister. There is little happiness in death. And in my mind, you are what led him to it."

Yamina thought about a reply, yet before she could form the words, tears burst from her eyes as Becca strolled away.

•

When Yamina had regained herself, she thought about what Becca had said about Shachar. The idea of seeking help began as a question that soon blossomed into a desperate need. In what felt like days, but was only minutes, Yamina decided to walk down the hall.

"Shachar, are you home? This is Yamina, your neighbor. I see the door is open. Can I come in?"

"Yamina! Hey, girl." He motioned her into the apartment, patting the seat on the sofa next to him. "I'm smoking some ill shit and it's got my head rolling." Yamina didn't move beyond the doorway.

"Yes, Shachar, the whole neighborhood is aware of your marijuana habit. But I have not come here to ask you about it."

"Oh, for real, Yamina, then what's up? Want to pet my dog?"

"No thank you, Shachar, I am allergic," she said, tears again beginning to form. "I shouldn't have come. I'll go."

"Wait, wait. Please sit down, my neighbor. I won't bite, and, unless I say otherwise, my dog won't either. So, what's up? How can I help you?"

"Yossi," Yamina stiffened, "is dead. They say he was killed by a terrorist in the settlements."

"I am sorry to hear that, Yamina. A lot of fucked up shit goes down in the territories."

"That's the thing. Yossi didn't get into fucked up shit. He was boring as shit. And I loved him for it." Yamina moved toward the sofa. "But now he's gone, and I don't understand why."

"I feel for you. What you need is a therapist. Luckily, I've got a Rolodex full of them."

"I don't mean existentially, 'Why is Yossi gone?' I mean literally he had no business being where he was killed. They said he must have taken the bus there, but why would he do that when we have a car?" Yamina sat, disconcerting the dog. "Yossi hates the occupation, why would he seek to join it? To consider moving us there when we wanted to move to Germany? Tell me Shachar. Explain it to me."

"Even when you know people…when things get hot and get difficult…when you got fear, love and confusion…anything is possible. But I see you are grieving and need closure. I can ask a buddy of mine. Maybe he knows about what goes on in that settlement. We go way back. He owes me, and I don't have anything better to ask."

"Thanks, Shachar." Yamina rose and prepared to go. "How much will it cost, the investigation?"

"No cost. What are neighbors for, right? Though I wouldn't mind some home cooking. I smell good things from your party."

"My what? *Shiva?* It's not a party, its a gathering of mourners" Yamina scoffed.

"Sure, sure, call it what you will. People come, people chat, people eat, people go. I'll call my friend and see if he's got anything to tell."

CHAPTER 2

Captain Boaz Oded of the Third Battalion pressed his palms into his eyes. It had been a long couple of days, moving weapons out, bringing in scrap metal to melt down in their place. The five soldiers who helped, middle-aged reservists, were only too happy to exchange a bit of extra labor for several-thousand shekels. The reservists knew little and would be keen to avoid destabilizing their family lives by snitching. Besides, Boaz reasoned, they would also be risking their lives. With that established, Boaz turned his thoughts to his commander, General Ram Cohen. Commander Cohen seemed like a good sort, an old school Sabra, which meant he demanded discipline while remaining aloof to the possibility that someone might not be following the rules. According to the regulations, because the weapons were faulty they were to be destroyed. Oded was simply following protocol, and Commander Cohen might even suggest a promotion for this ridged adherence to the rules.

General Cohen frowned as he looked over his maps. The last thing he needed was to thin his forces to cover for some incompetent captain. The mismanagement of these weapons would need to be meticulously investigated, with Captain Oded most likely earning a demerit for his inability to maintain readiness and discovering, only when the weapons were needed, their worthlessness.

•

With the exchange made, Ronit was left flush with diamonds and drugs. Moving the drugs was easy, as Dan was already out making the deliveries in exchange for hard cash. The money would be used for local payoffs, bribes, equipment, and a small array of henchmen. Ronit laughed to herself at the word "henchmen," and reveled in the freedom that being the bad guy engendered. Ronit had grown up in one of the few remaining kibbutzim. Everything was shared that socialist paradise. As a girl Ronit had dreamed of becoming a veterinarian. But when she finally left the kibbutz she found an Israel not as she had been taught, that did not align with why three generations of her family had toiled and sacrificed. Instead, it was both capitalist and religious, each a feature of life the kibbutz shunned. Ronit felt betrayed not only by Israel, but by the kibbutz itself. Cast out of the army, *a socialist with no social life,* as she liked to reflect, Ronit decided that if Israel wanted to be a culture of accumulation then she would participate to the extreme. She would beat them at their own game by living the good life she had been denied, and exposing the unethical state of unequal development. Years passed after she made this pact with herself, and Ronit had embraced her role as an outlaw, even as a criminal. Thus, henchmen were preferable to employees, though really they were just goons: losers who took a bit of cash in order to continue their lives of violence after they concluded their army service. To further stress the imbalance of power between she and her men, she assigned each goon with a biblical moniker, irrespective of their actual names, and referred to them as such.

"Naphtali, get over here."

"Yes, your highness."

"Take Issachar and Gad to provide backup to Dan. He is already with Zebulon."

"Yes, your highness."

Being a criminal is great thought Ronit as she dialed up her contact in Antwerp.

"Toujours Diamants."

"Fabien please. This is Ronit."

"Ronit, my pet, my love. How are things?"

"Very well, thank you. Fabien, I have something that may interest you."

"Ah yes, always quick to business. But alas, my business has grown since we last spoke. Perhaps now I am too big for what you can bring me."

"Not this time. What I have is worth your attention."

"Truly? I am sure, Ronit. However—"

"Fabien! Must I remind you of the last time we met, of the people who are no longer with us? You will be happy with this, I guarantee it. If it does not please you, I will not bother you again. But if it does, I expect better service."

"Ronit, I will hold you to that. If what you have is not to my liking I will consider all debts paid. If it is, I will remain your most loyal servant."

"I am sure that you will. Dan, my most loyal servant, will get in touch with Marta to arrange the details."

•

Surrounded by heavy furniture and peeling paint, Monsignor Jerome sat in his office just off Manger Square in Bethlehem. He stared out the window contemplating whether he would link Lauds, the early morning prayer, with the mid-morning Terche. Jerome usually combined the prayers but he knew this was not encouraged. Feeling guilty about the practice, he was startled by the ringing landline.

"Monsignor Jerome. I have not seen you in too many

months. This we must remedy."

"Cardinal, your eminence," his chair squeaked as he leaned forward over an oak desk that had been imported centuries ago, "it would be an honor to be in your presence again."

"Naturally. How are things progressing?"

"On schedule, your eminence."

"Excellent. You are doing a good service to the church and the faithful. Wooden crosses from the Holy Land make for excellent souvenirs for the pilgrims in Rome. But I am sure you are well aware of the blessings the lord has bestowed upon your land, and your trees."

"I have thousands of crosses ready."

"Of each type? Hollow and solid?"

"Yes, and the hollow has been filled to the correct weight. I have seen to that myself."

"Excellent Monsignor Jerome. And when should I expect my little scintillante crosses?"

"The glitter will arrive within the week. It is arriving by ship into the Port of Taranto. They will then proceed to you by truck. It was all arranged by my partner."

"That Jewish she-wolf?"

"Eminence, was not Rome founded through the efforts of a she-wolf who nursed Romulus and Remus?"

"Myth."

"This wolf is real, and she doesn't nurse, she bites."

The Cardinal mumbled what sounded like the use of the Lord's name in vain, then ended the call with a click.

CHAPTER 3

The airplane touched down and the steward announced, "Welcome to Israel." A few people clapped while others returned their headphones to their ears. Remy grabbed his bag, carry-on only, and stood to deplane. The queue in the passport control area could only have been described as chaos with endless pushing and ever shifting lines that eventually led to the passport control booths. Upon reaching a booth the guard issued a single command: "Passport."

"Hello. Here you go," Remy said, as he handed the book over, already opened to the correct page.

"Purpose of visit?"

"Research."

"No."

"Yes. I'm here from my university in London to do research on hummus."

"No, you are not. I do not see a visa for research. Therefore, you are not here for research."

"I guess you are right about the type of visa but—"

"To you, I am god, and so I am always right. I give you tourist visa. Three months."

Remy thanked the passport control officer and moved further into the airport. Suitcases of fellow passengers were retrieved from the belts. The crowd then advanced toward customs control. At customs, officials in military garb stood with attack dogs. Remy continued on to exit the restricted part of the airport. Without a moment to orient himself, his ears were assailed by offers of transit.

"Taxi here!"

"Bus this way!"

"Train tickets there!"

"*Sheruit, Monit Sheruit.*" The *sheruit* driver grabbed Remy's arm. "You are coming to Jerusalem in my car."

Is this a question, Remy wondered? "I am going to Jerusalem, yes, but I was going to take the train."

"Ah, you say yes, good, the train is slow, expensive, you come with me."

Remy relented. It was too early to check into his room and he reasoned this unexpected diversion provided an opportunity to learn about local life. Another eight passengers packed into the minibus, and then they were off. The *sheruit* hastily joined the highway and soon left the fertile plain behind as the minibus climbed the hills toward Jerusalem. Rocky grass was punctuated by pine trees and signs to villages. When the *sheruit* reached Jerusalem, Remy told the driver where he was staying. The driver might have nodded, Remy wasn't sure, and then Remy was driven to a spot where the passengers disembarked.

"This is your stop," the driver said and gestured Remy to get out.

"Where am I exactly?"

"Jerusalem. You are fit enough to walk to where you want to go. I am going back to the airport. Get off here unless you want to come to the airport again. If you want to go back to the airport, I can give you a good price."

Remy declined the offer of wasting and instead paid and hopped out. There were a few tourist signs, and he used those to get a rough estimate of his location. Remy pulled out his map, traced a route, and set-off. The day was warm, dry, and sunny: the opposite of London in almost every way, save the bus exhaust.

As Remy walked toward his little rented room a half-mile outside Jerusalem's old city he fell into deep thought. *How should I go about researching hummus?* He decided to start, as Professor Roy taught, at the most general level. *Okay, so I am researching hummus*, he reasoned. *And hummus is a food. So I am doing a piece on food. I am a food reporter.* With that in mind Remy came across an orange juice stand and realized he was parched. He ordered a glass, and, as Remy drank, it occurred to him that he was consuming a food. Remy turned to the seller and asked, "Where is this fruit from?" As an aspiring journalist Remy often asked questions like this.

The juicer, a man in his late thirties wearing a black t-shirt and jeans, and smoking a cigarette, looked into Remy's eyes, and answered, "Don't ask me difficult questions. I don't know these things. Next customer."

Remy was handed his change, a half-lingered glance suggesting the strangeness of the inquiry. *Odd* Remy thought. *I usually receive more information when I show interest in a vendor and their work.* But it was a warm day, and another customer might soon approach. After enjoying the fresh-squeezed juice Remy tried another vendor, for research, and thirst.

A juicer around the corner had a similar operation, yet there the proprietor was mid-fifties: though age and location were perhaps the only difference between juicers as this one had a similar outfit, was smoking a cigarette, and showed disdain for his customers. Remy ordered a juice and again stated his question, "This is great juice; might I ask where the oranges are from?"

"Ask the oranges," was the reply.

Remy remained still and narrowed his eyes, challenging the juicer into a more helpful answer, yet instead the juicer calmly lit another cigarette and sat back as if to give Remy a moment with the fruit. As Remy began to look through the oranges he got a sense of their weight, noticed their varietal skin type, color, and texture, but before Remy could continue his interrogation of the fruit he heard a sharp voice through the haze of smoke.

"Get the fuck away from my oranges."

Remy complied, and resumed the stroll to his room to stretch, unpack, and plan the next move. Asking about oranges didn't result in much information, but he got a taste of the locals, and, more importantly, had something refreshing to drink.

Later that evening, Remy decided to take a walk to the Old City, entering through the Jaffa Gate. There he came across a strawberry stand laid out on an ancient looking wooden cart. Two vendors, each in their early twenties, wearing t-shirts and jeans, one with a cigarette and one without, leaned against the cart.

"These strawberries look great. Where are they from?"

Without a second glance or a blink of an eye the one without the cigarette answered, "Palestine, where else?"

"Who grows them?"

"Palestinians of course."

"Where in Palestine are they grown?"

"That you will have to find out for yourself."

Remy ordered a kilogram of strawberries, paid, pocketed the change, exited the Old City through the Damascus Gate, found a step to sit on, and enjoyed the strawberries while he took in the flow of people coming and going to shop, work, pray, and visit. Later, as he lay down to sleep, Remy reflected about how researching in the Middle East was not as difficult or dangerous as it had once seemed.

•

"What is your name?"
    "Remy."

"Remy, my friend, why do you ask stupid questions?"

Remy's questioning of an Israeli greengrocer was not going well. "I merely asked where some of your produce grew. If you do not want to talk about it—"

"I do not. Get lost."

Remy had decided to spend his Friday morning at Machne Yehuda market in Jerusalem. *Perhaps I should have selected a less busy moment.* But he was so eager to begin. The market was packed with shoppers and sellers moving hundreds of goods in a frenzy before the Shabbat bell rang and everyone rushed home to prepare for the evening's meal. Giving up on tracking produce, Remy decided to join the crowds and source some dinner. He saw a *kugel* stand and decided to purchase some. "What is the difference between these two?"

"This one some people like more, and that one other people like more."

Remy bought both; one with black pepper and the other sweetened with raisins. He also bought a couple of pastries, bread, and several containers of dips. That done, Remy walked away from the market and found himself in the narrow lanes of Nachalaot.

There was a pretty little park not far from a synagogue, and Remy decided to enjoy the sights and sounds of the coming Shabbat, undecided if he should have a picnic or go back to his room. In due course, a man approached and said *shalom aleichem*, to which Remy answered *aleichem shalom*. The man further wished Remy a *Shabbat Shalom*, and after introducing himself as Noam, he asked if Remy had any plans for the night.

"I don't," Remy answered.

A quick chat about where Remy was from and what he was doing soon led to an invitation to dinner. Remy accepted but pointed to his *kugel*.

"*Kugel* is always welcome in our house, and tonight so are you." A wonderful dinner with Noam and his family ensued.

"Remy, what do you think we should do?"

"Do with what Noam?"

"Our conflict, with the Palestinians."

"Resolve it."

"How?"

"Share."

"It is not so easy."

"Why?"

"We want the same thing."

"Which is?"

"The land."

"Isn't there enough for both peoples?"

"No. And even if there was enough land, physically speaking, each people maintain an ideal whereby there is not enough, and that moreover there is an ethical imperative to hold it all."

"But how can that exist within a reality whereby there are millions of Israelis and Palestinians; and in roughly equal numbers between the river and the sea."

"River and the sea is a statement meant to disguise a Palestinian dream of committing another holocaust. To push us Jews into the sea."

"Apologies, I meant it only geographically."

"It is the reference to geography that seeks to obscure the meaning."

"Then why not a single state? Everyone gets to be part of a country that holds all the land."

"That won't work. We are like biblical brothers, we cannot share, only fight."

"Then what is the future?"

"Fighting, unless you can think of another solution."

"There must be something, you can't just fight forever, you can't hold one people subservient to another."

"Why not?"

"Because it is unethical, and because it will damage both peoples. Neither will be able to enjoy the land they love."

"There can be only one owner. There are too many Palestinians, we cannot combine peoples, they will vote us out."

"What about instead of fighting it out with the Palestinians, you buy them out?"

"Buy?"

"Isn't that what the early Zionist settlers did? Buy the land."

"Yes, but then there were willing sellers."

"Perhaps the prices are higher, but who is to say there aren't sellers today? If you buy-out enough people, then you can give rights to the rest."

"I don't want Gaza. What is the price for Judea and Samaria?"

"I couldn't possibly say. $1 million per person, including children?"

"Israel could never afford that. Will America pay?"

"For argument's sake, let's say America will help. Let's see, there are 3 million Palestinians in the West Bank."

"There are not that many."

"For argument's sake, let's say there are 3 million. But you don't need all 3 million to leave. In Israel now the Palestinians are what, one-fifth? Would it be OK if they were one-third?"

"Tolerable, for argument's sake."

"If there are 7.5 million Jews, including settlers, and 5.5 million Palestinians including Israelis, but not Gazans, this would mean Jews consist of 58% of the people. If you needed two-thirds to be Jewish, that would mean you would have to subtract around 1.5 million Palestinians. At $1 million per compensated Palestinian, that would equal $3 trillion."

"That is six-times Israel's economy!"

"To end the war? To have peace? That would drive the economy forward by enhancing trade and investment."

"It could hurt our military industrial complex. Still, I

will concede that peace is preferable."

"Then have we found a solution?"

"As a representative of nobody but myself, I will say perhaps. If you can find $3 trillion to spend, and 1.5 million Palestinians to accept it, you will have my thanks and a Nobel Peace Prize."

After dinner, and despite the late hour, Remy found he had plenty of energy and decided to take a stroll through the Old City. The streets were empty, the shops closed, and the tourists tucked safely away in their hotels. He wandered and wandered, through tunnels and over rooftops, eventually finding himself lost in alleys that never tired of twisting. He went around another corner and found himself in the courtyard of a home. Three Palestinians were engaged in a relaxing conversation that ceased upon seeing Remy approach. Remy stammered an apology and request for directions. Instead, he was offered an *as-salamu alaykum*, a seat, and a cup of sweetened black tea. Remy answered, "*wa-alaikum-sa-laam*," and accepted the invitation, sat, and proceeded to have a chat that lasted until the small hours of the morning.

"I recently had a conversation about an idea to resolve the conflict, and I wondered your thoughts on the matter."

"Ask."

"Would people move out of the region for money?"

"No."

"What about for $1 million per person."

"I say no. You cannot buy my soul."

"I say yes. Life here is too difficult, and this would be a way out. I have 8 children and a wife. With $10 million…."

"I say maybe. Where would we go?"

"There will be many countries who would want educated and moneyed immigrants. This could be part of the negotiation."

"I would choose America where the streets are paved with gold. Maybe Canada."

"Too cold!"

"But very friendly."

"The Netherlands?"

"The people are too cheap. I've listened to them bargain at the market."

"Britain?"

"We'll never need to pray for rain."

"Australia? Sunshine. Lots of space. Nowhere near the conflict."

"Nowhere near anything."

"People would never agree to losing their heritage. Anyone who took the deal would be an outcast, or worse."

"I think many would take the deal. Especially Gazans and refugees."

"What if the deal only included people in Israel and the West Bank?"

"What would you do with the refugees and Gazans? That is millions of people. It might work in the West Bank, though you will be left with the fanatics. And with the refugees and Gazans…no this plan cannot end the conflict unless you expand it to include all Palestinians."

"That would cost too much."

"Then you have not found a solution to end the conflict, at least not for all."

By dawn Remy was back in his room. Exhausted, he reflected upon how nice everyone was, aside from those who sold food.

CHAPTER 4

Marwan woke to the sound of the call to prayer from the mosque around the corner. Ever since the mosque's high-quality Hi-Fi system went down, replaced by a cheap speaker, the melodious sounds of the *muezzin* had been reduced to a loud, feedback riven, and only somewhat comprehendible squawk. It didn't help that the previous muezzin had been replaced by his apprentice. Afterwards Marwan had a light breakfast of bread and hummus spiced with za'atar and olive oil along with a cup of strong tea. Marwan scrolled through his phone, dialing the number of Major Rafiq al-Khana of the Palestinian Customs Police.

"Major al-Khana."

"Raffy! It's Marwan. How are you, my friend?"

"Marwan, hello. I am so glad to hear from you. When I heard about where the Israelis were doing their demolitions I hoped it would not effect you."

"It was a neighbor."

"A noble and blessed man."

"Yes, of course, but he has left a homeless and grieving mother and brother. Did you know the brother of the martyr has a kid in my son's class? They are friends."

"I was not aware. How can I help, Marwan?"

"The family asked me to make a few enquiries. They did not think this son, brother, husband, and father could have done such an act of violence."

"Did you tell them that when this happens the family is always the most surprised?"

"Of course. But the brother of the martyr Ahmad insisted. I agreed to make a few calls, just to give them peace of mind. Do you know anything about the Har Kesem settlement?"

"Only what the TV tells me."

"Raffy, *come-on*. It's Marwan. Give me more to take the family of the martyr."

"Marwan, your son must have grown so much since I saw you last. I must see him, and visit you."

•

Raffy knocked while he opened Marwan's unlocked apartment door. Marwan was sitting on his sofa and switched off his rather large TV when he saw Raffy enter, and then rose to greet his dear friend.

"Raffy, please come in. Will you take some tea?"

Marwan's apartment had a new leather sofa which sat awkwardly in the middle of the otherwise unadorned room. The type of décor that is found in the homes of doctors, police, and bachelors. Raffy felt at home.

"Coffee, if you have it."

"Of course."

"Is your boy or Mehmet nearby?"

Although the apartment building was only a ten-minute taxi ride from downtown, it felt a world away. The stone facade building was only a few years old and not fully occupied. The hallways had wires for lights and outlets, but neither had covers. The main door had a place to install a security system, but instead there was only holes and a door that was always propped open.

"Not yet. They have chess today, clever boys. It should be finished soon."

"That's fine. You asked about Har Kesem. As you know, the Customs Police monitors what goes in and out of settlements, to the best of our limited abilities."

"Frustrating business, watching without doing. This is why I preferred traffic duty."

"It *is* traffic duty, Marwan. Just one with considerably more paperwork."

"Okay, so tell me what the paperwork says about my settlement."

"The settlement has a lot of army patrols. It also seems to make deliveries late at night, but once they go into Israel we cannot follow, so we do not know where the deliveries go, or what is in the containers."

"That is normal for an industrial settlement, no?"

"Har Kesem is listed as a residential settlement, yet it does not seem to have many residents. It gets more army protection, so what is really strange is that this martyr, Ahmad, was able to gain access. Then he found a prospective resident to shoot? I agree with the family that it is, at the least, peculiar, but I do not know anything more than that. I can try to get in touch with the Major; perhaps he can tell you more. I am sorry I cannot be of more help, Marwan."

"Thank you, Raffy. I hear the boys coming. Let's go out to greet them."

•

Shachar groaned when his phone rang. He tried to ignore the call by burying his head in the pillow, only there was no pillow. Shachar looked around at his Spartan studio with the mattress on the floor and a sofa with two broken wooden legs. And torn fabric. The phone rang again. *Where could the pillow be?* More ringing compelled Shachar to pick up the phone. He thought about throwing it against the wall, being free of ringing forever, but instead answered the call with another groan.

"Hey Shachar! It's Ephraim returning your call."

"What time is it?"

"A bright and sunny 6:01, my man."

"Why the hell would you call me so early?"

"You said to call as soon as possible, and I just got home."

"Fabulous."

"Yes, that is how I would describe my night. But how are you?"

"Fine. Listen, Ephraim, can I call you back? I need to piss, make coffee, and hate you less."

"Sure, Shachar, so it's not urgent?"

"It's about this Har Kesem business. I know you spent time in the region."

"Why don't we meet up and get some coffee together? I'll be there in, say, fifteen minutes."

"Just enough time to piss," grumbled Shachar.

•

Shachar stumbled out of his building into the bright morning sun. He still stumbled as he reached Café Rothstein. Ephraim had chosen an outdoor table and had ordered three coffees, two of them for Shachar. After a quiet breakfast, the two friends began a stroll down the tree lined Rothschild Boulevard.

"Ephraim, I can't believe a coffee costs that much."

"Where you been, Shachar? That is quite reasonable these days. Plus, they gave you chocolate powder on top. Still like powder?"

"It's still early."

"I didn't mean now! But if that's how you still roll then why ask about Har Kesem?"

"The murdered guy was a neighbor. Lived in my building. His wife came by and said it didn't make sense that her husband was in the West Bank at all. I told her I would look into it."

"Shachar, I am serious now. Har Kesem is not something to discuss. Really. It's not safe, and nothing good can come of it."

"Come of what, Ephraim? Asking? Who is paranoid now?"

"No. Just be smart about this."

"You are going to have to give me more, and you know it."

"It's not safe."

"What are you afraid of? We are in the middle of Tel Aviv, strolling down a boulevard drinking lattes and cappuccinos at 7 in the morning. Where is the threat? The man selling newspapers? The lady walking her dog? Those two sitting in a blue van? Maybe the pigeons are bugged. Hamas thinks we have militarized our dolphins."

"Don't joke, Shachar. I am deathly serious."

"As am I! Killer dolphins. I might never swim again. Look, here comes the dog-lady, maybe she needs to borrow a baggie. Let's then buy a newspaper and see what's in that van."

"Enough, Shachar. I'll tell you what I know."

"Hold that thought. Good morning, miss. What a beautiful dog you have."

"Thank you, Shachar. Ephraim, you have disappointed us."

The dog walker raised her newspaper putting two bullets into Ephraim's head. The dog leapt at Shachar who managed to place a forearm between the dog and his neck. As the dog tightened its jaw on Shachar's arm, he felt the painful sensation of bone beginning to break. He dropped to the ground, landing on top of the dog. The dog's breath was thumped out by the impact, and it released Shachar's arm. Shachar snatched a piece of loose pavement and smashed it into the dog's head until the beast lay still. Shachar's arm was shredded,

Ephraim was dead, and the dog walker, newspaper seller, and blue van had all disappeared.

CHAPTER 5

General Ram Cohen snapped out his orders to the members of his staff who had gathered in his office. "The belt around Ramallah will be tightened. From Qalandiya to Dolev, Talmon, Nahliel, Halamish, Ateret, Ofra, Beit El, Psagot, Kokhav Ya'akov, Geva Binyamin, and back to Qalandiya."

"Yes, sir."

They stood before him at attention in the concrete room. The walls were grey, the floor, ceiling, desk, lamp and chair grey. The only color in the room was the outdated maps covering one of the walls.

"Bethlehem will be hemmed in by Har Homa, Gilo, Har Gilo, Betar Illit, Neve Daniel, the forward base of Givat Hatamar backed by Efrat, Tekoa, and the Herodion National Park, which is located just off Route 398 that runs back to Har Homa. The Judean Wilderness will, as always, act as an eastern defensive line."

"Yes, sir."

"Around Hebron we will reinforce Kiryat Arba and the Cave of the Patriarchs, but also Ma'ale Hever, Carmel, Ma'on, Sussia, Asael, Shim'a, Otniel and Beit Hagai. In the north around Jenin, we will strengthen defenses around Malkishu'a, Meirav, Ma'ale Gilbo'a, and the Gilboa Council including the front line towns of Gan Ner,

Sandala, Ram On and Ma'ale Iron."

"Yes, sir."

"And we will stiffen the noose around Nablus. I want extra units in Elon Moreh, Itamar, Yitzhar, Har Brakha, Har Gerizim, Khavat Gil'ad, Kdumim, and Shavei Shomron. Let's also bolster Ari'el and Shiloh to keep Nablus isolated from Ramallah."

"Yes, sir."

"Dismissed."

The staff filed out to pass on the orders. General Ram felt the aching in his legs that reminded him it was time to get some rest. The terrorist had been neutralized, and the family punished. The incident brought cover that would enable them to capture or kill other persons of interest, even though it was obvious their activities were unrelated. *Who could question the actions of a nation under siege from terror? If America could invade Iraq for no reason other than because it was Muslim, then surely the world wouldn't mind a few less Palestinians, especially if they were Muslim.* With that happy thought General Ram began to slide into sleep. But that calming notion led to another more alarming one. It was fine to lose Palestinians, but it was not okay to lose weapons. The general reached for his phone.

"Captain Oded? This is General Cohen. I am coming down to your base to observe the destruction of those weapons. Your work might end up in a field manual."

"General, sir. That is excellent. However, I must warn you that the soldiers I used for the job have been sent home after such labor. Perhaps you would care to visit another time?"

"Captain, I will review the bases under my command whenever I deem it pertinent to review them. I will be at the gate in twenty-one minutes and expect to see you there."

As soon as the general had hung-up, Captain Oded began to mutter to himself. *Damn those old Sabra warriors, those prickly fucks, don't they ever sleep?* Captain Oded ran his fingers across his desk. A million excuses danced in Oded's mind. But he knew, in the army you either obeyed or were insubordinate. Oded stacked his papers neatly to one side. Stacks of paper made Oded feel organized, in control. Oded knew this visit was a possibility. And had planned for it. There must always be contingencies. But this one was not preferable. There were a couple of Palestinian contractors who worked just off the base. They could serve as sacrificial pawns if General Cohen needed to be retired early. Captain Oded slid back his chair, swapped his service pistol for his personal one, checked the positioning of his long knife, and went to meet General Ram at the gate.

"Good evening, General."

"Captain."

"If you will come with me I will show you to the weigh station where we have left the melted-down weapons."

"Lead on, Captain."

Walking in silence the pair of officers made their way through the base past empty guard booths, warehouses with doors open, and barracks left with the lights on. The lack of alertness across the base only heightened Cohen's.

At least this room had guards posted, General Cohen thought.

"Here they are, General."

"But they are all sealed in crates."

"Yes, they have been packed and are ready to be driven to the recycling facility. They are all here and accounted for. I've had them weighed."

"Very good, Captain. Now if you would please open one of the crates so I may see the condition of the munitions."

"Allow me, General."

Captain Oded pried open a lid on one of the containers and stepped back. General Cohen leaned forward.

"There is much metal here, Captain."

Oded gave a thin tight-lipped smile.

"But this looks like scrap metal," the general said, and turned to confront Oded. As he did, the captain drew his personal pistol. General Cohen sensed the danger and whipped his heavy hands onto Oded's wrist, bending the wrist down toward Oded's foot.

Anticipating the maneuver, Oded deftly stepped away. As Ram tightened his grip on Oded's pistol arm the gun clattered to the floor. The guards outside the room shifted nervously. Neither had an interest in getting between two officers, no matter the result. Oded swung his other arm, connected with Ram's jaw which rocked his head back. Oded stepped closer and elbowed the general in the nose. Ram staggered and dropped to one knee. Oded stepped forward and began to pound him with flying punches to the head.

Ram put his arm up in a feeble attempt at warding off the blows, but enough got through that he began to see stars and knew he must make his move. With some effort Ram swung his fist up into the groin of Oded. Ram rose quickly, catching Oded, and seeking to put his head in a vice. Younger and faster, Oded narrowly slipped his head out of the danger, took two steps back, withdrew his long knife, and lunged at Ram. The blade nearly caught the artery between his shoulder and upper arm. Ram clamped his arm down on the knife, momentarily trapping the blade against his body. As Oded pulled back the knife Ram felt searing pain as it sliced into him. Accepting the injury, he was able to briefly delay Oded's withdrawal of the knife. Ram used that split-second to step forward and smashed his forehead into Oded's face, knocking the younger man back. Ram followed the head-butt with a series of punches which Oded, shocked by the turn of the fight and stunned from the head-butt, was unable to stop. Ram swung and swung until Oded slumped against a folding table. Before

Oded and table crashed loudly to the floor, Ram was already hauling his subordinate into a chair and zip-tying Oded's arms and legs. As Oded came to, a cut, bruised, sore, and heated Ram began his questioning.

"Oded, what have you done?"

"General, it was merely for money. Nobody got hurt."

Ram backhanded Oded. "I didn't ask why! I asked *what*."

Oded clamped his mouth and stared defiantly as blood trickled from his mangled nose.

"Captain, you have forfeited your life to me, and I will have it. The only question remaining is how much pain you will experience before I dismiss you to hell. You know our methods well. And you know no man can withstand it forever. You will talk. Perhaps you would like to do it before —"

"General, please, I will tell you what little I know."

"That's good, Oded. I pride myself in always taking efficient care of my men. I am listening. You may begin."

CHAPTER 6

Marwan pulled-up outside of the Headquarters of the Palestinian Customs Police. The building had been a three-story apartment building, the gardens now covered in pebbles to accommodate unused police cars and dusty pickup trucks. Marwan stated his purpose but instead of being brought up to an office, the colonel came down.

"Colonel Awadallah, thank you for meeting me. I hope I am not taking up too much of your time."

"We have much information to gather, but nothing to do with it. As you well know, Marwan, we cannot follow goods into Area C, which is most of the West Bank. We can merely observe from our Area A."

"Of course, even in my department we cannot even chase criminals. Officially we can liaise with the Israelis, or get their permission to enter, but they never agree."

"It is the same for us. I am glad you understand. Major Rafiq al-Khana said you were interested in Har Kesem. To tell the truth, we do not know for certain what goes on there, but we suspect something strange. We have stopped trucks that have come back or through Area A and we have questioned the drivers. But they don't know anything about their cargo. We ask the shipping company who they work for, but the answers are the same."

"Is that unusual, Colonel Awadallah?"

"Not really. But what is odd is how much business they seem to do at night, after curfew, when the Israeli army is out. They think we are unable to see them at night, but, just like their army, we can use the darkness. That is the only time we can take positions outside of Area A. We can crawl closer, but the goods are all in sealed crates, and the trucks drive straight into Israel along Area C roads, where there are Israeli soldiers and we cannot stop them."

"I wish we could use the night like that, but most of what we do is urban, where the fences are high, electrified, and monitored."

"Marwan, I would like to know more as I see you do. I believe it is a dangerous place, but we cannot prove anything. There is not much information, but what you might find interesting is a meeting with a hydrologist friend of mine, Dr. Muhsin."

"A water scientist?"

"Why not? We have to be resourceful. Wait here and I'll arrange things for you."

•

Marwan hesitated outside the offices of the Institute of Hydrology wondering if he was actually making progress on the case, feeling either it was a run-around or was increasingly beyond his depth. Seeing he was already there, Marwan gave himself an internal shrug and pushed open the doors. A man in a suit sat at a table peering into a microscope. Marwan looked around for a receptionist but there was nobody else there.

"Be one moment," the man said.

After a moment of an awkwardness felt only by Marwan, the scientist swiveled his chair away from the table and introduced himself as Dr. Muhsin, director of the Institute of Hydrology.

"Thank you for taking the time to meet with me doctor. I must say I am a confused about why Colonel Awadallah has sent me to you."

"Marwan, or *Lieutenant*, if you are here on official business."

"I am not; Marwan is fine."

"Good. The case of Har Kesem is an interesting one. We have long taken samples of the run-off from there. We do this around most settlements."

"Why would you do that?"

"Because we have three main aquifers here in the West Bank, and we must protect them. The Israelis seem to treat our land as a dumping ground with chemicals seeping through to the aquifers. At least the aquifers they don't harvest. We need to know what might be reaching our water."

"I see. Your work is very important."

"This is why the USA has given us so much funding."

"What have they given you?"

"Machines and computers mostly. They have also provided us with server space to save the data. There is a lot of important information there. At Har Kesem we had seen a lot of animal waste in the early years but then we started seeing fertilizer and then other chemicals which wiped out the trees nearby. It was similar to the chemicals that were being released in the north around Jenin."

"Ah, yes. I remember there were rumors about the farmland around Jenin. About melons?"

"Correct, Marwan. They had the best melons in the entire world, scientifically speaking."

"Anecdotally as well."

"The chemicals killed off the melons and the farmers lost their lands. Do you know what they are being used for now?"

"Drug production. Poppies mostly but also marijuana. Of course, we cannot do anything about it since they are being protected by our own Palestinian Authority."

"Our endlessly corrupt ministers. How they have lost their way! I pray for them. Sometimes."

"I would like to arrest them, but their connections run deep. They even get funding for agricultural production from Australian Aid, which we can prove, and some say the Americans as well."

"In the case of Har Kesem, unlike other settlements, we have found that all of a sudden everything has stopped."

"What do you mean?"

"I mean the wastewater be it from animals, fertilizer, or other chemicals. There is nothing, barely even water. If we did not see it was busy, I would say it is abandoned. Or at least the water says it is."

•

Ronit looked serene standing in the basement bunker, so Dan reminded himself that she was furious.

"Captain Oded seems to have disappeared. From asset he has become a liability. Much as I hate to lose the source, I think we will need to closedown that operation."

"I understand Ronit. I have the addresses of the reservists who worked with him. Although I would be surprised if they came forward."

"I would rather be certain than surprised. Use the acid for the remains."

"Okay. I will get it out of self-storage. Good thing you had me rent that unit."

"Good thing you follow orders."

"Always Ronit."

"Take the henchmen you just did the deliveries with. Who was that?"

"Gad and Issachar."

"After they have dealt with the reservists I would like them added to the body count. They know too much already, and this is a good opportunity to clean house.

Get help from Zebulon and Naphtali, then offer them a raise."

"Zebulon is related to Gad; they are brothers in fact."

"Then toss Zebulon into the acid as well. The loss of three idiots will reduce our costs. Without Captain Oded we are going to need to conserve our cash until a new source of weapons can be found."

•

General Ram Cohen lurched out of the warehouse and drank in the cool night air. Guards posted at the door stood stiffly at attention, trying not to tremble. Ram glanced at them and knew that he would have these guards attest that the captain, upset he had not been promoted, had attacked his commanding officer. Ram explained this to the guards, who were only too happy to be offered a way out of the machinations of senior officers. That would take care of the official side the general decided. Now it was time to investigate Oded's true motives. Obviously, he could not move that much metal and weaponry on his own. First on Ram's list was finding out who had helped him.

"Sergeant, who was detailed to Captain Oded before his assault? Perhaps they know something about the captain's mind before his tragic end."

"It was five reservists, general. They were dismissed and sent home shortly after the weapons were reported damaged."

"Names and addresses. *Now.*"

"Yes, sir." The sergeant dashed over to the filing cabinet.

"And on the computer." The sergeant complied.

"Excellent. And now delete and destroy the records."

"Come again, sir?"

"I want these soldiers protected from further scrutiny. They must already be shaken, and we don't want to ruin their families' lives by having them continually harassed by prosecutors, journalists, and others who benefit from the sorrows of others."

•

Shachar staggered as he climbed up the steps and banged on Yamina's door. He leaned against the door and felt glad to hear the sound of the nurse's footsteps growing louder upon the tiled floor.

"Shachar, what happened to you?"

"A minor flesh wound, I was hoping you could help me bandage it."

"This is a serious injury, Shachar! There's a lot of blood here, and, let me see, these marks run deep! Are they from a bite? You must get yourself tested for rabies."

"The dog did not have rabies; it was ordered to attack."

"Ordered by whom? Who would do that?"

"People that killed my friend, people that don't want us to know what happened to Yossi."

"Are they the same people who killed my Yossi?"

"Yamina, this is something I will be risking my life to discover."

"Your blood is soaking through the bandages; let me put pressure on it."

"Thanks."

"What is your next move?"

"I don't know; this is getting serious; we might assume Yossi's murder was not just a random act of violence. I'd like to get into that settlement to have a look around, but following the attack, the state of emergency is restricting access to the West Bank. Perhaps I can get permission from the captain of my old unit. Boaz Oded was the name. What I really want—"

"Captain Boaz Oded? He's reported to have died. And the state of emergency has ended as well."

"What?"

"It was on the news; the army said the state of emergency—"

"Not that. What of Oded!"

"Ah, I saw a report on TV that Captain Oded had attacked his commanding officer, a general, Cohen I think. And your captain was killed in the struggle."

"I wonder if Oded had any operational connection to Har Kesem. Or that general perhaps."

Yamina, startled, kneeled on the floor to beg. "Shachar, it's too dangerous for you to go anywhere near that settlement."

"What I'd really like to do is interview the family of that terrorist."

"Terrorists? Those people who murdered Yossi? *Animals*. There is no reasoning with them. They'll kill you Shachar. That's not an option, and you know it."

"I know it; I just wish there was somebody who could act as an intermediary."

"I doubt the US ambassador is available to you."

"We'll just have to pray, Yamina."

"Shachar, you're not religious."

"Even atheists can pray. Especially if they need to see a rabbi."

CHAPTER 7

After that pleasant Friday evening, Remy spent Saturday exploring a quiet Jerusalem. By Sunday, he was ready to return to work and had decided to take the strawberry sellers up on their challenge. *Where did the strawberries come from?* By Palestine were they referring to the entirety of historical Palestine, did they mean the Palestinian Territories of the West Bank and Gaza Strip, or was it a moment of poetry from a guy pushing a wooden cart?

Remy decided to try his luck in the West Bank. He packed his notepad and backpack, walked through the Old City to the Damascus Gate, and soon reached the Sultan Suleiman Terminal bus station in East Jerusalem. When Remy asked which bus went to Ramallah, a ticket seller pointed him in the right direction. The bus was quickly loaded with passengers, and set off.

The bus sped through northern Jerusalem toward the Qalandiya gate, that infamous opening that controlled access between Ramallah and Jerusalem, a distance of only twenty kilometers, just over twelve miles. There was some traffic moving through the gate toward Ramallah, but the way from Ramallah back into Jerusalem was packed for miles. Remy hopped off the bus and walked to Ramallah's Al-Manara Square in the heart of the city. What he found was a busy, dusty, dirty traffic circle surrounded by markets, tea and juice sellers, and big buildings, one of which hosted a huge advertisement for Stars & Bucks Café. He wandered, bought a Nescafé with creamer to sip from a street vendor, and eventually made his way to the market to see if these fruit and vegetable sellers were any more helpful than those in Jerusalem.

The market was not nearly as busy as in Jerusalem, and it was, especially for the bustle of the city, quite small. Moreover, the produce was not appealing. In some places the food was simply spread out on blankets or tarps on the ground. These sellers seemed different from the well-dressed people Remy had just seen when walking around Al-Manara Square. He must have looked bemused because a young man walked up to him.

"Hello. I am Husain, and I am studying English at Birzeit University. Do you know it?"

"Hi, I'm Remy. I am a journalism student studying in London. And yes, I know of Birzeit University. It is one of the best in the West Bank."

"In all of Palestine, I think," he said, beaming. "Tell me, what are you doing staring at the vegetables? Do you need a drink of water? Do you need directions?"

"No, thank you, I am trying to research where produce comes from. I was just noticing the differences between the market here and the one in Jerusalem."

"In this area of the market you are seeing only poor villagers." He swept his hand over the market. "They cannot compare with the rich merchants of Jerusalem. If you want better produce in Ramallah, you go to the supermarket. This is a Western city, you know. Would you like me to take you to a supermarket?"

"I'd appreciate it, thanks," Remy replied, while wondering if he had tested his pens before setting off that morning.

•

The blast of cool air hit them as soon as the automatic doors opened. Like most other supermarkets Remy had visited, this one opened into the produce section.

"This is MaxMar," said Husain. "It is one of the finest supermarkets in Ramallah and, therefore, all of Palestine."

"Beyond posh. Am I reading these prices correctly?"

"Yes, it is very expensive. But remember in Ramallah we have all the government ministers living here; we have all the Western donors living here, and those who work for Western companies, bankers, lawyers, plus the usual professionals of doctors, professors, and people doing big business. There is plenty of money here."

"I see that."

"Is there anything else you would like to see here?"

"I guess not." Remy turned on the spot where he stood, looking around the large, clean, orderly, and well stocked store. "I wanted to find out more about where they are getting their produce."

"Ah, you want to know where the supermarkets are getting their fruit, not where you should buy them?"

"It's helpful to know where people shop, but I was hoping to get further into the supply chain," Remy said as he picked up a box and attempted to read the label.

"Remy," Husain said, taking the box from his hand and putting it back on the shelf, "my Baba is a Director in the Ministry of Economics. I'll take you to him."

"Now?"

"Why not? Let's go! We can get an ice cream along the way. Have you tried Rukab's ice cream? It's a very famous parlor. Do you like ice cream?"

"Of course. What makes it so famous?"

"It has a unique taste and it's local, not like the other ice creams made by international conglomerates that manufacture Great Laughs or Brad & Gary's. Have you heard of Duoliver? They own those brands. Rukab is local."

"What about the taste?"

"It is not the taste so much as the texture. It stretches."

"How does ice cream stretch?"

"It has gum of course. How else?"

"Why would they put gum in it?"

"The ice cream takes longer to melt. This is ideal on a hot day. We have lots of hot days here."

"I noticed."

"Rukab's is for Ramallah, but there are other Palestinian ice creams, the best being Al-Arz in Nablus. They are similar in style to Great Laughs, which is also very popular here despite their connections to Israeli subsidiaries."

"I'll have to try some, after Rukab's of course. You seem very knowledgeable about ice cream."

"I did a project about it at university. Besides, it is good to know about the things you love. And I love ice cream! I'll call Baba from the parlor to tell him we're coming to his office."

•

After the ice cream, Husain and Remy walked over to the Ministry of Economics which was housed in a tower made of glass. A motionless glacier in the middle of a desert. Security waved them through and, without stopping, Husain warmly greeted the secretaries and pushed open an oak door that seemed out of place is such a modern building. The minister was seated in a leather cushioned swivel-chair behind an equally imposing oak desk.

"Baba, this is Remy; he is a journalism student visiting from Britain and interested in where we get, or grow, our produce. I thought you could help. I need to get back to campus because I have a class. Can I leave him with you?"

"Director, your son Husain has been very kind to me."

"I wish he would be more kind to his studies, but I am glad to see that he is so welcoming. Now, how can I help you? I too have a meeting in a few minutes." The minister checked his watch, glanced at the clock on the wall and looked down at his intercom. Remy noticed this and began without further pleasantries.

"I'm conducting doctoral research on food. I started with hummus, but I have since become interested in fruit and vegetables. Your son has explained the market and the supermarkets here in Ramallah, but where does each acquire its produce? Is some of it locally grown and others imported? And if so, from where?"

"Much of it comes from Palestinian farms. There is an issue here with quality in that many farms have contracts with Israeli wholesalers. The Israelis take the best for themselves to sell in Israel and the rest comes here. In the case of flowers and strawberries, some are sent to Europe. Have you ever seen Israeli produce in England?"

"I have seen strawberries, yes, and Medjoul dates. In major supermarkets, upmarket mostly, and also in other shops."

"Those are most likely Palestinian with Israeli labels. They take our best products to their settlements and put on a new label that says, 'Made in Israel,' and go and sell in Israel and beyond. Most Israelis don't even know." Remy flipped open his reporter's notepad. The minister noticed but did not stop. "This is the case for many products. Did you know that seventy percent of Israeli eggs are produced by Palestinians in the Occupied Territories?"

"Would the Israeli consumer care?"

"They will not if they want eggs that are cheap, high quality, and available."

"How do the wholesalers reach so many farmers?"

"Some Israeli companies contract with cooperatives that are run by village leaders; others work directly with farmers. The companies will provide some technology such as irrigation hoses, knowledge of certain techniques, and the seeds. They then use our water, land, and labor."

"Why do farmers work with the Israelis?" Remy pressed.

"As I said, the Israelis provide the equipment. They also provide an easy way to sell. The farmers have little choice in that they have lost their crops or their olive trees and are left nearly destitute; so ripe for exploitation to grow low value crops like potatoes and cucumbers. If they are successful and their land proves productive they might be given the chance to grow the higher value items such as tomatoes, strawberries, or flowers."

"Where does the part with the settlements come in? Are a lot of products relabeled?"

"Oh yes. This is a big problem for our political economy. We do get some money this way, but Israelis and the world do not know how much they are connected to us Palestinians, and the high quality of our products."

"I suppose there are many people in the world who want to help Palestinians but don't know how. Perhaps the way would be to buy Palestinian products, if only they knew which ones. This relabeling thing seems big."

"It is *everything*. And because of the trade regime, and because we are surrounded and do not have access to a border, *everything* labeled Palestinian or Israeli must use an Israeli firm at some point."

"Why?"

"Logistics. To cross all the internal and external borders. Remy, I do not know if this has been helpful to you, but I do need to attend to my next meeting. If you want, I can refer you to the Palestinian Customs Police; they can tell you more about relabeling if that is something that interests you. Hold on, I'll make the call now. If you are able to go there right away. I know it is almost evening, but this might be a good opportunity for you."

"Yes," Remy said, "thank you; I will go right away."

CHAPTER 8

"Remy, I am pleased to meet you. I am Colonel Awadallah, and this is Major Rafiq al-Khana." The three of them stood outside of the Customs Police building surrounded by pickup trucks being loaded with gear. "The state of emergency the Israelis declared has ended. We are going on a reconnaissance mission tonight, you're welcome to join us. Otherwise, you can return tomorrow, and we can answer your questions then."

"Is the mission dangerous?"

"Not really. Here take this flak jacket and helmet. Major al-Khana is usually correct with sizing."

"I'm not sure if this is such a good idea."

"Be brave, my friend. How is the fit?"

"It is the right size, but my professor advised me to take care."

"Your professor seems wise to the practicalities of the world. We are taking the best of care, which is why you have the flak jacket and helmet. Now into the truck; we need to be in position before the Israeli soldiers rotate for night duty."

•

The pickup trucks loaded with customs police officers drove through a valley with their lights off. No one spoke including Remy. At length, the trucks stopped and everyone jumped out. They were behind a steep rise.

"Remy, are you okay crawling?"

"Sure, about how far?"

"Just over that ridge. Where the light is coming from."

"I see it. Where is it?"

"This is Har Kesem settlement. We have been trying to monitor this one in particular for a long time now."

"Why?"

"We were given a tip."

"By whom?"

"A driver we arrested and beat in the basement of one of the governors' offices. He told us to watch this settlement. We think it might be for relabeling."

"Do you get much reliable information that way?"

"Most certainly! The Americans trained us well in interrogation techniques. They trained us in weapons, tactics, and interviews. We *interviewed* the driver using these methods, and he became *helpful*. Wait, it looks like the trucks are on the move."

"Where do they go?"

"A few go straight into Israel, where we cannot hope to follow. Most go to other settlements nearby. We are already breaking laws by doing police work here in Area C. If the soldiers or even settlers see us they can shoot, and we would be in the wrong."

"Did you hear that? Is that thunder?"

"No, truck engines. And I see vehicles speeding out of the settlement. That is unusual; they turned our away instead of—we need to go right now. Now! *Now!*"

Colonel Awadallah turned and slid down the hill with Major al-Khana close behind. For a brief moment Remy watched them go before sliding down the back slope and began a slow run across the rocky terrain. Remy tripped on a rock and stumbled, regaining balance, but getting some pebbles stuck in his shoe. *Damn.* The police had discussed detection as a remote possibility, something Remy thought they would talk more about on the ride or the long march to the observation point. The plan was to get to a rarely used shepherd's hut and wait out the night. Or at least until just before dawn when the next army shift change occurred. The key, al-Khana had stressed, was getting over the road. The patrols were mostly along the roads, and the roads acted as borders. Get over the road and the chances of a successful escape increased exponentially. As they approached the road Remy felt a hand across his mouth. It was al-Khana, and he pulled Remy to the ground.

"Get down. A patrol approaches."

"That isn't a regular police car is it?"

"No, it is *the Zev...the Wolf.* An armored personal carrier."

The Wolf moved slowly and rolled to a stop. The searchlight illuminated the darkness and swung around.

"Remy, close your eyes and get down. They can see the reflection off your irises. And they are going to be using night vision."

The searchlight abruptly switched off; the vehicle creaked and then began to roll forward. Relief flooded through Remy. Then the searchlight came back on just a few feet away followed by a burst of gunfire. Soldiers had jumped out of the back and were shooting into the dark.

Awadallah signaled to al-Khana to make a move toward the front of the Wolf. The opposite side of the road featured a deep ravine where the Wolf could not follow. It might give them enough time to get away before more troops arrived.

Major al-Khana moved swiftly to his feet while pulling Remy with him. He then dashed in front of the truck, and Remy followed closely. Colonel Awadallah then followed Remy. The soldiers in the rear were being blocked by the bulk of the Wolf. Major al-Khana launched himself over the edge and moved downhill at an incredible speed. Remy paused to look where to step when the tires squealed, Awadallah gave him a rough shove, and the Wolf slammed into the colonel. Awadallah was gone, and the soldiers had reached the edge and were pouring fire down the ravine, but al-Khana had waited, and he flattened Remy against the stone embankment.

"They will go soon to try to cut us off from the nearest village. We might have gone there as Awadallah has…had a cousin."

"I'm shaking."

"Keep calm or you'll send yourself into shock."

"He saved me."

"Awadallah is lost. Let's finish the job and stay alive."

When the soldiers had gone, al-Khana dragged himself up and scampered back across the road. "They'll look the way we were heading. We'll have to take another route. There is a cave not too far away. It's damp, cold, rocky and where we are going to wait out the night. And while we do, you can call me Rafiq."

•

"General Cohen?"

"Yes, Captain Levy."

"We caught a Palestinian officer outside of Har Kesem."

"Seems your plan to lift the state of emergency while keeping a strike force at the settlement paid off. I am glad I promoted the right man."

"Thank you, General. Sir, what should we do with the Palestinian officer?"

"In what unit does he serve?"

"He appears to be Customs Police."

"Rank?"

"Colonel."

"Really? What's the name?"

"Awadallah."

"Has he been questioned? If not, I can do it."

"My apologies, General Cohen. He was killed upon being struck by a Zev."

"We need to keep this away from the media. I can spin a ball on my nose better than our diplomats can spin the death of a Palestinian in uniform. The Palestinians will not want to make this into an incident any more than we do since they would have to explain why their people were trespassing near the site of a terror attack."

"What should we do with the body?"

"We don't want it, Captain Levy. Return it to the Customs Police. They can clean up their own mess."

•

Awadallah's body was deposited outside the police station. Nothing out of the ordinary was reported. It was a simple heart attack. Everyone in the police department knew. They'd seen it before, but there was more danger from it becoming public. No matter what they did, nothing could bring Awadallah back.

Rafiq and Remy sipped sweetened tea while sitting under a large tree near the station. Remy absently wondered about the tree, thinking about who planted it and what it had seen in its many years. A police officer who was smoking a cigarette outside of the building coughed violently, snapping Remy out of his reverie.

"Rafiq, I can't understand how this can be. How this can stand. How we can all turn away."

"It does not matter if you, or I, understand why it

happened." Rafiq scratched his stubble. "But we do not have the luxury of turning away. Our families are here. Our jobs. We cannot feed our families without our jobs. And if we declare war on the Israelis, nobody is safe."

"I am sorry; you are right. I have nothing at stake here. I did not mean to offend you."

"It is a difficult situation. If you could, I am sure you would like to help our people."

"I can help. You cannot go to the settlements, but I can. Tell me where to go, and I'll check it out."

"No."

"I am a journalist you know; I go where the story is. If the story is in Har Kesem then I should go there."

"No."

"I owe it to Awadallah. He saved my life."

"You do not owe a debt and it is not your duty."

"I must do something." Remy's lip began to quiver. "I need to do something." Remy's eyes began to water. "I insist."

Rafiq did not want to use Remy; he was out of place and out of his depth. But it was a good opportunity. Rafiq felt a wave of hurt for Awadallah and decided to accept Remy's offer. "If you want you insist, need to go to Israel, then you can take Israeli transportation to the settlement. I'll give you a dummy phone for us to contact you. After I call you with the license plate numbers of the trucks to follow, ditch the phone. You also won't want to attract attention by crossing back and forth between the West Bank and Israel. I have an acquaintance who knows the route to get into Israel without much fuss. It's usually for Palestinian VIPs who can use the airport, but he owes me a favor."

CHAPTER 9

The cigarettes arrived in the Mauritanian capital of Nouakchott. Shipments to Morocco, Algeria, Spain, and Western Europe came through here or Western Sahara's Laayoune. But the importance of and destination for this particular shipment meant there was no other option than Nouakchott, the most westerly point on the trade routes of the Sahara Desert.

When the flight touched down in Nouakchott, George was there to meet it. The two Colombians stepped off and were immediately blinded by the brilliant light of the desert sun.

"Welcome to Mauritania. I am George, your liaison."

"We are ready to depart, George of the CIA."

"May I have your names? We are planning a long journey together."

"My name is Sanchez, and my partner here is also named Sanchez."

"Are you brothers?"

"No."

"Great to meet you two. Our guides are waiting for us across town. We can load up the packages in a tourist van I've arranged for us, then zip over to the caravan waiting at al Taqwa Mosque in Aoujeft. Shouldn't be more than a few hours."

•

"Hi there!" George said to the man standing as still as a statue next to the camel sitting in front of the car rental agency that doubled as a jumping off point for their trek across the Sahara. Usually the caravans came here for the gold mined nearby in Akjoujt, but not this time. "I'm George. This is Sanchez and Sanchez. Who might you be?"

"I am Mohammed," said the man as he nodded and then gestured toward the man standing off to the side, by a few camels, "and over there is also Mohammed."

"Does anyone have a real name here?" George asked jovially.

"Is your name George?" Mohammed asked, masking his amusement.

"Of course, my trustworthy friend."

"Good, George. We set off shortly after the pack animals are loaded. I hope you three are fit because a journey through the Sahara is not for the weak."

"I'm always ready for anything. The Sanchez twins will not be going all the way, as I'm sure you've been told. Which route are we taking?"

"We have decided to take a southern route to avoid the more common routes."

"Is that not a route for cigarettes? Like we have?"

"There are many routes. The one we take is the one we take. The Sanchezes will not object to taking that route?"

"The route doesn't matter to them. And the pack animals? Are there not trucks we can use?"

"We will use the animals for most of the stages. It allows us to avoid the roads."

"But how much longer will it take to go by animal?"

"Longer by days, of course. Like I said, you must be very fit," Mohammed said as he spit into the sand along with the camel. "We go through Casbah des Aït Maouin and Aguilâl before we reach Araouane in Mali. Here your

Sanchez family can take an eternal rest or a tourist 4x4 to Timbuktu. You'll choose of course. But we will move northeast of there to Timétrine where another decision needs to be made. There is a popular route that moves north into Algeria via Tamanrasset."

"I know Tamanrasset. It is a big place for the movement of refugees."

"We prefer to refer to them as living cargo. But yes, we do not need to mix with those traders. Better to head southeast to Kidal and then to Tin-Essako. There we will encounter one of the most difficult stretches to Niger where we visit Tassara and Tamaya before we bypass Kao Kakil and Kandel Bouzou as we make a hard push to Fachi."

"What is the situation in Niger?"

Mohammed shrugged. "It matters little. Fachi is so remote. Besides, we have a longstanding relationship with the tribes there. This is good because they are now flush with Libyan weaponry."

"How do you keep in contact with the tribes?"

"We have family and other ties to these people. In fact, most of the areas to this point we have relations. There is no other government but them. This is also why in Fachi we have another big choice to be made if we are to reach the Red Sea safely. We could go north through Libya via the Djado Plateau or east into Chad and Sudan. Our cousins in Niger have some connections with the Toubou people in northern Chad, so preferably we will take that route."

"Another detour. Is Libya not faster? We could take a road directly to Egypt."

"The safety of the routes changes with the winds. You hired us for this journey; you must trust that we know the way." George gave a sharp nod as Mohammed continued his explanation. "For a time, Libya was the primary route. As long as Gaddafi got his tax you were seen through. But with the civil war and the weakness of the

Chadian government, the north of Chad became open to whoever could hold it. The Toubou have their routes, and, though they are an inferior race, they smuggle with honor."

"Honorable smugglers."

Mohammed opened his mouth into a big toothy grin. "Not so different from an honorable spy. We move from Fachi to Dao Timmi. This is when we meet our Toubou contacts. They will guide us away from the Qadhadhfa tribe that dominates the western half of Libya and take us through the Tibesti Mountains in Chad. We will be vulnerable there and must be vigilant. At that point, being far from the other Berber tribes, we can enter Libya via land that is deserted—even by the standards of the Sahara. We will cross into Libya at Bikku Bitti and then across to the oasis of Ma'tan as-Sarra."

"I see," George said. "The name Ma'tan as-Sarra seems familiar."

Mohammed scowled, "It seems then you, and your friends, already know about our air-strip there. I wonder if you know about any others." George shrugged and asked, "Do we then move directly east to the Red Sea?"

"Normally, we would move to the south of the Kufra District to Mount Uweinat at the intersection of Libya, Sudan, and Egypt. That provides opportunities. But things in Sudan are too unstable, which you pay me to know, so we plan to go deeper in the desert by swinging southward from Ma'tan as-Sarra into Chad toward Lake Yoa, then through the Mourdi Depression into Darfur to the Sudanese village of Wahat an Nukhaylah. We will travel northeast from there to Laqiya Arba'in, and then finally to Taqab where our Sudanese friends will pick up you and your cargo, and where I will turn back to the desert."

"And from there?"

"From there you are under the protection of those Sudanese. They are allied to both the military and the paramilitaries. Or, at least, feared by them. From there they have organized a Nile crossing by boat. Perhaps, due to the chaos, they will stay on the west side of the Nile until the bridge at Atbara, and from there a quick seven hours by the main road to Port Sudan. Now I have told you *my* route, and where I can get you. You tell me, George, after Port Sudan where will you journey?"

"From Port Sudan, my trusted friend, the cigarettes will be loaded onto an Egyptian ship sailing north to the Sinai town of Dahab."

"The Egyptians won't mind your presence onboard?"

"Oh they *do* mind. That is why I'm taking a flight to Sharm el-Sheik. I think I'll deserve some relaxation while I wait for the boat. Then I'll head to Dahab where there is already a well-developed network of bribes and threats that enable fast transport by road from Taba to Al-Kuntillah, then to Al Qusaymah, and then finally into the Israeli town of Ezuz in the Negev. Once in Israel, loaded onto an Israeli lorry, the shipments will move at speed to Hebron where some crates are unloaded, and then onto Bethlehem for the rest."

"Will you be going into Israel with the merchandise?"

"Most certainly. Just like in Egypt, I will enter the country from a different route. This time by flying into Tel Aviv. I will then be waiting for the trucks in Hebron and then accompany them to Bethlehem. And when I get there I will finally be in someone's company who looks a lot better than you."

"Possibly, my friend, but I find being around camels improves one's looks, at least comparatively."

"Well said, Mohammed."

"Good looks though…this is no sand-worn face you are referring to; this can only be a woman? After such a journey it will be nice for you to be somewhere safe."

"A woman, yes. But being anywhere near this one is extremely dangerous."

CHAPTER 10

"Remy?"

"Yes?"

"I am Sultan, your driver. Major Rafiq al-Khana sent for me, and said you are headed to the airport. Please step inside my van."

"Certainly," Remy said stepping inside where he encountered another passenger. "Hello, how are you?"

"I am well. My name is Amira."

"It is nice to make your acquaintance."

"May I ask what you are doing here in sunny Palestine?"

"I am a journalism student, conducting my doctoral research."

"And that is?"

"Food. Well…not food, but ingredients. Well…not so much ingredients but the resources. Okay, not resources but, well, understanding where things like fruit and vegetables grow, and how they are brought to the market."

"I see. You are interested in trade then?"

"Yes, that's right."

"Silly boy, why not just say that?"

"A good academic is always confused and confusing."

"Then you must be very good," Amira said with a smile as the van pitched forward into a pothole.

"I thought there would be more passengers. Does the

van usually run so empty, Amira?"

"Few people have VIP status, and so few can use the Tel Aviv airport. And even fewer use these back routes. When is your flight?"

"Not sure. I'll decide when I get there. And where are you headed?"

"I'll be hopping out at Rantis just before the Israeli border to visit with some friends. Sultan will join me after he takes you to the airport."

•

"Marwan," he said, standing in the doorway of the modest home.

"Raffy! It is so nice to see you at my house."

"Can I come in?"

"Of course. What's up my friend? Is everything alright?"

"Colonel Awadallah is dead."

"Your supervisor? The man who I just met?"

"Yes," he said, hanging his head as he struggled to hold back tears.

"What happened?" Marwan asked in a worried tone.

"We were investigating Har Kesem," Raffy whispered.

"Who was?"

"The Customs Police, along with a journalist."

"What happened?" Marwan asked more forcefully.

"As you now know we think there is something peculiar going on up there, so we were trying to learn more. The state of emergency had ended, so we decided to go and take a look. Apparently, we were spotted."

"And they caught Awadallah?"

"He was killed by an army truck as we fled."

"I'm sorry, Raffy."

"It's like they knew we were coming."

"Is that possible? Who else knew about your plan? Who is this journalist? Do I know him? Do you?"

"His name is Remy. He is doing a doctorate in journalism in London. He was sent to us by a director in the Palestinian Authority."

"Why would someone from the Authority send him to the Customs Police?"

"I'm not really sure. Awadallah spoke to the official. When Remy came we were already prepping for the mission. Maybe it was the director who passed on our plans to COGAT?"

"Raffy, this is serious. Are you suggesting collaboration between the Palestinian Authority and the Israeli army?"

"That would surprise nobody."

"Everyone knows there is contact and corruption, certainly. But this is a direct connection that resulted in the death of a colonel!"

"We were ambushed Marwan," Raffy said in anguish.

"Have you spoken to this journalist? Where is he now?"

"We spent the night together, on the run. He seemed genuine. Very shaken by Awadallah's death."

"Shaken from guilt?"

"I know what you mean Marwan. Remember we are both police. I did not sense anything duplicitous, but of course if he was a spy on such a dangerous assignment he would need to be well trained." He paused to rewatch the events in his mind. "No, it was too dangerous, too chaotic...."

"Unless he was tracked so they knew who not to target?"

"It was dark. There were guns. It would have been too risky for a spy."

"Maybe for the Shin Bet, but what about the CIA?" Marwan said as he leaned forward.

"I am not a linguist but now that you mention it, he did use some American slang."

"How would you know any American slang?"

"Because I am a cultured gentleman Marwan. I watch all *The Fast and the Furious* movies."

"Fine. So now we've got a potential CIA agent, posing as a British journalism student, liaising between the Palestinian Authority and the Israeli army, based around something going on in Har Kesem, which has resulted in between one and four deaths."

Raffy counted on his fingers, "Awadallah, your neighbor Ahmad, the settler..., but who is the fourth?"

"An Israeli captain. Fought a general to death on a base that covers the territory that includes Har Kesem."

"Fought to the death?"

"Apparently, in hand-to-hand combat."

"Why are the Israelis always losing their minds?" Raffy asked rhetorically.

"Where is our spy now?"

"He is going to Israel. I sent him."

"You sent the spy back to Israel?" Marwan asked incredulously.

"I sent him to investigate Har Kesem."

"I guess, if we see him again," Marwan shook his head, "we'll know he is what he says he is. Moreover Raffy, if you needed someone who can go into Israel, into the settlement, you could have contacted me. I have questions to ask."

"I am sorry Marwan. I was acting quickly after Awadallah. When I hear from him next I will be sure to contact you immediately."

•

Driving west, Remy, Amira, and Sultan reached a checkpoint. The car rolled to a stop as the guard spoke, "Name?"

"Sultan," the driver answered.

"Is that a first name or a surname?"

"Both."

"Let's see your documents."

"I am driving a VIP."

"Who is that then? I did not receive a notice."

"It is an American. Going to Ben Gurion airport."

"I see. Open your trunk and then be on your way."

•

"Name?"

The van headed east had stopped at a checkpoint.

"Sultan."

"Is that a first name or a surname?"

"Both."

"Let's see your documents."

"I am driving a VIP."

"Who is this VIP?"

"An American. I picked him up from Ben Gurion Airport. His name is George."

"George? Please enjoy the rest of your journey."

•

"My brother Ahmad was not a terrorist. Marwan you must believe me in this."

"Perhaps Sami," Marwan said, taking the cup he was offered, "and thank you for the tea, but we should explore the possibility before we creep deeper into a world of shadows. I asked for help from a good friend, who introduced me to his commanding officer."

"And what did you find out?"

"That water is telling and—"

"And everyone in this region knows water is important. So?"

"Never mind the water." Marwan set down the cup. "The officer is dead."

"Doesn't this indicate something out of the ordinary surrounding the circumstances of my brother's death?"

"Not really. I am a detective; we use fact-based investigations, not conjecture. This is why it is so important that I develop other possibilities, otherwise I would be susceptible to tunnel vision."

"Speaking of which, did you see that news report about the Gaza? Truely awful."

"Sami, I need to know how often Ahmad went to mosque, and with whom?"

"No!" She shook her head at the implication, "This is too much Marwan. Ahmad was a good man."

"How often?" he said, pressing her, "And where?"

•

"It is so nice to see you here Marwan. I can't remember the last time you came for Fajr."

"Yes, Imam Ibrahim. The new muezzin sang so beautifully this morning. How could I resist a predawn prayer?"

"You seem to have resisted quite well for several years now." He chuckled a little as he said it. "And of course, it is not just Fajr, but you've been here for all the prayers—Dhuhr, Asr, Maghrib and now Isha! You went from being lost to us to a man who might sleep with us. You know the mosque is always open to you, and you are indeed welcome to sleep here, but is there anything else I can help you with?"

"I have been thinking about my neighbor Ahmad Naser who—"

"Was killed by the occupiers. I know. His nephew Mehmet has been spending a lot of time with us."

"Does Sami know about that?"

"Why would it concern her?"

"Because she is the parent of Mehmet."

"The Holy One is the parent of us all."

"Yes of course, Imam."

"But enough about Mehmet. Ahmad's murder weighs on us all, as have the many before him. Why, Marwan, why have you finally decided to come to me?"

"I want to know if you knew anything about Ahmad. If there was anything about him that might suggest he would—"

"Attempt something heroic."

"Yes, Imam."

"Are you asking me as a police detective or as a fellow man of the faithful?"

"Neither, or both; I am asking for direction, Imam. I want to know which way to go if I am to follow in his path."

"Are you interested in doing something heroic, Marwan? Are you not satisfied with police authority and the shisha lounges?"

"I am not like that, Imam."

"I know you are good, Marwan."

"I need to know if Ahmad was following his true path when he was killed."

"Come, let's say our evening prayers, and then we'll talk."

●

"Shachar, I am glad to see you. I was surprised to hear from you."

"Has it been that long, Rabbi Avraham?"

"Enough that I was surprised to hear from you. What brings you out to me?"

"I am thinking of making several life changes."

"Yes, I heard things were not so good with you. I stayed in touch with Ephraim and several of the others."

"Ephraim is dead, Avraham," Shachar said, bowing his head.

"I know. Is this why you have come?"

"In part. I needed to come here, and to get away from Tel Aviv."

"I understand."

"Do you, Avraham?"

"Of course. By the way, you are welcome to stay here for as long as you wish."

"It is beautiful here in the West Bank."

"Yes, indeed. I feel the spirits of our ancestors here in the *Shomron*."

"I feel that too."

"Do you, Shachar?"

"Of course. And I would like to stay here. Take walks. Enjoy the freedom, the fresh air."

"Do be careful of our Palestinian squatters. Always go armed. If you do not have a rifle, we have plenty to spare."

"Thank you. Tell me, what are all the lights on those other hills around us?"

"Those over there are residential settlements. Many of their occupants work in the Tel Aviv suburbs. And over there are people more like us. They are here, *to be here*. To settle the land and to live according to the Holy One's plan. There are also industrial settlements."

"Do people live in them?"

"In the industrial settlements?"

"Yes."

"Nobody lives there, though there are always guards. That one there is Har Kesem, where there was a terrorist attack."

"Wasn't the victim supposed to be looking for a house?"

"I guess he was in the wrong place, and very much at the wrong time. But right now it is time for our evening prayers; will you join us for *Maariv*?"

•

In their holy places, on their opposite sides, the two men

prayed.

Marwan finished his formal *Rakats* of the *Salat al Isha* and added a personal prayer, "To the Compassionate, the Merciful God."

Shachar finished his formal *Amidah* of *Maariv* and added a personal prayer, "To the Lord our God, the only God."

And their murmurations continued, in their separate places, from their separate lips.

"Please guide us on the straight path, the path of those who have received your grace."

"Please cast your blessed light on my journey."

"That I may bring peace to the family of the slain."

"That I may bring comfort to those who have been murdered."

"That I might know the truth."

"That I can stop wickedness."

"For the Palestinian people and the Ummah."

"For the Israeli people and the Diaspora."

"Amen."

"Amen."

CHAPTER 11

What struck Remy, upon being dropped off by Sultan at Ben-Gurion airport, was just how hot it was. The airport, located in Israel's coastal plains, was a different world from the hills of Jerusalem and the West Bank. The heat announced itself immediately and prompted Remy to strip off his jacket to prevent soiling it, and so as not to stick out like a sore thumb. The jacket was a thin leather shell with a nylon interior, much better for the cooler evenings in the hills to the east. Remy had taken pains to find a jacket that appeared rugged and yet had a touch of formality. A jacket which would not be too out of place in an office meeting as well as in the fields. Like the good journalist Remy aspired to be, he had a tailor sew in an inner pocket the size of his reporter notepad plus two pens: a primary and a back-up. While only mildly proficient in Arabic and Hebrew, Remy took some comfort in at least knowing the intricacies of shorthand. Responding to the heat, Remy stuffed the jacket into his backpack and looked for the bus.

Remy considered embarking on a series of buses that would take him directly to Har Kesem, however, upon reflection decided to pass through Jerusalem once again to spend time in the Old City. As he had already explored the East Jerusalem bus station outside of Jaffa gate, Remy thought it could be useful to know the West Jerusalem bus station as well. *A pitiful excuse for taking a break from the intensity of this research* Remy reflected as he disembarked. A bus is a bus, a station a station. That is, unless of course one bus has air-conditioning, and the other doesn't.

Upon arrival in Jerusalem, Remy walked the thirty minutes to the New Gate, eyeing but not stopping for fresh orange juice. From the New Gate, and focusing on not missing the important sights this time, Remy explored the darkness of the Church of the Holy Sepulchre and then proceeded to the Western Wall to enjoy the quiet chaos as tourists mingled with the devoted. Remy turned to the right of the wall and joined the queue to reach the Temple Mount to visit the Dome of the Rock and the Al-Aqsa Mosque. At security Remy noticed some settlers pushed their way through the line, tossed their bags over and around the scanners and then set off back down from where they came. Remy decided to file that tidbit away while walking up to the Noble Sanctuary and quickly noticed the peacefulness of the place. It was also immediately obvious that whatever anyone's opinion of the value and ownership of the site was, this particular rock had an incredibly nice dome.

The taste for the Old City satiated, Remy found his lodgings and collapsed into a heavy sleep. In the morning, Remy, now missing the warm air of the coastal plain and not quite wanting to resume the investigation, decided he might check-out another one of Israel's attractions: the Tel Aviv beaches. The weekend was approaching, and Har Kesem would be shut, or at least that is what Remy told himself as he decided to try the train. An hour on the train, including a short delay, he arrived at Tel Aviv's HaHagana Station and walked due west. The path took him into Florentin where hip cafés and bars lined the road. He continued on and reached Jaffa. There was a great looking takeaway near The Clock Tower and some sweets shops walking south. As Remy moved deeper into Jaffa, he realized it was starting to feel just a bit like Jerusalem with its ancient cold stone and tourists of all kinds. *Distinctly not the beach.* Remy turned back and headed north, finally reaching the sand and the sea; but noticing the lack of buildings as he went. It was as if Jaffa and Tel Aviv were magnetized, their poles pushing each other apart. Remy recalled an Israeli film he'd seen at a festival. It was 1973's *Kazablan,* thought to be a silly musical, a type of *Bourekas* film, a puff with melodrama, song, and dance. The film was shown as an example of the genre, but what was most interesting about the movie was that it showed the slums that once existed there. The area was once known as Manshiya, a predominantly Palestinian neighborhood home to Arabic speaking Jews and Muslims. It was a cultural mix that tied people together through poverty and perseverance. The area had been cleared, and with it a bridge that linked Jewish Tel Aviv with Arab Jaffa was forever severed. The city still had not recovered, and the land lay empty, only partially covered over by the grassy expanse that is the Charles Clore Park.

When Remy reached Aviv Beach there began the succession of some of the nicest beaches along the Mediterranean: Aviv Beach with its surfers, Jerusalem Beach with its many *matkot* paddleball games, Frishman Beach filled with beach volleyball courts and the Calypso café, and the umbrella clad Gordon Beach with its saltwater sea pool. Remy relaxed on one and then another. He walked into the city, ate, then returned to enjoy the day. Dizzy from sunshine and happiness, Remy flowed into the Carmel Market. Everything was being bought and sold: fresh fruits and rotting vegetables, baked goods, fresh meat, mounds of spices, knockoff clothing, pirated music and movies, and tourist trinkets of all shapes, sizes, and prices. Aimlessly walking, Remy sleepily remembered Professor Roy Vandermere and his wife Gloria back in rainy London. *Taking trips is much more fun than funding them*, Remy mused. A sense of guilt washed over him as he recalled Roy's support of his research and the importance of the time he was wasting being nowhere near some of the most interesting tips a journalist could imagine. Remy vowed to get back to work, tomorrow, but, in the meantime, he would buy Roy and Gloria a little bauble: perhaps a keychain they would never use. A small stall beckoned, run by what looked like a father and son. Remy approached and began to look through the merchandise. He frowned as he noted that each item was more chipped and bent than the next. Soon the father leaned over and remarked, "Are you going to buy anything?"

"Yes, of course, I am searching for one in good condition. It is a gift for—"

"You're accusing me of selling junk?"

The father grabbed a handful of trinkets and hurled them at Remy. A piece of sharp metal opened a small cut on Remy's hand.

"What the fuck?"

"Did you say *fuck* to me? *Fuck you!*" The father rushed around from behind the counter and ran up to Remy, and without delay, smashed his head into him—luckily aiming too high to break a nose—and followed that with wild windmill strikes.

Remy came to life seeing, and feeling, the danger. His quick wrists caught the father's on each swing, pushing the arms away while retreating down the lane. Remy continued to catch and release the father's attempted strikes. In a flash Remy noticed the son, a truly muscled figure, running forward with his fist held high. The son leaped up and Remy began to move away, ignoring the father who was finally was able to get his chance to slap and scratch at Remy's face. Just as the son was about to lower his fist and hammer Remy into the ground, a man stepped in front, faced Remy, and received a massive blow to the back. His eyes said, "Go!" and Remy nodded with his, running from the scene as the mysterious hero fell beneath the scrum.

Remy fled the area, now feeling even worse. His head ached, and his face was covered in small bloody scratches as if he had been assaulted not by a trinket dealer but an angry cat. *Did that just happen? Is Tel Aviv a place of purgatory vacillating between visions of heaven and hell? Might as well be in Jerusalem*, Remy thought. He found himself on Allenby Street and continued south until he reached Rothschild Boulevard. A street with a lovely garden down the middle, a street any Parisian would appreciate. A beautiful stretch of avenue on which to stroll and try to calm down.

Remy found himself surrounded by white apartment buildings and recalled the architectural style as Bauhaus, a modernist take on the architectural styling of the Arts and Crafts movement. In this neighborhood built in the 1930s, while waiting at a light to cross Remy saw two cute little dogs on the other side of the street. The woman walking them wore a towering hat made from ostrich and peacock feathers that stretched to the cloudless sky. Amused that the hat could still be considered fashionable, Remy's heart rate slowed and his muscles began to relax. At that moment a van took the corner between Remy and the hat lady, but made the turn too tightly, and Remy heard a scream as it jumped the curb just enough to run over one of the dogs. The other dog panicked and raced off down the road. Remy moved swiftly and launched himself toward the loose puppy. The dog danced across traffic and ran down the road. Remy frogged his way across the street and sprinted after the poor pup. The dog went another block then turned into an open doorway and headed up the steps. Remy reached the entry and slowed down, gasping for air and hoping there was no other way out. He climbed the steps to find the dog cowering in fear. Remy bent down, put his hand out, and moved slowly to the dog. The dog smelled Remy's hand and allowed itself to be lifted. The dog trembled as Remy held it to his chest, went down the stairs, and walked back to the woman. A crowd had gathered around the woman and her dying dog. Someone asked Remy if the dog belonged to the woman, and when he nodded yes, he was pushed forward, but before he reached the woman the petrified dog was ripped from his grasp and quickly given to the woman who clutched it as she cried , profusely thanking the man she assumed had caught her runaway dog. *Tel Aviv*, Remy thought, *made no sense, which is probably why there are stories to tell here.* Remy realized Tel Aviv needed its own investigation, but decided he was not the journalist for the job, and continued walking quickly toward the train, finding HaShalom Station and an eastbound train for Jerusalem.

Back in Jerusalem, Remy breathed in the cool evening air. There was a scent of settling dust that pleased him and a crispness that made Remy cuddle himself into his jacket. Tomorrow he would board the bus for Har Kesem.

CHAPTER 12

General Cohen sighed as he sat back in his office chair: a chair that was missing a wheel but was propped up by a book. The vaunted Israeli army was, at least in the arena of office furnishings, severely lacking. General Cohen looked at the latest reports. Hebron was peaceful. Bethlehem had protests again on the other side of Rachel's Tomb. A hose of wastewater had scattered their cocktail party. The stranglehold on the north remained in place, though it was relaxed to allow a trickle of traffic between Ramallah and Nablus. Route 60, the Patriarchs Way, *that was a fun one to dominate* General Cohen relished. The Rand Corporation had imagined an arc of development for a new Palestinian state radiating from this ancient highway, but in the meantime the only thing that radiated from it was Israeli hard power. Just then the general had a thought, *If the Palestinian Authority was so interested in Har Kesem that they would send their Customs Police to check it out, then maybe they were responsible for the murder of that poor Yossi character after all. Or perhaps*, he thought, as he reached for a mug of three-day old coffee, *there was something going on in Har Kesem that was worth knowing.*

•

Shachar rose with the sun, stepped outside of the caravan, and drank in the landscape. Samaria, the northern West Bank, did have a special feeling separate from the hectic dust of Jerusalem, the dilapidated grime of Hebron, and the dry scrubland of the Judean Wilderness. The settlement was on a hill looking down at the Palestinian farms below. Deep shades of green were interspersed by villages and patches of red and purple flowers. Har Kesem loomed longingly across a valley covered in knots of olive trees, though some of them had been burned or dug out. In his early days in the army Shachar had seen the removal of trees, and knew where some of them had ended up: universities, museum grounds, to the highest bidder or the most connected, but now he felt a pang of loss when looking at the parts of the valley that had been cleared for profit, fear, or firing lines. *It was time for morning prayers*, he thought, and then there would be a brisk walk to Har Kesem before the heat of the day.

•

Remy left before dawn as he was so eager to get back underway. The first bus dropped him at a station with fifteen minutes before the departure of the next bus. Remy walked swiftly to the bathroom for a quick decant of the previous night's tea and the morning's coffee when he heard the final call for the bus. He raced out only to find the bus pulling away. Remy saw the bus took a roundabout path out of the lot, and so he cut across the barriers to breathlessly stand in front of the bus. The driver seemed to consider running him over but then, with a shrug, stopped, and let Remy board.

Eventually the bus reached the bottom of Har Kesem, and Remy hopped off. The bus was mostly empty. Nobody else disembarked. Remy noticed a man walking up from the valley. His path would take him right past Remy and up to Har Kesem. Remy considered which was preferable: walking ahead of the man to reach the entry first, hanging back and following him to the gate, or attempting to befriend the lonely stranger. Remy decided to try to make a friend, especially considering he had just as much an idea of what was in Har Kesem as he did the gentleman's name. At least he could find out the latter.

"Good morning," Remy began.

"Good morning," Shachar replied. Shachar had briefly thought about pushing past this strange figure that had leapt off the bus. He had not expected anyone to disembark, or he might have jogged to ensure he was clear of any passengers. *How unexpected. How peculiar.* Shachar considered slowing his steps and dropping behind the new arrival, but it would be frustrating to follow this new man up the hill to Har Kesem. Shachar realized it might not be such a bad idea to arrive at the gate with a new friend. *Perhaps this guy knew the guards, so rather than needing to talk my way in I could be invited.* A cheery prospect.

As Shachar approached he noticed the man in front of him was about the same age as he was, possibly a touch younger, though the person in question was not Israeli nor Palestinian. His jacket could have passed as Palestinian, but the shoes were more practical than fashionable. With a lack of sunglasses, he was most certainly not Israeli. The satchel suggested Europe. But what made it most obvious was the sun addled skin. Hopefully he was one of those diaspora Jews who were so fond of moving to the settlements to reclaim their so-called birthright. They were simple enough to manipulate.

Shachar had long adopted the opinion that Jews needed somewhere to go, and Israel, or Palestine as it were, simply provided that opportunity. In school Shachar had been fascinated by some of the other options that had been put forth to be a homeland for European Jewry. Birobidzhan in the Soviet far east, Uganda in eastern Africa, and the

Jewish cowboys, *gauchos*, of the Argentine plains. But of course, it was the land between the river and the sea that was practical and desirable due to its proximate location and undeniable cultural affiliations.

"Are you headed to Har Kesem?" Shachar probed.

"Yes, and yourself?" Remy answered.

"Yes. My name is Shachar."

"Remy."

"If you don't mind I'd be glad to walk with you up this unfortunately steep hill."

"It would be my pleasure."

"So, Remy, from where are you coming?"

"I've just arrived here from Jerusalem."

"Yes, but before that?"

"London, where I've been studying."

"And before that?"

"What do you mean?"

"You don't have a London accent."

"There are many accents in London."

"Of course, but you don't have any of them."

"I see…I'm American."

"From the states?"

"Yes. Well from Washington, DC."

"I once went to Florida with my family."

"That's nice."

"Yes, we went to Disney World and then visited friends in Miami."

"Miami is nice."

"You've been?! Maybe you know our family friends, Sheila and Michael Moritz?"

"I don't think so. There are a lot of people in Miami."

"I suppose there are. Tell me, what brings you to Har Kesem?"

"I'm a doctoral student researching trade. I was told that this was a productive industrial settlement. Now let me ask, where are you coming from?"

"I've walked from just over there; can you see the settlement on the hill across the valley."

"For sure, but where did you grow up?"

"What do you mean?"

"That settlement is about as old as you are, if not younger. And you don't exactly look like a settler, which is odd considering the political stance of most of the settlements around here. So, it is reasonable that I ask why you are headed to Har Kesem."

"I am staying with some friends in the settlement over there, and they recommend it as a good place to set up a new business."

"What type of business would that be?"

"Logistics."

"Is that so? We are after similar information then."

"So it seems, Remy."

"Do you know anyone in Har Kesem?"

"No, but as I say it was recommended by a friend."

"Who is that?"

"The rabbi who lives over there. And what about yourself?"

"I was told to come by some fruit merchants in Jerusalem I happened to interview."

"You know, it's funny that you people from The States like to say you're American, because when I visited Brazil and Argentina I thought I was in America."

"Oh," Remy laughed, "South America. Yes, that's a place too, and located in the Americas, but by America I am talking about the USA. Where else have you traveled Shachar?"

"Many places, some near, and others far."

"What were some of your favorites?"

"I visited Thailand, as many Israelis do, but I particularly liked Brazil, Italy, and South Africa."

"Is that so? I especially enjoyed visiting those countries as well. I also liked Turkey; have you been?"

"No, no I haven't. Here is the guardhouse. Would you like to lead?"

"I'd be glad for you to give it a try. After-all the guard might not speak English."

"Maybe not Hebrew either." Shachar frowned. "Might be a ruffian."

"I think I've seen the type in the Carmel Market."

"You've been to Tel Aviv as well? You are quite industrious."

"Hardly. I was at the beach mostly."

"And that is a problem why?"

"Shachar, is the gate usually open at industrial settlements?"

"No. And there is no guard either."

"Should we wait for one?"

"Are you crazy? We might wait until they finally make peace."

"And the pigs are flying."

"I don't know anything about pigs."

"Never mind, Shachar. Let's go in."

"The layout looks normal enough. Several tin-roofed warehouses. All grounds paved and ready for cars and trucks. Lots of trash."

"Not trash so much as packing boxes. Here, this Hebrew, what does it say?"

"Donny Lesley, that's an Israeli grocery store that operates a lot of branches in the West Bank. Palestinians and Israelis both shop shoulder to shoulder. Isn't that nice?"

"Marvelous. Maybe Donny Lesley should be leading the peace negotiations to success before pigs fly."

"Again with the pigs. Here is a box in Arabic. What does it say, Remy?"

"*Al Minquar.*"

"Which means?"

"The Beak."

"Which means?"

"I don't know, but when I get back to Ramallah I'll get it checked out."

"Ramallah? I thought you said Jerusalem?"

"Yes, well you asked from where I came, and I had taken the bus from Jerusalem."

"Then why Ramallah?"

"Because I was tipped off by the Customs Police to check this place out. Why are you *really* here? You aren't in business."

"I'm investigating a murder, for the family."

"What murder?"

"The terrorist attack. Yossi Seigler was killed. And so was the terrorist."

"That was here?"

"How did you not know?"

"Because I am researching food logistics for my doctoral dissertation. I'm not investigating homicide."

"Is your mind trapped in an ivory tower? Take your nose out of the book and look around. This is a crime scene."

"Okay fine, but what next?"

"You're the journalist. Who should we question? Where else should we look?"

"We?"

"Why not? I know about murder, and you know about investigations."

"Research. I know about research."

"Great. Then we are agreed. I'll help the bereaved, and you'll help your career."

"Hey that's not fair. I'm willing to help, but that does put my career, and my life, on the line. And what did you mean by, you 'know about murder?'"

"Be cool, Remy."

"I'm the definition of cool."

"Then you don't need to know."

"Shachar, if you think I am going to partner up with someone who discusses murder like the weather—"

"Remy, in this country everyone is a solider, and when you are a solider, murder is your business."

"Murder?"

"Label it however you wish. It is a violent death. I know something you don't, that you might need to know if you are going to solve this case."

"Is there a case to be solved?"

"You tell me. We both ended up here. If it is the Customs Police then you are here for smuggling. I am here because people were killed. There are packing boxes from the leading settlement grocery, something about a chicken—"

"Not a chicken, I said 'The Beak.'"

"Yes, whatever. And there are no guards. No gate. No security."

"Even after all that just happened."

"Exactly."

"Okay, let's say I ask the Customs Police about The Beak. What are you going to do?"

"I'll look into security, or the lack thereof. I can ask the neighboring settlement. They must know something since a terrorist attack just happened. Forget about settlement security—where is the military?"

"Fine. And perhaps we should go before we are found. What's your phone number?"

"Use this dummy phone. I'll call you on it."

"Does everyone travel with extra dummy phones?"

"Like I said, we are all soldiers here. I'm going to walk back over. I don't need security to ask me any questions either."

"Guess I'll be catching the bus back to Jerusalem."

"To Ramallah via Jerusalem, to be precise."

CHAPTER 13

Remy began to tire waiting in the increasingly hot sun. The bus stop provided no shade, and he began to understand why so many Israelis hitch-hiked. On the other side of the road two Palestinian teens reached the road. Remy supposed they had been on an unmarked path, possibly from one of the villages in the valley below the settlements. The youths donned *kippot*, nicely crocheted skullcaps, blue with flecks of white. They would not be out of place in a settlement. A few minutes went by and an Israeli car with its yellow license plates stopped when hailed by the Palestinian youths. The drivers, unaware that they were giving rides to Palestinians, drove off toward another village down the road. *This land*, Remy reflected, *is full of idiosyncrasies. And the most pertinent at this moment*, Remy grimaced, *is that the bus isn't running on schedule.*

•

"Need a taxi?"

"Sultan! It's such a coincidence to see you on my way back."

"Remy, wasn't it? I'm returning to the West Bank after dropping off a client. Would you like a ride?"

"I'd love a ride."

"For you, no charge. After all it is on my way and nice to have the company."

"That's too nice. I can at least cover petrol. How is Amira by the way?"

"You can ask her. She is in the van. Get in."

"Hi Amira."

"How was your trip Remy?"

"It was informative, I guess. Where are you headed?"

"I am meeting with a governor."

"Which governor?"

"The Governor of Nablus."

"Is he coming to Ramallah?"

"No. He is in Nablus. At his office. You will meet him."

"Yes, I'd be glad to, though right now I am headed to Ramallah to meet up with some colleagues."

"I think you should meet him now. The ride is under an hour even on these roads."

"I really should get to Ramallah; my friend will be worried. I can visit Nablus soon."

"It's really not an offer Remy, it is more like an order."

"An order? From whom?"

"The governor. To be enforced by Sultan and myself."

"Enforced? Have I done something wrong? If I have offend anyone—"

"Don't make me use this knife 'Remy, the journalism student.' Sultan, let's go."

•

A series of concrete office buildings surrounded by high concrete walls hosted the Mukataa of Nablus. Rumors of torture facilities in the basement held Remy's attention, and he let out a deep breath of relief when he was led up the steps to the office of the Governor of Nablus.

"Remy. I invited you here to warn you. Your friends at the Customs Police are not what they seem. They are one of the most corrupt branches of our governmental apparatus."

"Your invitation included a death threat, which is hardly a way to deliver a warning, though I thank you nonetheless."

"Who threatened you?"

"Amira."

"Ah. She did not mean it."

"She brandished a knife."

"All for show. You see, I asked her to bring you here for a chat. We wouldn't have been able to have much of a chat had you been stabbed."

"I suppose that is true." Remy considered it.

"Certainly, it is true! I asked her to bring you here, and she delivered. She always delivers, so she said whatever she needed to say to get you to me. Anyway, that's all over now, and here you are, safe and sound."

"And in Nablus. So, tell me. Why am I here discussing the Customs Police, who are in Ramallah, while I am in Nablus?"

"This is my office. Simple as that."

"Is it?"

"It is."

"Then how is it that Sultan knew where to find me?"

"The Customs Police told him where you were going."

"Why would they do that?"

"Because one of them works for me. Remember, I told you they are corrupt."

"How would they know when to pick me up?"

"We followed you and then checked the bus schedule. There aren't that many at this time. We tracked the bus. Found that it was thirty minutes late, so picked you up fifteen minutes into your wait. It was not very difficult."

"You've given me your warning. May I go now?"

"Almost. Don't you want to know why I am giving you this warning?"

"Not really," Remy said sourly.

"But you will listen."

"I don't have a choice."

"You are embarking on a dangerous path going to the settlements. Some people here might think you are a spy working with the Israelis. If you would like, I can arrange for tours of markets and farms. That would make a good story. *And be far safer.*"

"I appreciate your offer, your interest in my research, and your concern for my well-being," Remy said, resigned to following the governor's advice, at least for the moment.

"Good, then I will make the necessary calls."

•

Remy walked outside and shielded his eyes from the sun as a dozen guards looked on. Sultan waited in his van to drive Remy to his new appointment: ostensibly to a farm outside of Salfit that grew flowers. It sounded dreamy after the constant threats of violence. And while Remy decided to acquiesce to the governor's offer, he was even more intrigued by whatever was happening in regard to Har Kesem.

The large metal gate began to open, grinding to the left. At two stories tall the immense door squealed on its metal teeth. The heavily armed guards shifted into a new formation. The whole scene seemed unnecessary, and served only to highlight the enduring power of the governor. Another group, paramilitaries perhaps, lingered outside the walls with their backs against the big doors, their eyes fixed forward looking carefully ahead at the passing traffic.

Remy strolled over toward Sultan's van, which waited on the sidewalk on the opposite side of the gate. Sultan waved at Remy, motioning him into the open door. A twinkle attracted Sultan's attention. Remy turned to follow Sultan's eyes just in time to notice a truck approaching. The truck stopped at the gate for inspection. Remy boarded the van, and Sultan pushed off.

"Apologies, Remy, that I did not pick you up nearer to the gate. Those paramilitaries frighten me."

"Is Amira here?"

"No, or else I would not have admitted my fears to you."

"Understood."

"Another delay, apologies Remy. First I could not come closer, and now a checkpoint."

"Israeli? Here in Nablus?"

"No, Palestinian Authority thugs."

Sultan slowed the car and lowered his window. There was a movement in the bush nearby. The officer merely waved them on as a cat bolted from the bush and skidded to a stop underneath a dumpster.

"Sorry, Remy, the traffic here is a nightmare."

"Just glad to get through checkpoints. Doesn't matter who controls them."

"A fair point. What is slowing us now? School children? What are they doing here?"

"Looks like they are out for a walk."

"And getting in our way. Good, they are across, and we are away—what is this guy doing? Parking?"

"The emergency flashers are on, but I can't see anything around. Hope they are okay."

"Yes, yes look, two of them have just gotten out and are waving us past," Remy said just as a pickup truck crashed into the back of Sultan's van which sent it careening into the vehicle in front. A machine gun sounded; a tire blew out. Someone grabbed Remy's hair. The man, Remy noticed, wore a balaclava. *Odd to wear that in this heat,* thought a stunned Remy. At the same moment another van screeched to a stop. Remy was pulled from Sultan's vehicle and tossed inside the van. As they raced away, and just before the bag was placed over his head, Remy caught a glimpse of Sultan's bloody arm hanging limply outside what had been his shiny black taxi.

CHAPTER 14

Remy stumbled as he was pulled out of the van: tripping on pavement, brushing against a door, feeling cool musky air. The interior of the van had been stifling hot, and the hood over his head made the heat unbearable. Remy was pulled forward, into a building, through hallways, and up steps. A metal chair scraped across the floor and Remy was made to sit. The chair was cool to the touch and Remy took comfort in that rather than imagining what was to come. Footsteps, hushed tones, and an angry whisper he could not understand. The hood was pulled off and Remy found he was sitting at a metal table. At the opposite side of the table a leaned a bearded man who sat with his head tilted slightly to the side. Remy waited until the man spoke.

"Why have you come to Palestine; why have you come to Nablus, to my city?"

"I'm here as a student."

"Of what kind?"

"Doctoral."

"In what subject?"

"Journalism."

"I see. And what is it that you intend to report?"

"I'm interested in the logistics of food: how it goes from one place to another, where it is grown, and how it is transported to the consumer."

"Then what were you doing in the governor's office?"

"The governor invited me—"

"You should know about the governor. He is one of the more corrupt officials in the Palestinian authority."

"That's funny because he brought me to his office to warn me about the corruption of others."

"It's true we have more corruption here than we would like. But everywhere has corruption in some way or another, and only God knows how much. Perhaps we Palestinians are just worse at hiding it from the eyes of the world. Do you know we are at the mercy of others economically?"

"Yes, I read a bit about it before I arrived in the region. International donors pay the majority of the costs of the Palestinian Authority salaries, and give huge subsidies for certain preferred companies. The key question there is who is preferred, and how."

"Very good. Then you'll know that Ramallah is a den of thieves. Ramallah grows through the stripping of the other great cities: Nablus, Jerusalem, and Hebron, which have been severely weakened by the growth of an internationally funded Ramallah."

"Is this why I've been taken, and taken again? To teach me about an authentic Palestinian city?"

"I do not know why you were brought to Nablus. You claim it was at the behest of the governor."

"I know who brought me to this city. But I don't know why I'm in this room."

"Some of my men thought you were in danger, that you were boarding a van that was to take you to your death. The governor is no friend of ours."

"I noticed."

"Yes, well, an enemy of his may well be a friend to us."

"And who is this 'us' that you're referring to?"

"A group of concerned citizens. We care about education, healthcare, and growth of the local economy. We stand for moral and ethical values."

"Given my rough treatment and the treatment received by the governor's men, I wonder how ethical your values could be."

"Alas, these are difficult times. You see there are two main political parties amongst the Palestinians. The governor, the president, and other governmental officials are all Fatah—"

"And would that make you Hamas?"

"Why would you say that? Why do you think I am Hamas? Because I have a beard? Not all bearded men are members of Hamas. It is discriminatory."

"Are you a member of Hamas?"

"Yes, but not because I wear a beard. Look at my men here, do they look like they dress in devout clothing? No, they look like everyone else."

"But they all have beards."

"Nevertheless, we want what's best for the people of Nablus and of Palestine! And this led to great difficulty with the Palestinian Authority and their Israeli and American allies."

"Other than explaining to me the intricacies of Palestinian politics perhaps you could explain to me why I am still here."

"As I said, we rescued you."

"Is it possible that I was simply being taken to a farm to conduct my research on agricultural goods?"

"Many things are possible. But our intelligence saw enough of a threat that we decided to take the admittedly drastic steps of bringing you here."

"Okay, so what now? Are you going to drive me to the airport?"

"The opposite: we would like to invite you to come to my family's picnic after Friday mosque."

"Your what?"

"Picnic. It is when you eat outside. Don't worry it won't be raining. You see, after mosque we stop for sweets. Have you ever tried our local delicacy, *knafeh*? It is made from warmed cheese with a crunchy shredded semolina on top then covered in a sweet syrup. We are renowned for our *knafeh*."

"No but—"

"You will love it! We will go eat a hot plate of *knafeh*, purchase some sweets for the family, and then go meet them in the fields where we will have lunch and relax under our olive groves, taking tea while leaning against my family's ancient trees. I am Anan, by the way."

"That's a nice offer. And it sure beats the room you've got me in now, but what happens if I decline?"

"In Islam there is no declining, only submitting."

•

George stretched after the long drive. *When did I start getting stiffness in my knees and shoulders?* George wondered. *Is this what it feels like to get old, to think about retiring?* He savored the coolness of the glass, the ice in the water, watching it slowly melt away, losing its strength, its definition. The condensation wetted George's hand giving him a slight shiver. When Ronit walked onto the covered porch he rose to greet her and wiped his palms on his still dusty trousers. "Ronit it's lovely to see you, how long has it been?"

"George, my prince, it has been too long. Yet you are looking very lean and tan. How did you find the desert?"

"Divine, though I'm not sure I'll ever wish it was hot again. I think I might move to Alaska."

"George, you're too much; I know you can take the heat."

"We are not what we were, when we were in our animal primes."

"Speak for yourself, George; my hunger is boundless."

"This I know Ronit."

"Business, George. Let's talk about it before we move on to more personal matters."

"The route through the desert is full of peril, but at the same time the guys knew where to go. Without them, it would be impossible. But with a mix of clan diplomacy, bribery, threats, and tradition…products should keep moving. Desert tribes know which caravans not to fuck with."

"So, this is a long-term relationship, George?"

"There's interest on our side. We think this represents a good long-term opportunity. Between your contacts and mine we can build a road straight into the heart of Europe."

"A road paved with diamonds."

"And cocaine."

"I love how you Americans just come out and say it. It feels good to be bad does it not George?"

"I am merely a servant of my country, Ronit. Between you and me, I'm having a great time. But now it's your turn tell me about your preparations."

"They are running smoothly. I'm sure you got a glimpse of the facilities in Hebron on your way here to Bethlehem."

"I did not receive a formal tour."

"It is a simple operation there. Almost brutish, like the people there. Not like what we're doing here with master craftsmen."

"Okay so tell me how it works in Hebron."

"It's quite simple. A huge percentage of the Palestinian economy is based around stone: marble and granite of many hues. These Holy Land stones are destined to be used in churches, mosques, and synagogues around the world. Domestically, it is used for religious buildings but also facing on houses and apartment buildings; the Israelis love to use it to build their governmental buildings, universities, and even some of their military installations."

"Truly?"

"Yes. The Israelis take the stones to build their buildings, and rip out trees to decorate their courtyards. Their growth is fueled the expropriation of Palestinian resources."

"Which you are too happy to facilitate."

"Of course, George; I don't mind who is doing the destruction as, unlike some of your agency friends, I care little for nation building."

"The agency is a diverse workplace with many over-lapping and conflicting strategies and goals. Tell me more about Hebron."

"As I was saying before I interrupted myself, due to such large flows of stone into Israel and to the ports, the shipments of stone get waived through the checkpoints, border control stations, and right past customs officials. We've developed a method of removing stone from inside the blocks to create hollow pockets in which we can tightly pack the powder from South America that you so kindly escorted."

"And then from the Israeli port we can ship anywhere."

"Correct. There is a special trading relationship between Israel and Europe. Through the international marble markets the possibilities are endless."

"Where are you thinking Ronit?"

"Greece, Italy, and Turkey have large marble exchanges. It is easy to make connections there. Sending anything from Greece to Cyprus is automatic, just like sending anything from Russia or Turkey to Cyprus is; and so, we have a path to Russia and Turkey through Greece and Cyprus. Or even just directly to Cyprus."

"Then Italy places our products in the middle of Europe."

"And the marble market in Turkey allows for distribution networks to a whole host of other countries that would otherwise be less accessible, including Iraq, Iran, Bulgaria, Russia, and lands further south and east."

"You seem to have dreams of running a global enterprise

Ronit. Truly the Holy Land is at the center of the world."

"That is only for starters, George. We are also developing Lebanese contacts. Soon we will also be diversifying the products we can distribute. Have you heard: heroin is quite profitable. Would you like to see that operation as well? We could always use your insight, financing and muscle, at least the appearance of muscle."

"Let me check with my people. I'll get back to you. In the meantime, tell me about your plans for the diamonds."

CHAPTER 15

"Captain Levy, execute Operation Rachel's Dream."

"General Cohen, order to execute confirmed, Operation Rachel's Dream launching now."

The soldiers peered around the wall. The mission was a quick strike to capture a wanted criminal. The target was in a warehouse in Bethlehem. Israeli commandos were tasked with entering the Palestinian-administered city through a door in a massive concrete wall located next to Israeli-administered Rachel's Tomb. The gate separated devout Jews from everyday Palestinians, and was often the site of protestors on both sides. The main guard tower suffered bricks and Molotov cocktails while returning the barrages with raw sewage. As the door opened Captain Levy wrinkled his nose, hoping that there had not been a recent protest.

The group moved quickly down the street. It was dark and the streetlights had been disconnected. They often were so that the Palestinians never knew if an operation was being conducted or if there was a simple electrical fault. Having cut his teeth in an engineering unit, Captain Levy was fully aware of the sophistication of the electrical system and, as such, the low possibility of so many outages happening in Palestinian areas. Of course the electrical networks were entirely the same. *Did nobody realize it made no sense to have outages only in a few select locations?* Captain Levy shook his head. And it sure made the Palestinian Authority look incompetent; not that they needed much help....

"Captain Levy, sir, we've reached Phase Alef."

"Thank you, Lieutenant Uriel. I can see that. Check positions."

"All in position. On your command captain."

"Go, go, go."

The explosive blew the door off the warehouse. The commandos filed in. Pistol shot was returned while the commandos took cover. The team moved forward only to find casings from a Desert Eagle .50, casings from a 9mm P229, as well as splinters, pebbles and the body of Lieutenant Uriel, shot through the helmet by a .50 round.

"General Cohen, sir, the primary target escaped."

"Inexcusable, Captain Levy."

"I will need a new lieutenant."

"That, at least, is some good news. Uriel was too close with my previous captain. We must keep our ranks close."

"Yes, sir."

•

"Ronit, what the fuck was that?"

"Commandos."

"Yes, I figured as much. What were they doing shooting at us?"

"I think they wanted to kill us, well me at least."

"And why would they do that?"

"This I will have to look into. Someone may have gotten a sniff and wanted more. Or perhaps our military has developed a level of ethics we never thought possible."

"Sarcasm is only fun when we are not being shot at."

"It was them who were being shot at. I took out an officer. What did you do?"

"Laid down covering fire because I had no idea what was going on."

"*Typical.* I'll handle it all then. Go back to the apartment and shower off. You smell as if a dead camel ate a rotting fish."

"What are you going to handle?"

"I am going to find out who ordered that raid, why they did it, and then make sure they never get the chance to do it again."

•

"Shachar, how was your walk?"

"Very nice, thank you, Rabbi."

"These hills are truly blessed. God's gift to the world, and the descendants of the Israelites most particularly. What route did you take?"

"I walked down through the valley and up toward Har Kesem. It was not very busy there; in fact, it was empty. Is it still in use?"

"Yes, but not frequently. But even still it is valuable to the settler community. We call it Magic Mountain because it turns products that are Palestinian into Israeli. The Palestinian goods come in, and *poof!* out comes an Israeli product."

"Is that a common practice?"

"Certainly, settlements derive a good portion of their income from re-packaging. Our self-reported industrial output far exceeds the relatively meager resources that we have in our settlements. In time, when we push out the squatters, we will be able to harvest the fruits of the land ourselves. But, until that time…."

"I do see why Palestinians wouldn't want to leave such a landscape."

"Shachar, you'll never make it home before Friday night. You'll have to stay with us for Shabbat. Sarah is cooking us a feast and a number of the schoolboys will be joining us as well. Should be raucous with some song and drink, activities with which I know you are familiar."

"Not so much recently, Avraham."

"When you drink for the Shabbat it can never be a bad thing. Yet if you find yourself fatigued from your long walk and want to turn-in with the women after the meal that's okay. In the morning, after prayers, you'll join us for our Shabbat walk. It will give you another opportunity to appreciate the landscape."

After the evening prayers Shachar joined the group, enjoying Sarah's soup, salads, roasted chicken, and the cake that followed. Shachar stuck with the wine, avoiding the free flow of liquor, but sang through the night nonetheless, and, just as the evening prayers were said under the stars, morning prayers were said against a brilliant blue sky. It was a fine day for a stroll.

•

The doors to the mosque were flung open as the faithful begin to stream out after their Friday prayers. Remy waited on the steps and spotted Anan, who was speaking with the Imam. Anan saw Remy and bid the Imam farewell so as to join his new friend. "Remy, I found what the Imam said very interesting, provocative even, but there will be time to discuss it later. Let's get to the *knafeh* shop before the queue grows and the supply shrinks."

Anan and Remy turned right, and then right again stopping in front of Al Aqsa Sweets, a small *knafeh* shop set into ancient stones. The place was crammed with people coming from the mosque.

"Remy take these two plates; I'll take the other two."

"Are more people joining us?"

"No, but when you taste this you'll want another. Eat them quickly before the cheese begins to cool."

Just like the other diners they ate quickly, felt satisfied, ate more anyway, and went on their way.

"Come, Remy, let's walk through the old market together. On the other side is a wonderful chocolate shop. We can go there, and get some for the family, then we can drive out to meet everyone under the trees."

The two men walked through the market, noting the goods and nodding at the proprietors. They then stopped at the chocolate shop, and bought a few extras for the ride out of town. The car had been parked near the chocolate shop, so, after they'd finished shopping, they got in and sped away.

"The Imam connected purity of the soul with the purity of the land, what do you think he meant Remy?"

"Maybe he has found environmentalism?"

"I'm not sure if we have that luxury. Living under occupation brings many environmental hazards."

"What do you mean?"

"Israelis use wastewater against protesters, but they also expel pollutants from their hilltop settlements into our agricultural valleys."

"The West Bank seems so verdant. Are they doing this everywhere?"

"Everything the Israelis do is highly selective. They buy many goods from Palestinians: agricultural products such as eggs, dairy, grapes, strawberries, tomatoes, cucumbers, and potatoes, but also industrial products such as plastic toilets for their loos, water tanks for their roof, straws for their drinks, metal wire and, well, the list goes on. They don't always have enough of their own, so they must buy from us. They buy the best and leave the rest."

"I noticed that in the Ramallah market the quality was much lower than in grocery stores there, while the same is not true in Israel where the markets burst with freshness."

"They buy and buy, except when Israeli farmers can compete: that's when they move in to destroy Palestinian production."

"Do you have an example, or are we to speak only in generalities?"

"On this drive we will pass through farmland on our way to the olive groves. Although most of this land has not been spoiled, you will be able to see where the runoff from settlements has damaged the environment."

"How will I know?"

"The land goes from green to brown, from vibrancy to death. What we will see is small scale; as we drive I will tell you about one of the most famous fruits, the story of the Jenin melon."

"Are you from Jenin?"

"No, but I am a chemist, and so like you I conducted a detailed investigation for my doctorate. At the time, the Jenin melons were disappearing, and I decided to research why."

"I love melons. Particularly from North Carolina. The ones from Spain are a bit different, maybe too sweet. Never mind. Jenin melons, I'm listening."

"Everyone savors a delicious memory of the melons. But my question about why it was declining was answered with a range of explanations. I remember one person described them as 'tasting like smooth sugar.' I spent time with a water scientist who tried to prove, scientifically, that the Jenin melons were the finest. I also spoke to a professor that was conducting a survey to find that Palestinians preferred the taste of the Jenin melon irrespective of their origin, which he claimed dismissed the notion that the decline was due to preference.

"One theory was the lack of water, or at least a decline in quality. I found that, at the time, Jenin had plenty of water, but much of it was drawn by nearby Israeli towns of the Marj Ibn Amir, which some people call the Valley of Megiddo or the Jezreel Valley. Water is also taken by Bisan, which the Israelis now call Beit She'an. The wells in Jenin were blocked for Palestinian use by stones and concrete which led to an artificial water shortage. It was reasoned that since water became scarcer, the price of water in Jenin and nearby the Israeli towns became different to the point of giving one side an overwhelming advantage.

"This was confirmed by a hydrological study that found that in the Jenin region 720 million cubic meters of water were produced each year, of which Israel took 600 million cubic meters. Israel then was selling 120 million cubic meters of water back to the farmers in Jenin! Unlike settlers, Palestinians in Jenin, like the rest of the West Bank, are not permitted to dig wells and build irrigation and so the ability to grow melons was severely restricted. With less water and no fertilizer, since that was also restricted, this would logically lead to fewer melons.

"With Israeli industrial farms, irrigation, water, the use of chemicals, and bioengineering, the Israeli melons can be grown as quickly as in a couple of weeks while the Palestinian melons can take a couple months. Furthermore, just before the Palestinian melons were ready the Israeli melons would arrive to market. These melons would not be as good, but they would be cheaper and available. By the time the Palestinian melons came to market in June and July everyone had already eaten plenty of Israeli melons since April and were less motivated to buy more melons, especially since those from Palestine were more expensive. Whereas when I was younger the lands around Jenin were covered in melons. Now, there is not one dunam of melon being cultivated for sale.

"But there was another theory I investigated: how disease and pollution ruined the melon crops and injured the land. The land then lay fallow, as nobody wanted to get back into the melon business. Many of the workers crossed into Israel to help with their melons! There was also a lack of knowledge about the sustainable use of chemical fertilizer, so the land slowly died. This is in contrast to the

Israeli practice of crop rotations and the ability to cleanse the soil through constant irrigation.

"A botanist professor was convinced that the melons suffered from widespread viral disease. He identified the 'Squash Leaf Curl Virus' and the 'Watermelon Chlorotic Stunt Virus' are responsible for the devastation. Working with the botanist's team we were able to sequence the viruses. But we also noticed that the virus did not have an impact on the Israeli melons, some of which were located just a few steps away. Were the conditions in Israel different enough to explain why the virus did not spread? Did conditions in Jenin encourage the virus to attack those plants? Was it that Israel was using a disease resistant variety? An Israeli botanist told us that Israel had a vaccine. As a result, there was speculation that Israel may have released the virus. In any case, the end result was that the virus further prevented the Palestinian farmers in Jenin from growing melons.

"Israel is at the forefront of agricultural technologies, and they have the water. Farmers do not grow melons because of a possible combination of disease, water shortage, and the influx of Israeli melons. And it has only gotten worse. Palestinians can only build in urban areas, Area A according to the Oslo Accords. So now places that were farms are becoming urbanized: no water, no land, no workers. Many of the farms closed entirely, and they sit fallow even today. Others were bought or now grow other crops."

"Like what, Anan? What else do they grow in Jenin?"

"Poppies. We have reduced Jenin to the lowest rung of drug production. If there are any melons grown by Palestinians they are grown for themselves, for tradition."

"A fascinating study Anan. But you didn't say the result of the study. Why did the melons disappear?"

"I could never prove anything definitive."

"Did your academic supervisors mind?"

"Very much. They had me do another study. But that time I chose a very easy subject."

"And what was that?"

"The importance of water. I conducted tests on the West Bank's Mountain Aquifer to help determine its division into three main basins. My research was appropriated by the Technion in Haifa to help Israel better harvest Palestine's water resources. That was not the purpose of my research."

"What did you do after that?"

"I learned about other types of chemistry. Perhaps one day I will have an opportunity to demonstrate my expertise."

CHAPTER 16

Marwan was desperate for news, and increasingly concerned for the safety of his dear friend and so decided to stop by Raffy's office at the Customs Police. The receptionist waved Marwan through without bothering to inform Major al-Khana about the visitor. Marwan guessed that the receptionist's apathy was caused by the death of Colonel Awadallah. Raffy's door was closed, unusual for the typically jovial officer, so Marwan knocked softly as he pushed open the door.

"Raffy, may I come in?"

"Marwan? Of course. Sorry I did not return your calls."

"That's okay. When you had told me that you would contact me when the journalism student was back, I had thought you said it would only be a couple of days. Then I became worried for you when I did not hear from you."

"Apologies my friend, I was still planning on calling you as soon as this guy comes back to us. We've lost track of him."

"So, he was a spy then?"

"Just because he has not come back does not make him a spy."

"Does it not?"

"No, it does not. Perhaps he found the assignment was more difficult than we all anticipated."

"Possibly."

"He also might be chasing up other stories, other contacts."

"Has he not checked-in Raffy? Even a short call?"

"He only has one dummy phone. Maybe he is keeping it for later or is somewhere without reception."

"Yes, I hear that the cellular service in Israel's intelligence agency building is problematic. Strong backs but weak signals."

"He will turn up Marwan, have faith."

•

Dan drove through towns and villages without a destination. He had no idea how long he had been driving, though absently noted that the car's gas tank needed to be refilled. He aimed his car for the cat that scampered across the road, but missed. *Maybe next time.* His despondency was broken as his phone rang. He saw it was Ronit, steered the car to the side, closed his eyes, and answered, "Dan here."

"Where the fuck have you been?"

"Driving."

"Driving? Never mind, there is a leak in our ship. Bring all the men to me so we may discover the identity of the traitor."

"It will be done," Dan murmured.

•

Surrounded by maps, coffee mugs, and empty picture frames, General Cohen stared hard at his subordinate Captain Levy, who, without an invitation to sit, remained standing. "Do you have any questions?" Cohen asked snappishly.

"General, how did you know which building to raid?"

"I tell you this, captain, because I need you to know who not to kill on your next raid, which I hope will be done with a higher level of professionalism than in Operation Rachel's Dream."

"Yes general. I put the fault on that reckless Lieutenant Uriel. Now that I can pick my own subordinates—"

"You will no longer have any more excuses."

"Yes general."

"Excellent, I am glad we understand each other. Here is the photo of our contact. I found his number in Captain Oded's desk, taped underneath his keyboard tray."

"That was clever."

"It is what an amateur might do. I ran the number through several databases, finding the voice in one and linking it with a name in another."

"He certainly looks the part."

"I had him stopped at a checkpoint, and then held until I could question him. But I can't risk such exposure in the future. Captain Levy, you are the liaison with this man."

•

Disgusted, Ronit looked at the collection of men huddled against a wall in a concrete bunker. *A gathering of fools,* she thought as she stomped out to the next room to confer with Dan.

"They are all here Ronit."

"Thank you, Dan, let's begin the questioning."

"Surely you don't suspect them all?"

"No, but they all must be questioned to ascertain the Judas in our midst."

"How can you say such a thing?"

"Judas? He was one man, not an entire people. Who could disagree with that most obvious truth?" Ronit called each man into the room. She questioned them, but none admitted to any wrongdoing. As the last man walked out,

Ronit controlled her breathing, internally furious. Knowing their innocence, Dan tried to defuse the situation.

"I guess we'll have to set them free, Ronit. The military must have used another way. We'll just have to change some of our operations, keep watch, and hopefully the traitor, if there even is one, will reveal themselves."

"I think not. These people are quite replaceable."

"But Ronit they've been with us a long time. Think about Naphtali. His family depends on him, just like most of the men's families. I know about—"

"Alas, those families will suffer due to the actions of their relatives."

"Ronit, we don't even know which one of them has betrayed us. You will be punishing dozens for the sins of one, or maybe the sins of none!"

"It is done, Dan. *They* are done. We will recruit new people, hungry people, people without families. Dan, give me your weapon, I've always wanted to use two guns at once."

"Do you really need two guns to kill one man?"

"No, I will shoot two people at one time. They won't be armed of course, but it's good practice all the same. Now handover your piece Dan."

"Take it, Ronit, but be careful; the safety is off."

•

Many olive wood carvers in Bethlehem lined the back alleys that surrounded the Church of the Nativity. These shops had a singular layout, with the gift shop to the front and the workshop to the rear. Monsignor Jerome scoffed at the scores of tourists who came to Bethlehem for the pictures and souvenirs rather than for contemplation and prayer. He lengthened his stride as he continued southeast for another twenty minutes until reaching Beit Sahour; where the city slowed to a peaceful pace, and the olive wood carvers were able to meet larger orders. He reached the first shop, and paused to drink from his water bottle, before stepping inside.

"Greetings Monsignor."

"Hello Youssef, my most expert of carvers. Will I be seeing you in church tomorrow?"

"That would be our wish Monsignor. It's just—"

"Just what Youssef?"

"We have so many orders to fill, would it not be better to continue our work, even if it is on the day of our Lord?"

"Where are you in your production?"

"Things are going well Monsignor, but we are starting to run low on olive wood."

"Why did you not say so immediately, Youssef? I cannot give you more time, but I can give you more trees. I'll make a call, and we'll have more when the opportunity next allows."

"Thank you, Monsignor."

"I expect to see you in church tomorrow."

"But like I said, there are only so many hours in the day, and we must fulfill the quota."

"Then you will work through the night Youssef, but you will not skip your duty to God. You will meet your quota, or you will find yourself in the afterlife, but if you miss church, when you reach the afterlife, you will not be happy with what you find."

•

Dan looked at the bodies of what had been their gang and suppressed his rage. After all, he had recruited and trained them, whereas Ronit had treated them with cruelty.

"Ronit did you have to torture all of our men before you shot them?"

"We had to be sure, and find out whom in the military knows about our operation. If they know one thing, they could know more."

"We have to develop some other locations."

"We will move on three fronts. You're going to recruit new employees. I'll contact the Monsignor to find a new location for our operations, and I am going to investigate our breach in security."

"At least the breach has been filled."

"Which is why I am going to see George. I will take him on a journey north. He'll never admit it, but I think the poor chap is a bit shaken."

"Where would you like me to focus on our recruiting efforts?"

"Same as before. Keep things spread; I don't want to have to deal with any previous alliances or allegiances."

"Does that mean you wish to include Arabs?"

"I don't care who they are as long as they stay loyal through their love of money and fear of death. Our operation is going global Dan. Our organization should reflect this. So, when I say I want a spread, I want our people to look like the United Nations. We never know when we'd need somebody to go undercover."

"That will take us more time."

"No Dan, that will take *you* more time. I want Arabs; I want Jews. I want a Christian Arab, a Muslim Arab, and a Jewish Arab. I want a Druze, a Bedouin, a Baha'i, a Samaritan, a Russian Jew, a Bulgarian Jew, an Ethiopian Jew, a French Jew, a British Jew, a Jew from South America, and a Jew from North America. Wait, I don't want one from North America. Those people are crazy. I don't need the aggravation, the *tsuris*."

CHAPTER 17

After a light breakfast, they sat under a covered patio out-side of Anan's kitchen and sipped sweet lemonade. It was early in the day, yet the sun was already intense.

"Yesterday was delightful; your family is so kind, so gracious."

"Thank you, Remy. It was nice sharing the day. I hope you will tell your American friends that not all Hamas are terrorists."

"I suppose you want me to leave out the part about the shootout."

"You mean *rescue*, of course."

"Maybe it's the air, or Stockholm syndrome, but I do feel comfortable here."

"You are in no danger, Remy; we are all friends. After breakfast I'll be visiting another friend, a farmer. His wife died, and his son is angry. But perhaps he would enjoy meeting you. Will you come?"

"Yes, I'd be glad to."

"After that, since you're interested in the logistics of food, while we're out there we can stop by to see another friend who runs an industrialized farm. This outing might be beneficial for your research."

"Yes please. It would be interesting to see what is grown in small plots and what comes from larger operations."

"Good. Upon returning we can rest, then walk back into the fields. I love my family's olive trees; they connect me to my ancestors. However, I'd also like to show you the trees of my uncle. Their age and beauty speak to the soul."

•

Anan turned off the pavement onto a rutted dirt road. The road clung to the side of a steep ravine as they wove their way up to the crest, the car barely making the summit. The views of valleys, trees, and farms went on for miles. Anan stopped suddenly.

"Here we are. My friend's farm."

Nabil, a weathered middle-aged man, stepped out of his house wearing a sport jacket, deep brown in color, made of wool, and almost as weathered as the face of the person who wore it.

"Remy, meet Nabil and his son Jehad. Nabil is a farmer who had his olive trees removed."

"This is true. Though removed is too weak a word. The trees were stolen, and with them our only source of income. When we found out our trees were going to be taken my wife died of sorrow."

"What will you do now?"

"I would rather perish on my land than leave it. I could move-in with my other sons in Dubai, but then I would become a refugee. And look at those refugees: they have nothing."

"Are there other things you could plant?"

"My neighbor found a solution that is not open to me. He also had his trees removed. Same problem. But then the Australians sent their aid money, and they are building him terraces for farming."

"Why is this not a possibility for you?"

"He is an important member of the Palestinian Authority. Here, look at this pamphlet my son found. It is from Aussie Aid and says, 'Aid is for the development of an impoverished region in support of the Middle East peace process of which the Palestinian Authority is an integral part.' You see, they cloak their corruption through words of peace."

"Is there anything you can plant yourself then?"

"Ha. Without the trees my land is just rock. I did have Israeli agents come, not government, but from a fruit and vegetable company. They offered to give me the tools to grow cucumbers and tomatoes. Irrigation technologies, you know, drip, drip, drip. And little tents for the vegetables to grow. They said I would get a fixed price, and if I provided good quality they might give me a chance to grow strawberries for a better price. But then I am using my land, my water, my labor, and for what? Not even Shekels but Agarot! Pennies! Pence! I told them to *go to hell.*"

"How will you survive otherwise?"

"Well, I saved their number. Just in case. But I have food. My other neighbors bring me prepared dishes. Even though they have little, my community does not let me starve."

"Remy," Anan interceded, "why don't you and Jehad take a walk? Jehad can show you where the trees were. There is a nice view of Israel from there, and a view of the wall that slices us apart."

•

Remy and Jehad left the stone home, passed by the family well and a solitary lemon tree, and then Remy saw it. Hundreds of stumps dotted the rocky terrain. *It looks like a graveyard,* Remy thought. "Jehad, I have seen the beauty of olive groves. I am sorry to see this."

"Sometimes it makes me think of a story my mother would tell me, about when she was in university, like me.

She studied in Jerusalem, at Al-Quds University during the Intifada."

"The First Intifada?"

"The only true Intifada. The one led by local people, not foreign gangsters who came from Tunis, Cairo, and London. The only intifada that was about rights, not guns. The only intifada that could have led to a lasting change, or at least a happier one. My mother would tell me how when there was a protest, everyone went to support it. And sometimes everyone would throw stones. She had to do it, to show solidarity. It was just what one did, especially as a university student. They didn't think about it. Not really. She said they were too young to know how to speak."

"That is only natural, but it was also very dangerous."

"She said that. People on both sides could have been killed. And that was not why they were protesting."

"Violence is often used as a distraction."

"I suppose. Her parents, my grandparents, were very disappointed in her behavior. But what could they do? It is like now. What could my father do if I wanted to protest like that? My mother said she regretted it, but do I not get a chance to do it? To find out if I feel the same regret? Maybe I will regret not throwing. My Imam would also tell me a story, about Daud, the King who slayed the giant Jalut with a well-placed stone."

"Who? King David and Goliath?"

"As you say."

"Maybe if you decided you are bad at throwing, it would make it easier to find another way."

"I am not bad at throwing. I can throw farther than you."

"I don't think so. I played baseball in high school. Did you play any sports?"

"I wrestled. I could put you to sleep in under three minutes. Want to see?"

"Maybe next time Jehad."

•

Remy and Jehad's humor lasted until they reached the stumps of the ancient olive grove. Jehad lapsed back into an intense melancholy, and they walked to the house in silence. Anan was already in the car and motioned Remy to get in. Remy thanked Jehad for the walk, was ignored, got in the car, and barely had time to buckle his seatbelt before Anan sped away.

"I hope you enjoyed your walk with Jehad."

"He seems like a good kid. A bit troubled, but then again he has been through a lot."

"I fear for the health of his father. Nabil's spirit may wish to join his wife's rather than spend years yearning for her, and his trees."

"Jehad needs his father, I think."

"We could all benefit from being around such as man as Nabil. Even in his position he sent us away with tomatoes, cucumbers, and strawberries his neighbor brought. He says they hurt his stomach, but I do not believe him. Now we go on to my friend the chicken farmer."

"Chicken?"

"Yes."

"What is the name of his company?"

"The Poultry People."

"Oh."

"Is everything alright?"

"Yes. Yes. I had thought I might have heard of the company."

"Have you?"

"No."

•

This barn is huge, Remy thought as they pulled into

the grounds of The Poultry People. Tall shrubs blocked the view from the road, and around the parking lot the grounds were surprisingly well tended. This was particularly surprising considering it was a farm that raised and slaughtered animals. A touch disconcerted, Remy climbed out of the car and was met by smiling executives that offered hands, if not names. They toured the grounds, and the modern yet foul-smelling barn, before moving to an office adorned with portraits of poultry.

"As you can see on this certificate, our facility is inspected by Israeli officials. It is in Area C, and therefore under direct Israeli civilian and military administration. The Israeli health ministry approves of our operation, and as a result the chickens can be sold in Israel."

"Then your market is huge."

"Not quite. There is a problem. We cannot get Jewish officials to come and gain a certification to be kosher, so the religious Jewish market is unavailable to us. However, we are inspected by Islamic officials, and so have a halal certification."

"Right, so you sell in Israel and the West Bank, but not to Jews?"

"We sell to Jewish Israelis who visit shops that carry non-kosher goods. This is a lot of people."

At the end of the tour, waiting for Remy and Anan, was a room with tables, chairs, silverware, glasses full of orange juice, numerous salads, and a perfectly roasted chicken for each person. As it turned out, before and during the tour of the facility, one of the employees was roasting chickens over an open fire. Remy sat at the table with Anan and his friend.

"Next time you come we will prepare the 'the national dish of Palestine.'"

"Which is…?"

"Maqluba of course. Anan, where did you find this guy? It is made from chicken, eggplant, cauliflower, and rice. The vegetables go into the pot first, followed by the chicken, and then the rice. Stock, or water, along with garlic and other spices is added, and then it simmers. The rice is cooked with the flavors of the chicken and vegetables. When finished, the dish is served by flipping the pot over onto a large serving plate. The vegetables will then be on the top, led by the cauliflower that roasted on the initial simmer. After that the eggplant, the chicken, and finally the rice, the latter of which has by now taken on a rather dark and deep yellow hue and is full of flavor."

"Thanks for the tour, the magnificent lunch, and the recipe."

"My pleasure. And Anan, always nice to see you."

•

Remy and Anan stepped out into the midday sun. Remy felt dazed but didn't know if it was from the brightness or the calories. They sauntered and swayed to the car. "That was delicious. I don't think I've ever had chicken that good," Remy remarked.

"Nor will you ever. The hand that grew them performed the dhabihah, then prepared and roasted the meat."

"And those tomatoes and cucumbers we brought made for an excellent accompaniment."

"Remy, you are starting to sound like a cookbook. Wait until you try the strawberries Nabil gave us; we'll take them with us on our walk. I want to show you my uncle's olive grove."

CHAPTER 18

They stood at the edge of the hilltop settlement, looking down at the lush valley below. The rabbi, his face clad in a beard that managed to be both scraggly and full, stood next to Shachar, whose eyes shone even more brightly as they sat within his deeply lined face, a face far older than his age.

"That was a lovely service Rabbi."

"Rather unique, wouldn't you say?"

"Yes, the melodies were heartfelt, and the scenery certainly lends itself to movements of the spirit."

"I too feel it in my soul. These rocks, these holy rocks, when I gaze upon them my heart flutters. Now let's have some lunch, take a short rest, and be off on our Shabbat walk. The students are eager to go, but that's only because teenagers have not learned the value of rest."

"When did we become old Avraham?"

"Nonsense, we are not too old, they are too young."

•

The rabbi walked out of his small white house that overlooked the rolling hills of the West Bank. Avraham stretched his back and looked toward his front garden. The birds of paradise flowers were blooming, and the apples were almost ripe. He was surprised to find Shachar sitting on the grass. "Shachar, I didn't see you. Have you been sitting here all afternoon?"

"Yes, Rabbi. I would not want to waste a moment inside with such a view to enjoy."

"Then you should come back more often. You should live with us. You know you are most welcome."

"Thank you. I'll consider it."

"I've had my rest, and I think the students are more than ready to put down their books for the day; should we get going?"

"Sounds good. Lead the way, but I have one question."

"Yes Shachar?"

"You told me we must never go out unarmed, does that extend to Shabbat?"

"Do not fear Shachar, the Lord protects his faithful. We've reported our route to the army, and they will be with us to provide any protection we might need. Those Arabs are cowards: one look from a man with conviction and they scatter like dust in the wind. If you will follow me we may proceed on our walk."

•

Anan and Remy were walking together, enjoying the sweet cool air as they entered a valley covered with olive groves. "Anan, it is so beautiful here. The twists and turns of these ancient trees."

"They can live two-thousand years."

"Imagine the things they have seen."

"Yes. Look, there is a football match being played in that clearing. Quite a few young men, so it seems."

•

"Look at those barbarians, Shachar! Sport on God's holy day! Our mature student, Benji, is going to talk to them."

"Hey degenerates, heathens, animals," Benji shouted. "Go away and let us enjoy our walk."

The football match stopped, and sixteen Palestinians glared at the nine settler students, the rabbi, the six Israeli soldiers, and Shachar. Remy saw Shachar, but the latter did not see the former. The Palestinian 'footballers' scattered, each moving with purpose. The settlers laughed until they realized why they ran.

Stone missiles began to fly. Remy saw piles of rocks stacked behind the biggest trees and a jagged boulder. Two of the students were injured, one seriously. An Israeli soldier was also knocked down before the remaining soldiers opened fire. They pointed their weapons at the nearest target, the one who had felled their comrade. A blaze of blood sprayed from behind the tree, the venerable trunk no match for modern weaponry.

With that, the next phase of the clash commenced. Five Palestinians, each armed with sticks, rushed the students from the side away from the Israeli soldiers. The seven settlers moved into a semi-circle, ready for the fight. The first Palestinian got a boot to his stomach before another Israeli darted in with a rock, striking a killing blow to the head. The four remaining Palestinians split into two and battered the edges of the circle, taking out two of the settlers. Four Palestinians faced six settlers. The Palestinians rushed again as gunfire erupted. The lead Palestinian was dead, shot through the cheek by the rabbi, who wielded a 9mm. The rabbi stepped forward and emptied his clip into another as the students kicked, tripped, and stomped the last two.

At the same time, several of the Palestinians had grabbed guns hidden behind other trees in the grove. A shootout ensued, with two of the Israeli soldiers taken-out by surprise before three others could find cover. Two Israeli soldiers provided a brief covering fire while the third soldier slid into a crawl to get into a flanking position. The two soldiers alternated fire, picking off three Palestinians for their trouble.

Shachar had taken refuge behind a rock up the hill from the rest. He peered out and saw the rabbi reloading his pistol. Remy was frozen. Until he wasn't. The adrenaline spiked and Remy was off. The remaining Palestinians, two with rifles, two with pistols, and three with stones, began to withdraw. The young settlers kept their heads down now, thinking about tending to their wounded while eyeing the lifeless Palestinians nearest to them, wondering if they were indeed dead. The flanking soldier came upon two Palestinians, one with a rifle and the other a handgun, and dropped them both in a burst of fire, then moved on. The two remaining soldiers pushed forward. The remaining Palestinian rifleman stepped out, saw the students, shot one but was immediately killed by a soldier. A Palestinian pointed a handgun at the Israeli soldier who had just iced the rifleman, but the rabbi sent his entire second clip into the man. The three remaining Palestinians, stone throwers each, quickly fled.

The two soldiers, knowing the remaining Palestinians were without firearms, rose, and in a short chase ended three more lives. The fight seemed over but the flanking soldier heard a twig snap and continued to creep forward. He slid around a rock and found Remy, who immediately showed his sweaty palms and sun-burned face. The Israeli soldier slung his weapon, grabbed Remy by the ear, and dragged him back to the rest of the group. The rabbi had reloaded, thanks to a dead soldier, and was walking toward the captive. Shachar saw Remy and recognized the danger he faced. Remy looked around with wild eyes. Anan was nowhere to be found. Only bodies.

"Who the fuck are you?" the rabbi growled.

"Remy. I'm a student."

"Are you indeed? I think you will tell us what happened here, student, and maybe you will live. Or will at least keep your body intact."

That got Shachar moving. "Rabbi! Hold on. I know this kid. He is a student. I, uh, took a class with him at Tel Aviv University."

"Liberal bullshit of a school. Tell me, why he was with these terrorists?"

"Ask him, but don't kill him. He is American, via London. And I think innocent, other than being an idiot. What were you doing with them, Remy?"

"I wasn't with them. I was taking a walk through the trees with another friend."

"And where is this friend?"

"I don't know."

"Well, is he dead or has he run off?"

"I don't know."

"Let's take him back and lock him up in the canteen so we can question him further, after we get my people medical attention."

•

Back in London, Professor Vandermere was watching a news report. "This is BBC reporting from Jerusalem. A skirmish between settlers and Palestinians has resulted in the death or injury of eight Israelis, along with twenty-two Palestinians killed. The incident is being referred to as the Battle of the Trees in the local press as it took place in an area thick with ancient olive groves."

•

Looking forward to listening to his own voice on Israeli Army Radio, General Cohen switched on his old transistor. "General Ram Cohen reports that '...the trees were used as part of a terroristic ambush. They constitute a military threat to Israelis and to the settlements on the hills around the valley. For security reasons the trees will be removed.' General Cohen has directed the Combat Engineering Corps to uproot the trees and take them to be recycled as part of a plan to reduce the Army's impact on the environment."

•

"Monsignor Jerome, this is General Cohen." Jerome had just finished his prayers. "An opportunity has arisen to meet your request for olive wood." As he made a sign of the cross, Jerome reminded himself that *God works in mysterious ways.*

•

Secretary of State Sanders rose from his lacquered desk in his top floor office of the Harry S. Truman Building, the seat of the US Department of State, and approached the man who had just been ushered in by his assistant. They gripped hands and Sanders smiled at Ambassador Ruben Gebinir, even as he noted the lack of a necktie, an insult to the unstated rules of diplomatic protocol, and, therefore, of politeness. Sanders motioned for Gebinir to take one of the two wing chairs in front of a portrait of former president Truman, the first world leader to recognize the State of Israel. Sanders moved to a wooden globe, hand painted, with golden clasps, and, oddly to Gebinir, hinged at the equator. "This was a gift from Kaiser Wilhelm II, meant to keep the US out of the First World War." Sanders flipped open the top of the globe revealing a collection of whiskey. "It didn't work of course. Too many torpedoes from an alleged ally you see. May I interest you in a drink, ambassador?"

"Always."

Sanders chose the bottle, poured, and brought the crystal glass tumblers over to the chairs, handing them to

Ruben, ignoring the side tables at their elbows. "Each of those bottles cost more than my monthly salary. Here, hold this while I get comfortable." Sanders sat down and said formally, "Ambassador, welcome." Sanders reached over and plucked his glass from the ambassador. "Thank you, and thank you for coming."

"Of course, it's not every day that the Secretary of State summons me."

"Oh stop, Ruben, you know you're here for our own domestic politics; to look like we are doing something useful. Although, in truth, the reports about what happened at the Battle of the Trees, saying nothing about your security operations in the West Bank, is disheartening."

"Disheartening for whom?"

"Those who are seeking peace, ambassador."

"Ah, yes, peace. Many people believe Palestinians are most peaceful when they are laid to rest."

"Are you suggesting people in your government support genocide?"

"Don't be ridiculous Secretary, we have nothing against Palestinians per se; we only wish they would stop squatting on our land."

"And how can they be squatters if they were there before most of your people?"

"It appears, Secretary Sanders, that you have forgotten your Bible. My people were there long before the Palestinians. This is known to the faithful of your country, just as in mine, and it shapes the politics of both of our great countries."

"The sands are shifting Ruben, and recent events are not helping Israel's cause."

"Of whom do you speak Sanders, my dear friend? Your hit squad of those lovely ladies in your Congress?"

"Them yes, but increasingly others as well. Moreover, those squad women are not all fools. They are affecting policy far ahead of what might be expected of such junior members of Congress."

"I'll concede. Not all of them are jesters. The one from New York seems particularly sharp."

"She is, but unfortunately lacks experience."

"She is tactless, Sanders. Reminds me of that Palestinian woman, Hanan Ashrawi: smart, prepared, and a devastating debater. She gave us decades of problems…which I'm sure yours will give to you." He shifted uncomfortably in his seat at the thought.

"Back to the matters at hand. Could you ease off the Palestinians, even a bit? Even if just a statement of intent?"

"Ambassador, do you know that by summoning me you've limited our options? My government must be strong. It cannot ignore security for your elections."

"But *your* elections?"

"Are *ours*, and if our voters want us to keep them safe from Palestinians no matter the cost, then that includes resisting being strong-armed by our American friends." The ambassador lifted the glass of the amber liquid, made a subtle bow toward Secretary Sanders, and downed it in one gulp.

•

"Hi Sami, this is Marwan. I am having a bit of trouble with my investigation into your brother Ahmad's murder. Might I speak with Abu Ahmad? I have a few questions he might be able to help with." Marwan stood in the doorway of his flat, looking out at the setting sun.

"Marwan, I am not sure how much my father can help."

"And why is that?"

"Because he never approved of Ahmad. Ahmad was already dead to him."

"Why would he think that?"

"It is not my story to tell. But if you think it will help bring the murderer to justice, then I'll give you my father's address."

"Okay, and you will let him know I am coming?"

"No."

"I can telephone him before I go?"

"Marwan, my father is a very particular man. He prefers not to use a telephone."

"That's fine. The countryside is lovely this time of year. Are certain times better than others for a visit? Is there something I can bring him?"

"He loves sweets, so a couple hours after Friday prayers is a good time to find him, and bring the sweets. Unless, of course, you will be attending the same mosque as him?"

"My neighbor Sami, I have prayed for your brother before, and I don't mind praying for him again. Which mosque does he frequent?"

CHAPTER 19

"As-salamu alaykum." The prayer was over, and the men were slowly exiting the mosque.

"Wa-alaikum-salaam."

"Are you Abu Ahmad?"

"People have known me by that name. Who are you?"

"Apologies, my name is Marwan. I am investigating the death of your son, Ahmad."

"Ahmad is dead?"

"Yes, he was found murdered days ago."

"Days ago, you say? You are mistaken, my Ahmad died years ago."

"Perhaps your relationship with him did, but his body did not. Your youngest child asked me to look into the matter."

"And why would this man's death be worth investigating?"

"Abu Ahmad, *be merciful.* Whatever came between you two is over. He was killed in a settlement where an Israeli was also killed."

"So, my failure of a son tried to repent by becoming a martyr? I am happy to hear it. Thank you for bringing this news to me, Marwan."

"I'm glad to bring you comfort, but that is not the purpose of my visit."

"What then?"

"As I said, I'm investigating why Ahmad was murdered, why he was in to begin with."

"But you just said it was to martyr himself."

"I did not say that, what I said was he was murdered."

"How unfortunate, that his soul will be forever damned."

"I understand your relationship has caused you great pain. Ahmad may not have been a martyr, but his death may reveal the evil of others."

"What do you want of me, Marwan?"

"I am struggling to put the pieces together. I hoped you might be able to direct me where I might find who, or where, or what, could have led him on a path that got him killed."

"Before he was dead to me, long before he was dead to you, he would go to the Sahara Lounge. I did not approve."

"What is that, Abu Ahmad?"

"A place where young men go to meet, and to smoke shisha. Perhaps you will find the answers you seek there."

"Thank you, Abu Ahmad. My sympathies for your son, no matter when or where it happened."

"That is kind of you, Marwan. God willing, I wish you success in your investigation. Now before you go, do tell me what you are holding there. It looks like a box from Hassan's Sweets Shoppe. I think you must know that I love things from there. Would you care for some tea?"

"I would be honored."

•

A thick haze of smoke stung Marwan's eyes and nose. The air was heavy, yet a sweetness filled the mouth. The lights were dim, but Marwan could see sofas set in squares, with space for a shisha in the middle. Liveried staff moved from group to group delivering soft drinks, teas, coffees, juices, light snacks, and flavored tobaccos. The tobacco was stuffed into a vertical pipe, the shisha bowl, and hot coals were placed on top before the men began to take their smoke. A curt greeting was followed by a swift walk to a quiet corner where only a few customers lingered.

"May I bring you a drink while we prepare your shisha?"

"Yes, I'll have tea, two sugars."

"Very good. What flavor shall I get for you, sir?"

"What do you have tonight?"

"Strawberry, apple, peach."

"Apple."

"As you wish."

Marwan settled into his divan. The tea was brought and the shisha soon after. A few puffs later Marwan's vision began to swirl. He became increasingly dizzy, the air stifling. Marwan became desperate for fresh air, but his body would not respond, and he feared falling. His head lolled back, and he looked toward the ceiling, seeing the lamps dance in their colored glass chandelier. A sturdy voice addressed him, and Marwan snapped his head forward and reached for his tea.

"Are you well, my friend?"

"Yes, thank you."

"I am of the opinion that one should not smoke alone. I am alone. And so are you. Would you be opposed to having company?"

"Please take a seat."

"My name is Jamal. I am thirty-seven, and work in marketing."

"I am Marwan. I am with the police."

"I see…; I am sorry to have bothered you."

"I am not on duty. My time is my own."

"That is well." Jamal signaled for his shisha to be moved. "I have not seen you here before."

"I haven't come before. I only learned about it recently."

"And who, may I ask, told you about the Sahara?"

Marwan took a moment to collect his thoughts in the

heavy air of the room, "Ahmad Naser."

"You must tell me if you are working as police."

"I swear to God I am not."

"To God? Well, I might remember an Ahmad. How do you know him?"

"Through a neighbor who thought I might find this place interesting."

"Unique really. There is nowhere else like it in Palestine." He smiled at Marwan, and with that they relaxed into conversation: family, work, recreation.

"Do you like football Marwan?"

"Not as much as others."

"Is there a club you prefer?"

"Queens Park Rangers."

"I've not heard of that one."

"That's one of the reasons I like them."

"So, you are clever as well as dashing."

"What about you Jamal? Do you like sports?"

"Not that type. As a marketer I must be interested in art, in beauty."

"Then you are blessed. There is much beauty in the world if one knows how to look."

"And do you know how to look Marwan?"

Marwan looked at Jamal, and considered the question. "Yes," he said, his eyes drifting from Jamal's face to look up to the ceiling; seeing clouds where there were only stains. "I would say that I do."

The tobacco finished, and, rising from the plush sofas, the two men bid each other farewell. "It was nice meeting you Jamal."

"I feel the same. By the way, if you are interested in unique places I know a spot you might enjoy. Would you be interested in seeing it the day after tomorrow?"

"Possibly."

"Excellent. I will reserve a table for eight in the evening."

"Dinner? Where are we going?"

"Osama's Table. Do you have a pen? I'll write the directions."

•

Jamal had seen Marwan warily approaching Osama's Table, chuckled to himself, and decided to wait outside so the two men could enter together. "Marwan, so nice to see you. Have you been well?"

"Yes, and you, Jamal?"

"I did very well at work the day after we met. You must be lucky for those around you."

"A coincidence I am sure."

"Perhaps. I am glad to show you Osama's. Have you been?"

"I never knew this place existed, yet I have been in this part of town many times."

"It is not well publicized." Jamal walked to a table in the corner, and Marwan followed him, taking everything in with widening eyes.

"And why might that be?"

"They sell alcohol."

"Here?" Marwan's eyes narrowed as he looked around at the bare walls and wooden tables in disbelief.

"There are Christians in Ramallah and Bethlehem, are there not?"

"There are, yes of course. And in other places."

"Then there is alcohol. Does it bother you?"

"Not in the least. I was merely amazed that I did not know about such a place."

"*Such a place!* Marwan, it is a simple establishment serving food and drink, like many others in the city."

"That serves alcohol."

"We can leave if you wish."

"I'll stay."

"Then no more acting the schoolboy."

"Sorry, you are right. I don't mind, but the place does have a certain...aroma. Do you smell it?"

"It is old beer."

"And why is the floor sticky?"

"You are a schoolboy!! During the weekends Osama's Table becomes Osama's Bar. There are shows—"

"Shows?"

"Music, bands, singers. Last week was Maysa Daw."

"A woman?"

"Marwan, you are too much." Jamal chuckled. "I'll try to explain it, slowly. People dance, people bump, people spill. It is hard to clean, and then people will just spill again."

"That seems reasonable."

"I am glad you approve of their hygienic practices."

"Is the food as clean?"

"Is pork clean?"

"Are you serious?"

"Let me ask again, are there Christians in Palestine?"

"I understand."

"It is odd, you seemed to want to experience... differentness, at least I thought so when we met at Sahara's, but now it seems to make you uneasy."

"I am getting used to these differences." Marwan realized how stiff his posture was, and tried to make himself appear at ease. "I am not afraid of them, just previously unaware."

"Good." Jamal noticed Marwan's failed attempt to seem unperturbed. "Then you won't mind if I order extra bacon on my hamburger? *Ha! I am joking.* Did I frighten you?"

"Maybe a little. Do you love bacon so much that...you can pass on the pork pie?"

"Now you are getting it! I am getting the avocado on toast."

"Is that food?"

"A light snack that costs more than food. But still, I can't stop eating it. What about you?"

"I'll have the same."

"Now you are getting me. Well-done! Two avocados on toast!" Jamal pushed back his wooden chair with a scrape, and moved to make the order at the bar.

•

"Jamal, I had a nice time at Osama's. But I am not sure I am up to going out there tonight."

"The band playing is one of my favorites…but no matter, they will play again."

"Thank you. I've just been so busy."

"No worries my friend." The two men were walking down a path that had taken them to a scenic view that overlooked the sprawl of Ramallah.

"I am enjoying this walk. The view over the city is fantastic. I thought I knew my way around, but your knowledge seems to know no bounds."

"That is very kind of you to say but I must admit I am running out of secret locations. And yet," Jamal grinned, "I have a few more, if you are interested."

"I am."

"Excellent. Tomorrow night, when you are rested, meet me again at the Sahara Lounge."

•

"What should we do with him? Turn him over to the military or make him disappear?"

"Let him go," Shachar said as he turned away from the rabbi.

"Shachar, how can you suggest we let him go?" The rabbi was perplexed. "By letting him go I assume you mean turning him over to the military for arrest, imprisonment, or expulsion?"

"I mean let him go, rabbi." Shachar turned to look out the window. "Drive him to the airport if you wish; then let him go."

"I understand if your stomach is weak, but what about the military?"

"We can't turn him over to the military, or the police."

"Why not? He was there at the battle; they could charge him with terrorism or even murder. Then he would be in prison or expelled."

"He knows we were provocative. He might know *you* carried a gun. And we don't need more attention here. You don't want it. Not here, or across the valley."

"Why not disappear him ourselves?"

Shachar spun around to face Avraham.

"Could you do it, rabbi? Could you kill an innocent?"

"If they're standing in the way of God's work then they aren't innocent."

"You're assuming he's going to create problems for us."

"What good can come of him, Shachar? Nothing but problems."

"There is nothing good about keeping him. Or even disappearing him. Anything that brings attention that might highlight whatever is going on here does not seem to be in your interest. What we need to do is find a way that he can help rather than hinder."

"And how is that possible?"

"I think," Shachar tapped a finger to his head, "I have an idea."

CHAPTER 20

"Ronit this is beautiful country."

"Thank you, George." She gave a small sigh that was as loving as it was impatient. "I prefer the north to the south, so much greener, more water, more life. Have you been to Jenin, George?"

"Can't say that I have."

"And you won't be going today either."

"Where then?"

"As I said, north."

"How far north?"

"Lebanon."

"Lebanon?"

"If you want to see our northern operations."

"I thought you meant Jenin, Nablus, or Nazareth."

"Sometimes, George, your people are so busy thinking big that they end up thinking too small. We do business in Jenin and Nazareth: selling guns, buying drugs, distributing drugs, and washing money. But through Lebanon we have increased and diversified our global reach."

"I'm impressed, Ronit. You've come far since we first met. I have only managed a few raises in pay grade, and incrementally at that."

"Maybe you are working at the wrong place. Might you consider working with me?"

"I love my country, Ronit."

"I'm not so sure, George, you love the power that serving your country enables."

"You see through all disguises. Sure, I like being an agent who plays fast with the rules, but I still am a patriot."

"At least consider my offer. I would not be your employer. We would be a partnership."

"I appreciate the attractiveness of the offer." He took a moment to look Ronit in the eyes.

"Enough of that. Here we are approaching the border."

"And how am I meant to pass?"

"George, don't be silly. You know how well I work with border guards."

"And how do you propose I return? Give them your name and address?"

"You're resourceful!"

"I am?"

"Of course, you are. You can go through your friends at the United Nations Interim Force in Lebanon."

"UNIFIL?"

"Yes."

"How do you know…"

"Hush now," she put two fingers to his mouth. "Let's get you across. Your host is waiting for you on the other side."

•

"Shachar, you think he will do that for us?" The rabbi was staring at the screen of the desktop computer in front of him.

"Look at his university webpage. He wants to be a journalist. He investigates stories. Give him a story, and off he'll go. Let's give him a story, Rabbi."

•

"Remy. I've sorted things out with the people here in the settlement. As you can imagine they are very jittery." Shachar had come into the room where Remy sat on a stiff wooden chair, hands tied behind his back. "They want to let you go, so you don't have a problem with the military, or the police."

"Since I might tell the military, police, or press what I saw?"

"*You saw and know nothing*! Otherwise you might not ever see anyone again. Do I make myself clear?"

"Crystal."

"But they have a suggestion."

"And that is?"

"They want you to know they are good people. They want you to be successful. To move on from all of this. You are to take me to a place known as Osama's Table. It is a Palestinian joint halfway between Ramallah and Nablus."

"I am taking you?"

"Someone has to do the talking. And it can't be me. As it is I'll have to change my clothing."

"Ah, so you need me to cover for you?"

"I'm doing an investigation for the settlers. There are many whispers about Osama's Table. Something goes on there, but nobody seems to know what. I mentioned it might be where the thugs who attacked them might hang out. There might be nothing there, but it seems worth checking out. At least that is what I told them. There is a band playing tonight. We can go and see them, ask around, have a few drinks, and forget what we have just seen here. It will be just the two of us. It is the best I could do."

"Well done Shachar."

"Who knows, maybe we'll meet some nice people and enjoy an evening out," he said as he untied Remy's wrists.

"I find it hard to believe that we'll be able enjoy ourselves after what we've seen."

"Once you realize that you are listening to music at a club, and not dead, you might feel happier." Shachar stood back as Remy rubbed his wrists and got up from the chair.

"Then let's get going."

•

"Sorry, I did not see you there," Remy said, moving his foot off of the toe of the man next to him at the bar.

"No worries. I am also enjoying the music."

"Let me buy you another drink."

"And I will buy the round after. My name is Jamal. And you are?"

"Remy."

"Is that your friend over there? He looks rather sullen."

"He is quite harmless."

"Looks like Shabak or Mista'arvim. How do you know him?"

"What is Mista'arvim?"

"An Israeli, undercover as a Palestinian."

"Do they do that?"

"Sure. Many Israelis are Arab. And so many Arabs are Jewish!"

"If you say so."

"Where did you meet him then?"

"I've bumped into him a few times. I have found so much hospitality here, even just visiting as a student. Always being whisked from location to location."

"I would be glad to take you to some places I know. Let's go to Nablus. Do you enjoy hiking?"

"I do."

"Then let's go in the morning. There is a beautiful view to see. And you can leave that one home," Jamal said, nodding toward Shachar. "There is something I don't like about him."

"I think he is just surly by nature."

"I suppose there is some romance in that. Still, I prefer to show my places *only to you*."

"Then we can meet tomorrow."

"Great. We can begin with coffee at Amore's, near the university in Rafidia. Do you know Nablus?"

"Increasingly."

"Then you know it is not hard to get there, assuming they are not under a curfew."

"Let's hope not. What time should we meet?"

•

"Remy, what was that about?" Shachar asked as Remy came back to the table.

"I made a friend. Name is Jamal. We are going to take a hike tomorrow."

"What else did you find out?"

"Nothing. Does this look like a criminal lair?"

"No. It looks like a bar. The only odd thing is it is in the West Bank."

"Do you frequent the West Bank?"

"Years ago, as a soldier."

"Then you don't know much about most of the Palestinians who live here."

"True."

"Why don't you head back and find a motel in Israel. I am going to have my hike and then I can give you a call."

"Last time we departed you were going to get back to me but instead became a terrorist."

"I did not." Remy shook his head, "I had nothing to do with that."

"Then tell me who you were with."

"Anan Radwan."

"The Hamas Mayor of Nablus?"

"The mayor?"

"Former mayor. And Hamas leader."

"Perhaps he is that, but I don't think he was involved in the incident in the valley."

"Where is he now? Was he killed? I did not see him among the dead."

"He left when it began. I hid; he ran."

"Which way did he go? Did he try to take you with him?"

"I don't know. It happened so fast. What were you doing with those settlers? They looked like they came ready for a fight."

"I was their guest. I did not know any of that was going to happen. I was just in the wrong place."

"And I was there at the wrong time. Let's move forward. I'll contact you tomorrow afternoon after my hike, and we can make a new plan."

"Speak to you then," Shachar said, as he stood up to leave.

•

Remy and Jamal had just returned from the hike to the starting point, tired, but in good spirits. "Jamal what an incredible view! Thank you for taking me."

"It was my pleasure. Say, if you would like, I am going out tonight to smoke shisha at a laid-back place named the Sahara Lounge. I'm meeting a friend there after work. Would you like to come?"

Remy considered this idea, wondering about what that might communicate to Jamal, but decided going was an opportunity not to be missed. "Yes."

•

"Shachar. It's Remy." He stood at the desk in his hotel room, gazing into the mirror and realizing he needed a shave. "I wanted to let you know I am going out tonight with some friends."

"Friends? What friends?"

"Jamal and one of his friends."

"And where are you going?"

"The Sahara Lounge."

"I've never heard of it."

"You've never heard of anything here."

"I keep forgetting how different the Palestinian world is from mine. We inhabit worlds so removed and yet so close."

"I'm calling so as not to disappear on you again."

"I appreciate that. When you are done playing with your friends please contact me so we can get back to the investigation."

"Don't worry, I'll see you soon."

●

"Remy my friend. Please meet Marwan. Marwan, this is Remy. We met at Osama's Table. He was at the show I invited you to." Marwan extended his hand and Remy took it and gave a firm clasp, though he was startled, and a little embarrassed, that Marwan maintained a relaxed grip. Who he was embarrassed for, he wasn't quite sure.

"Hello, Remy. Did you enjoy the concert?"

"Yes, thank you. And I am glad to have met Jamal. He took me on a most wonderful hike this morning."

"Did he? How nice of him."

"It really was. And now he invited me here. This place is both hip and drab. How do they manage it?"

"Jamal, this Remy speaks the truth. Though I think drab and aged are better descriptors."

"Very funny, Marwan," Jamal said as he dropped down onto the sofa next to him. "I'm quite tired from the morning walk. Let's get the shisha going, that always revives me."

•

"I am going to turn in," Jamal said, after slowly pulling himself to his feet.

"What happened to the shisha-led revival of our dear friend Jamal?"

"Marwan you have become quite perceptive tonight. The hike, the night at Osama's, work, and the time with you two has left me fatigued, and I do not mind admitting it. Remy, it was nice seeing you. I hope we meet again."

"As do I. Have a good rest."

"Goodnight, Jamal." Marwan gave Jamal a wave.

"Nice guy, your friend Jamal."

"Yes, very hospitable. Though I have only known him a short time."

"Longer than me."

"Not by much. So, tell me, what brings you to Palestine?"

"I am writing a doctorate in journalism, and I've come to do some research. I am looking at food logistics."

"Logistics? And what have you found?"

"That things move in many ways, some obvious, others less so. What do you do, Marwan?"

"I am in the police. But I have taken a leave, so am not thinking of myself as police."

"I see. Do you know anything about smuggling?" Remy asked, as he leaned back while perking up.

"Why? Do you?"

"There is smuggling in every country. I thought maybe you would know about some here."

"I don't think it is a secret to say there is smuggling from the West Bank into Israel through the settlements. There is much disgust about it, but the people involved are—"

"Powerful. I met with the Customs Police, and they told me—"

"Customs Police? My good friend Raffy works there.

Major Rafiq al-Khana. Did you meet him?"

"Yes! I spent a lot of time with him!"

"Really? He told me about you! I did not connect you to his description. He thought very highly of you."

"I was impressed by him as well. How is it that I came up?"

"He told me you were asking about Har Kesem. I too came to him asking about Har Kesem."

"What interested you about it?"

"I am in contact with the family of the man who was murdered there."

"Colonel Awadallah."

"No, before that. Ahmad Naser."

"Seems there is a lot of killing going on there."

"Ahmad's family is certain there was foul play. And they asked me to investigate. I have made some interesting inroads, but the place I cannot go, where I wish to go the most, is Har Kesem."

"Where I have been."

"That, and to talk with the family of the other person who died at the same time as Ahmad."

"Yossi Seigler. I met someone who is investigating his murder. An Israeli."

"And where did you meet this Israeli investigator?"

"Har Kesem. He was there at the same time I was."

"Can you contact him?"

"Yes."

"I wish to speak with him. To find more about Yossi Seigler."

"I'd imagine he would like to ask you similar things about Ahmad Naser."

CHAPTER 21

"Marwan, Shachar, and Shachar this is Marwan," Remy announced.

"Hello, Shachar. Welcome to Palestine," Marwan said disdainfully as he looked at the Israeli.

"Thank you, Marwan. It is nice to be in Israel," Shachar replied as he glared at the Palestinian.

Remy rolled his eyes. "Knock it off you two."

Marwan dipped his head in acknowledgment. "Apologies. What did you find out from the Seigler family?"

"The media reported that Yossi was looking for a home in Har Kesem. But according to family, Yossi was trying to move abroad, to Germany, not move to the settlements. Further, there are no homes in Har Kesem. It is an industrial settlement."

"The family of Ahmad also does not see a terrorist. I do not either, though it is of course possible. But given they have serious doubts, and you have doubts...well we are both here investigating."

"Shachar, Marwan, could we even pretend to assume this is all a coincidence?" Remy asked rhetorically. "Especially given that I am also here because of a murder. Shachar learned more about the settlement across the valley and found they knew all about Har Kesem as a center for repackaging, smuggling, and little else. We also found some packaging that we hoped you, Marwan, could help with."

"Al Minquar? It means The Beak."

"I know that, but what I don't know is where it is from."

"Look here on the back. This is an address. And it is in Lebanon."

"Then should someone go there? Marwan?"

"I can't go. It's nearly impossible. I would need to go to the District Coordination Office, the local administrative center of the Israeli Army, to request a pass to go to and through the Allenby Bridge into Jordan. That could be rejected or, at best, take months. Then if the Allenby Bridge is open there is the long bus to Amman and then—"

"I get it. And you, Shachar?"

"Israel is still at war with Lebanon. Has been from the beginning, and it has never ended. With my passport I can never get to Beirut. Remy, you are our only hope."

"I have a friend who lives outside of Beirut; I can give her a call." The three men stared at each other and then nodded. Shachar gave Remy a handshake and one-armed hug, quickly released before Marwan stepped in for a big hug, which was surprising to all three of them.

•

"I'm home, Gloria!" Roy hollered as he swung open the wide wooden door, leading the multicolored Victorian glass panes in a dance across the Georgian tiled steps.

"Is that my husband I hear? The famous professor Vandermere?"

"In the flesh. How was your day my darling?"

"Cold and empty without you. And rather dull at the office."

"Isn't that a good thing?"

"Only if you care about personal safety, world peace, and general economic stability. And what about you?"

"Even less glamorous, if you can believe it. They should be building me a statue in light of my intellectual prowess."

"Academic contribution is what I think you meant."

"Yes, contribution, but a statue regardless. Instead of conducting cutting edge research nobody will read they have me spending time marking papers and meeting with unbearably unprepared children."

"They are undergraduates, Roy, not children."

"You aren't in these meetings, Gloria. These are supposed to be academic sessions. It's their opportunity to meet with—"

"Someone who is worthy of a statue?"

"Precisely. But instead I get, 'So and so broke up with me,' or 'What career should I do?' or 'Is it okay if I wear jeans to the school dance'?"

"They do not ask fashion advice from you; this I'm certain."

"I do get relationship questions. The best are the more typical questions where students are seeking the correct answers. Are they even listening to my lectures!? There is no answer dammit!"

"Calm down, Roy. Why don't you go take that extra energy to the kitchen and fix us some dinner."

"Gloria, you always know what to say."

"But seriously, Roy, not all your students are that bad. What about Remy?"

"He is a doctoral student; it's not the same thing. That's an adult project for an adult student. Moreover, Remy is different."

"And how is Remy, your *star* student?"

"Do you know what Gloria? I have no idea."

"Didn't you send him to a war zone?"

"Yes, signed him up for and helped pay for, at least through a mild misuse of departmental financial resources. But you're right, I should probably check in with him."

•

"Am I speaking to Remy?" Roy held the mobile phone in front of his face, not knowing if it was on speaker-mode, or just set on the loudest setting.

"Professor, it's nice to hear from you!"

"How are things in the field?"

"Very good. I'm learning a lot. I've even been discovering—"

"That's great, my boy, just great. I'm glad I could help you."

"Yes, of course, professor, you have always been a big help to me."

"And I've always given you a lot of responsibility, a lot of trust."

"Of course, professor. Is there something the matter?"

"Remy, remember I told you about the conference in Brussels?"

"Yes, you told me it was attended by nothing but time wasters."

"And I still stand by that statement. Which is why I want you to go and present a paper for me."

"You need me to cover for you at a conference?"

"I am giving you the *opportunity* to cover for me."

"I'd love to but here in the field—"

"Then it's settled. I'll have Mrs. Harfroid in the departmental office process your travel arrangements. How soon can you get there?"

"To Brussels?"

"Of course to Brussels. Are there any other conferences you are slated to attend?"

"No, professor, but I am engaged in some very high-level—"

"You'll be fine. It's true my papers are at a very high-level, but the attendees won't notice between their coffees and carafes. The keynote speaker presents tomorrow evening.

You'll be presenting first thing the next morning. If you do well, one day I might just mention you in one of my publications."

"To have a co-authored paper that would be meaningful to me and helpful to my career—"

"Whoa, Remy, sorry to burst your bubble, I said mention your work within the context of my theoretical engagements. Get yourself ready for the presentation in Brussels; I've already emailed you the paper."

•

"Marwan, Shachar, I need to go to Brussels before I head over to Beirut," Remy tried to hide both his nervousness and his excitement.

"Are you bailing on us?"

"No Shachar, my professor needs a favor that I can't readily refuse."

"Can't, *or won't?*"

"Does it matter, Marwan? I am leaving Israel anyhow, and I can't fly directly to Lebanon from Israel. Instead of flying through Cyprus as we discussed, I'll just fly through Belgium. While I am gone, what are you two going to be doing?"

"I need to get back to the settlement. I'll tell them you weren't particularly useful. From there I can monitor Har Kesem."

"And while Shachar goes back to his settlement—"

"It is not my settlement."

"I will try to find more about The Beak here in the West Bank."

"How are you going to go about that?"

"I'm going to return to the well that led me to you."

•

"*Toujours Diamants*. Fabien speaking."

"Father, it is Haydée."

"How are you, my most lovely of daughters?"

"Fine, Father. I got your message about dinner, but I am going to the conference in Brussels remember?"

"Beautiful and so very smart. You might be more thankful that I've bestowed you with such gifts."

"I am forever grateful. But, of course I still cannot attend the dinner. It is important for me to go to the conference."

"I support you of course. I am very proud of you, standing-up to those who use blood diamonds. For too long our family industry has been sullied by the immoral practices of others."

"I fear that the problem is only getting worse."

"Which is why you must attend the conference in Brussels!"

"Adieu, Father."

•

Remy, who had been absorbed looking at a conference poster calling for the reintroduction of horse-drawn carriages, did not notice the woman standing to his right. "Excuse me," the woman said, "I just wanted to say that I thought you did a great job presenting the paper of your professor. Rather esoteric material, but you made it as interesting as possible. By the way, my name is Haydée."

"Thanks. I'm Remy, but you know that from my talk. And I recall your name from the conference program. I missed your talk, but your work seems very brave."

"Thanks, I guess."

"Don't be modest. On the ground investigative reporting on blood diamonds. Grim."

"You wouldn't believe," Haydée smiled even as her eyes sparkled with anger, "the amount of people that get hurt for shiny rocks is truly unfathomable, unless a person has seen some of the communities affected."

"No engagement ring then?"

"That's easily avoidable, if there is no engagement. If I had to be shackled in matrimony, I'd rather tattoo a ring, or tie a piece of twine."

"Twine is rough," Remy winced as he felt the tenderness on his wrists, "How about a softer rope?"

"Like?"

"Hemp."

"Agreed. I will marry thou who maketh a ring of woven hemp. I'm glad we worked that out," Haydée laughed.

"Same here," Remy grinned, "you are a tough negotiator."

"You aren't too bad either. Honestly, I'm exhausted from it all."

"Our negotiation?"

"No, my presentation of course. Care to join me for a coffee?"

"A good academic must never refuse a coffee," Remy stated solemnly.

"What about the good academics who drink tea?"

"Can't be trusted."

"But you, I can trust?" Haydée's eyes locked with Remy's.

"I drink coffee," he answered in a whisper.

"Show me," she playfully commanded.

"Lead the way."

•

"Illegal diamond mining is that widespread?" Remy asked Haydée as she sipped her cappuccino. They had escaped the confines of the conference center, finding a café on a little cobbled square.

"Yes, Remy, it's at least fifteen percent of the total

market. It gets mixed into other more legitimately mined diamonds, although someone could argue that all mining is theft, and, practically speaking, no mining operations are conducted ethically; at least in regard to its environmental and labor practices."

"I remember reading that there was a process to reduce conflict diamonds after what was happening in Liberia and Sierra Leone."

"The Kimberly Process, giving the rocks passports. It just helped strengthen the control over the market by Antwerp and Johannesburg. They claim now only one percent of diamonds are bloody, but really that means ninety-nine percent have been given travel papers by the few trading centers that control the market."

"I still don't quite understand how the diamonds get mixed together."

"Some of it happens at the source, and some of it happens along the way, but a good portion of the diamonds are fixed here, in Belgium. Russia, Israel, and South Africa are also important diamond trading centers."

"Have you been to all those places, Haydée?"

"Not yet. I have contacts in Johannesburg, and my father deals in diamonds here in Belgium. That is probably why I've been drawn to the subject. As much as I don't like the trade in general, the prevalence of blood diamonds pushes what could be an artisanal trade into a core segment of international crime."

"But in your paper, you mentioned exploring the networks on the ground. Did you mean here in Belgium?"

"No, you understood my work correctly. I've been all over western and central Africa, and much of northern Africa as well. What doesn't go south to South Africa goes north through the Sahara, reaching the global markets from there. Russia is also involved and China is increasing its activity in Angola, Botswana, Namibia, and Zimbabwe."

"These sound like major operations."

"Nobody is stuffing a few rocks in their peg leg. But enough about me. I know about your professor Vandermere's work thanks to the presentation you gave... so tell me, what's your thing?"

"Me? I'm writing a doctorate in journalism."

"Covering what?"

"Logistics."

"I see why the movement of diamonds interests you."

"Initially I went to learn about the movement of food, hummus to be exact, and maybe I still am, but it seems that I've stumbled upon networks of elicit movements."

"I like that; elicit movements. So very precise and yet so very vague."

"That's academia for you."

"Or journalism."

"Crazy as it sounds, a few people have died during the course of my research. It's getting messy in ways I could have never imagined."

"That is unfortunately too common in the shadowy world of diamond dealing. Those first few minutes, hours, and days are the most dangerous for a miner who has something of value. It's not unheard of for two miners, working and living together for months, being friends for years, immediately resorting to deadly violence upon the discovery of striking what may or may not be pay dirt."

"How awful."

"Many are driven to it as they dream about how a find could help their families while others dream only of days of debauchery awaiting them in a back room in Bamako or Burkina Faso. Or they've just gone mad spending so much time underground."

"How do the diamonds get to Belgium?"

"It wasn't in my presentation, but I received an award for uncovering a network of diamond smugglers that were using the old missionary networks. The missions themselves were used as safe houses. That network was Catholic which tapped into old linkages to Belgium's colonial past."

"That must not have won you too many friends in Antwerp, or Rome."

"My father thought it was a risky thing to publish but he does not know how bad things are. It was just a small part of the world of diamond smuggling."

"If that network is closed, how else are blood diamonds moved?"

"Like I said, there are three primary routes. There is South Africa which is huge, eastern African ports less so, and the Sahara trading networks. There are many ports in east Africa and even more ways to get to and through the Sahara."

"But how do they get to Belgium from the Sahara?"

"Through northern African ports and the border with Spanish Africa, but there are rumors that the network connects farther east to the Middle East. I don't know if that means Saudi Arabia, Russia, China or—"

"Israel? They must get their diamonds somehow."

"I have not heard that, but it does make some sense. Then given Israel's connections to Europe it would be easy to get to Belgium."

"How else would Israel get diamonds? They have no domestic production, am I right?"

"Not on scale at least. Israel could be getting diamonds from Russia either directly or through Cyprus. With so much money on the table, there are bound to be a lot of trading routes."

"Haydée. I want to stay here with you, talking about a million things. But I am off to visit a friend in Lebanon."

"That's a lovely place. When you are done with your visit do you want to meet again? I'll be here in Belgium, in Antwerp, with my father most likely."

"I'll book a round-trip from Brussels then. What is your

father like?"

"A huggable sweetheart, though every now and again, I see a glimpse of something disturbing, even…nefarious."

"Nefarious?"

"Yes, he is so gentle to me, and to most others, but sometimes I see him take a phone call or give someone a look, and there is just something about it that scares me."

"Maybe we should meet somewhere else."

"No, it's fine. He is a perfect gentleman, really. I was just confiding. Strange, I've never said anything like that to anyone."

"There is a reason I am returning to you."

"And when you do we will go traveling. Have you been to Bruges?"

"I've always wanted to go."

"Fly back here, meet my father, we'll visit Bruge, and then…we'll see."

"Haydée, I've got to get going if I am ever to make my arrangements and get to Beirut. I'll be looking forward to my return."

CHAPTER 22

"George, is it?" A well-dressed man stepped out from under a dusty animal shelter made of corrugated metal.

"Possibly," George answered warily, already knowing this was his contact but being cautious nonetheless.

"Welcome to Lebanon! Did you have any trouble with the soldiers at the border?"

"Which ones? The Israeli or the Lebanese?"

"Either."

"No."

"Good. Ronit told me to explain everything to you as I would to a child."

"That isn't necessary. I already know plenty."

"Just what a child might say."

"Go on then," George grumbled.

"You've just crossed into Lebanon, a state that is at war with Israel. You did not bring your passport, or maybe you brought several, but you used no passport to cross an international border. Interesting, yes?"

"One might wonder about such things."

"It is simple enough. The Israelis place the right soldiers at agreed times, and the Lebanese know to stay far away. Miraculously the border opens to whom and what we, and the Israelis, agree."

"And who is this 'we'?"

"Ah, yes, well not everything should be shared, *even amongst friends.*"

"Is your name Samir Youssef?"

"Possibly," answered Samir, playing along.

"The owner of a poultry farm here in southern Lebanon?"

"Such an amazing guess! You do know much."

"I'm here to inspect the route, not to play *guess who*," rumbled George.

"Then you will know I am here to lead you on a tour of our operations in the Bekaa Valley and Beirut. From the Bekaa to the coast one must cross Mount Lebanon. You can pray at Our Lady of Lebanon where there is a beautiful statue of Mary with an excellent view. We can then visit the grotto where tourists help to hide our activities."

"The smuggling routes and grotto will be enough, Samir."

"Please, we are talking *trade routes*. Which is why once we reach Beirut you'll be taken to meet some of our financiers. As a hub for commercial banks Beirut has suffered from war, as a place to deposit less visible cash and commodities, it remains highly desirable. Happily, there are some excellent restaurants along the route and each one of them will swear to you that they were Ariel Sharon's favorite eatery during the Israeli invasion. If you know about Ariel Sharon, which I'm sure you do, it is possible that each one of these restaurateurs is telling the truth!"

"That sounds lovely, a culinary journey complete with the sights, smells, and trails of smugglers."

"Traders. But first we will meet your guide." A thickset man in a sport coat and neatly trimmed beard approached.

"That won't be you? I was just beginning to warm to your humor and hospitality."

"Sadly George, I have more pressing matters, but Hadi will prove more than adequate. Hadi, I have given our friend George an overview, perhaps you could fill him in on some details."

"Yes, Samir. We will be taking a route that passes through Kherbet El Doueir, where you have just entered, into Slaiyeb, near Samir's farm, over to Cheeba, which can sometimes be accessed directly from Israel, up to Aaiha—though you may stop to rest in Rachaya—to Kfar Qouq, which is a beautiful place. If you keep north there is a crossing to Syria between Yanta and Aaita El Foukhar; but if we stay in Lebanon the route moves east to join the main road to Zahle since this area is under the complete control of our allies. Then it is under an hour to Baalbek. If you want, we can go to Aarsal and to Jura Castle and then into Syria at Flitah, though I would most certainly leave you at the border if you would like to play with the Syrians. There are also several places in the Akkar District going to Syria and the port in Tartus. The situation in Syria is not always ideal so flying in and out of Beirut is often easier. Officials in Lebanon are easy to corrupt and or threaten: the result being the same for us. Then we go to the coast, over Mount Lebanon. None of the mountain passes are great. Again, Zahle is best situated to reaching Beirut as it is just over an hour, but we will go from Baalbek over Mount Lebanon as Samir has suggested."

•

"Hadi, these Roman ruins around Baalbek are exquisite. I usually hate to waste time on assignment, but thank you for the detour." They stood outside the classical columns of the well-preserved Temple of Bacchus in what was once the heart of a Roman city.

"The detour is also the journey, my dear George."

"How do you mean?"

"These ruins hide many secrets. They are full of storerooms, tunnels, and temples bursting with treasure the likes of which Aladdin could never imagine."

"True, though I'm not sure Aladdin imagined chests full of guns and drugs."

"Aladdin was a fool. After all, his best friend was a small monkey. With the cooperation of our friends at UNESCO, parts of the site are unfortunately unavailable for tourists since they are, what is the line? Ah yes, they are undergoing restoration. Didn't you ever wonder what was behind the rope?"

"I always check behind the pillow and under the covers."

"After that we will dine at what truly was Ariel Sharon's favorite restaurant, La Crêperie."

•

The sea shimmered gold as Cedars Airlines Flight 356 touched down at Beirut's Rafic Hariri International Airport. Passport control went smoothly, and Remy felt the lingering of the afternoon heat before the gentle embrace of a Mediterranean evening. Remy hailed a taxi and asked for the restaurant that Zeina had given, "La Crêperie please."

"There could be a hundred cafés with that name. Do you have an address?"

"An address? My friend just told me that it is overlooking the sea."

"Overlooking the sea. Why did you not say so? I think I know the place, so sit back, relax, and listen to the music. Have you ever listened to our Lebanese Fairuz? She is far better than that Egyptian Umm Kulthum everyone is always going on about! Here we are in the Port of Beirut. Much of it is being rebuilt. You know between civil war, war with our neighbors, and explosions due to corruption and incompetence, there's always a need to rebuild Lebanon."

"Very interesting."

"You seem surprised."

"I'm surprised that a historic café would be located in the port."

"Perhaps I've thought of the wrong café, but even though the meter is running, I'll give you good price on the final fare. At least I've been able to give you a nice ride."

"A nice ride all right. Do you have any more guesses on where the café might be?"

"Yes, I think I know the place. It's north of Beirut and housed in an Ottoman villa. I will take you there now."

•

"Zeina! I'm so happy to see you!" She stood in the garden outside the café, wearing a radiant smile.

"Remy! You made it! You're looking quite tan for one who studies in England. Oh, there goes your taxi. How much did he charge you? I wanted to speak with him."

"Whatever he charged me, he has now taken. In any event, I did get to see some of the city."

"How very stoic. I hope when I am mugged I will be as laid-back as you."

"Shooo Zeina, don't be mean; I'm just glad to be here."

"Shush, shush! You know I am just having fun. Now come inside, meet my father, have something to eat, and tell me about your travels."

•

"Remy, this is my father, Sheik Faysal."

"I am honored to meet a sheik in his home, or café as it were. Zeina has told me so many good things about you."

"Remy is it? A friend of Zeina?"

"Yes. We went to school, did our undergraduates together."

"Tell me, do I remember correctly that you were in

the US as an undergraduate, but in the UK for your doctorate?"

"That's right."

"Care to explain why you moved to the UK?"

"It's because of my supervisor, Professor Roy Vandermere; he's brilliant. Maybe a little eccentric, but those traits often go hand-in-hand."

"Your name, Remy, I like it; it reminds me of my first shaver. They don't make shavers like that anymore. I hope you will do honor to the name."

"Bring honor to the name of your shaver?"

"The name of my first and most gifted shaver. Now then, welcome to my café La Crêperie. Zeina, choose any table, the view is best near the balcony, and sit with him. I'll have the kitchen send you something to eat."

"Father, wouldn't you like to know our order?"

"Zeina, my child, I have run this café with all my heart. It's not just a business, it is who I am."

"And one of the things you are is somebody who orders for other people?"

"Yes, I order; and right now *I order* you to sit down with Remy and have a nice time."

•

"Remy, isn't this divine?"

"Not only the view but the food and company too. Zeina, what's down there?"

"It's a base for the Lebanese navy. I'm proud to say we have one of the smallest and least effective navies in the world," Zeina boasted lightheartedly.

"Very impressive." Remy pretended to be impressed. "I see at least twenty sailors."

"Yes, and that's a fifth of our fleet," Zeina giggled.

"Next-door to the base doesn't look so militaristic. That's a gorgeous pool."

"That's our country club. And much better than the Yarzeh Country Club our presidents seem to prefer. From our height up here on the cliff it is hard to make out, but it's quite beautiful, especially with the trees and gardens that surround the pool and property."

"So Zeina, what's new with you?"

"I've got a job at the American University of Beirut."

"AUB, a fine institution."

"And you'll also be interested to learn that I have a serious boyfriend."

"Oh, and what's his name?"

"Mohamad. And he's a doctor."

"So will I be."

"Not a doctor of thoughts, Remy, but of bodies. The kind of doctor that can actually help people."

"I can help people if they need editing."

"I knew you would do good in the world."

"Thanks, Zeina. Now who is this Dr. Mo?"

"We met in Ireland when I was studying abroad, and he was doing his medical training."

"And."

"And what?"

"Mohamad?"

"Yes, what of it?"

"Nothing, only that it's a Muslim name, and you are a good Maronite Christian girl, or so I thought."

"If the ring fits, Remy."

"You're marrying him?"

"No, it's an expression silly. Mohamad's a great person."

"Zeina, if there's one thing I know about you, you choose your boyfriends poorly."

"That hurts, Remy. I do my best. Is it my fault my beauty is so overpowering to the powerful?"

"I'm happy for you, and I'd love to meet the guy. How does your father feel about it?"

"Do you think I've told my father? Do you think I want

to be confined to my room for the next century?"

"What's the plan?"

"The plan is that there is no plan. I'm young; we're dating; what more needs to be said?"

"How do you meet up with him without your father finding out? He seems to think of you as a princess."

"That's because *I am a princess* Remy."

"Okay then, how do you slip your bracelets of privilege, *princess?*"

"This week it's easy."

"Oh?"

"Well, I've got my friend Remy visiting. I simply must show him around."

"Zeina, I would actually like to be shown around."

"There'll be plenty of time for that Remy, plenty of time for us to play. I've also found you a tour company that was able to squeeze you on their bus for trips farther afield, and our family driver, Waqas, will take you around Beirut."

"Sounds great. This is such an amazing restaurant," he said, taking a bite of the delicate lemon and sugar crepe arranged in front of him after he wolfed down his galette stuffed with eggs, cheese, spinach, and mushrooms. "How is it there's so few customers?"

"Times aren't what they were. The Lebanon of the sixties is long over. We've bled ourselves into a staid poverty."

"Not everyone looks impoverished."

"Looks can be deceiving."

"At least that one table is occupied. I'd feel terrible keeping the kitchen staff busy just for me."

"They would rather work than lose their positions. They love my father, and me, and they're proud to make our customers happy."

"That other table. There's something about the man eating there."

"What of him?"

"I am intrigued."

"Intrigued, are you?"

"Yes, he moves in a different way…did you see that movement? I think he saw us."

"Remy, I think you're the one seeing things. It's time for you to get to bed. Come, let me show you to your wing of the house."

"My wing?"

•

Zeina smiled as she poured her hot tea into a porcelain cup. "Hope you enjoyed breakfast, Remy."

"I did. *Labneh* with honey, fresh bread, cucumbers, tomatoes, cheese, olives, and a strong cup of tea. It was delicious, and I am ready for the day," Remy answered while catching a whiff of French lavender.

"Great. I've got to head over to AUB for a lecture this morning. You'll head off with Waqas, here." Remy followed Zeina's motion towards a large man standing in the doorway.

"It is my pleasure to serve you, Master Remy."

"Nice to meet you, Waqas. You can just call me Remy. Let's roll."

"I think we will drive. First, I will take you to see some of the scenic views of Beirut. Then we can stop in the city center for a *manakish* for lunch. I know the best place; they use a wood oven and they make their own *za'atar* blend. After that I think we can walk around the downtown and then come back to the house to change for dinner."

"Okay Zeina. Have a good day at the office. I'm sure Waqas and I won't get into too much trouble."

"You'd better not. I have plans for you tonight."

•

"This is the downtown? A lot of neo-Ottoman buildings. And it is exceedingly clean."

"Yes, and did you notice that the buildings all seem to have been built in similar styles?"

"Now that you mention it."

"They are all new, or at least rebuilt. The area was destroyed in the war. Even though they maintained the look, the same narrow streets, people think it is a Disneyland, a fantasy of what once was."

"Do you agree?"

"I believe that even if the buildings have returned, the spirit cannot."

"I see you've thought a lot about it."

"I knew the place as a boy. I would run from the tea house delivering hot sweet tea to offices all over this area. Later, I fought here, used my knowledge from when I was a tea-boy not to win, but to survive. Look, there is the manakish place I mentioned."

"It does look, and smell, very good."

"I'll order some and bring it over."

"Thank you, Waqas."

"I see a place to sit; go there," he said as he pointed to a table where their heads would be shaded and their feet tickled with sunshine.

"Wait, Waqas."

"Yes, Master Remy?"

"That man over there. I saw him at La Crêperie last night."

"I remember him as well."

"You do?"

"I notice military."

"So you think he is military?"

"No. I think he is more than military. I think he was military, but now he is something else. A monster."

"In a suit."

"He has seen us now twice. He knows we watch, and he

knows where to find us."

"I think we should go."

"No need. He is going and our food is ready. We will eat, tour, and hope we do not see that man again."

•

"Downtown Beirut has fewer holes and craters than the last time I was here."

"George, you amaze me. Where did you hide that suit, and why are there no wrinkles?"

"Planning and luck, Hadi, planning and luck. Hold, what's that?"

"George?"

"Don't look right away. I've seen these people before. One of them was dining with a woman at La Crêperie."

"I see. I remember the bodyguard. He looks formidable. If it comes down to it, you are welcome to take on that assignment."

"Hadi, you're not such a small man yourself."

"Thank you, George, I try. But I don't think we should interrupt our meeting. These bankers are busy people. Their minutes are worth thousands, and their hours are worth millions."

"You're right Hadi, of course. However, if I see them a third time, we simply must have a *conversation*," George said as he began to unconsciously loosen his muscles as he consciously studied the movements of their bodies.

•

"Then Waqas took me back here, where I've enjoyed yet another amazing dinner with my good friend. I could sit in this café and never leave."

"That is what my father does. I'm so glad the day was enjoyable."

"Everything okay, Zeina?"

"Yes, it's just work drama."

"Drama? Tell me more."

"Not fun drama, bewildering drama."

"That doesn't sound good. What happened?"

"After my lecture, which I thought went terribly until a student told me it was great, thank the lord for brownnosers, the head of my department asked me to step into one of our meeting rooms. These rooms are usually used for student meetings. But today I walk in, and there's a panel of administrators and academics from other departments that I didn't even know existed. *Could even* exist. They had me sit and explained to me that there has been a complaint against me."

"Oh, that's rough. What was the charge?"

"They said an exam question I assigned was too easy."

"Who said that?"

"There was a student complaint. They said it was an anonymous complaint, so they could not find out more from the student."

"That's ridiculous. They formed a panel on the possibility that a student of yours had a problem with an exam question? And that it was *too easy*? I mean I've heard of complaints about things being too hard."

"Last year I had the 'too hard' complaint. The difference there was that the students, plural, put their names on it. Plus, the question was too hard."

"Too hard, too easy, law of averages says you are doing fine."

"Who follows laws? Last year the panel eventually dismissed the complaint, because if they accepted student complaints all the time we might as well close the university."

"Or at least stop giving assignments, an idea which has its supporters."

"This wasn't about ideas. The complaint this year was

not that the question was actually too easy, it was why it was too easy."

"And that was?"

"It was culturally biased!"

"Culturally biased to be easy?"

"Yes."

"Against whose culture?"

"The university."

"The university's culture?"

"Yes. The university is all about inclusion."

"Naturally."

"Right, so the question, which asked about the collision of cultures, was allegedly culturally biased because the university claims to, in essence, reject the notion that there is a collision, because all are included."

"But doesn't inclusion mean, in essence, that there might have been people excluded if the university did not include them?"

"That was my argument."

"And what did they say to that?"

"They agreed with me, and then adjourned."

"How long did all of this take?"

"About fifteen minutes."

"They put all that together for fifteen minutes?"

"Sure. Most of the tuition goes to the administrators."

"And here I thought the bureaucracy was thick at my university."

"Tomorrow I've been able to get you onto a bus trip. It will be with other tourists; I hope you don't mind sharing, after the luxury of having a driver?"

"Of course not. Where will I be going?"

"Well, I couldn't decide between going to the Bekaa Valley in the east to see the Roman ruins, and to visit a winery where you can buy me a bottle, or south to the Phoenician cities of Sidon and Tyre. I thought we could go north to Byblos together, since it's got the most to do, or at least the most places to shop, eat, and dance."

"Sounds swell. What did you pick?"

"Well Bekaa has Baalbek, which gets hit by Israeli airstrikes now and again."

"Bekaa is known for its relationship with Hezbollah."

"It is a very fertile place. Where else are they going to grow drugs?"

"Drugs? Is that what Hezbollah is up to?"

"If there is a terrorist group not into drug dealing I'd love to meet them. They do take care of the Shiites who truly are the worst-off group in Lebanon."

"That reminds me, Al Minquar."

"The Beak?"

"Exactly, ever heard of a company with that name?"

"No. Maybe it is a chicken farm? Why do you ask?"

"Never mind. Just a thought about why I would want to visit the Bekaa."

"Super! I am getting bizarre meetings at work, and now my friend is asking about the body parts of birds. Now for tonight, I think it's time you've met Mohamad."

CHAPTER 23

"The buildings are certainly denser here in southern Beirut, with a lot more people on the street."

"Yes," Zeina said, impressed that Remy had noticed, "life for the Shia is not the same for the Maronite or the Sunni."

"I also noticed the anti-aircraft batteries sprinkled about on street corners," Remy said, pointing to the Soviet made ZU-23-2 anti-aircraft cannon and a Soviet made 2K12 "Kub" surface-to-air missile system.

"You know how it is, Remy. Lebanon, in general, and Hezbollah, in particular, are at the mercy of the Israeli Air Force."

"The batteries look quite old; are they successful in deterring attacks?"

"Maybe for drones or helicopter raids, but the Israeli Air Force flies so high and fast that only an incredibly lucky shot would even graze a plane, let alone down it."

"I guess you can't blame them for trying. Must be frustrating being sitting ducks."

"Oh, they are *not* sitting ducks Remy; they control half of Lebanon. And since that's not enough for their thirst for power, they also attack Israel, claiming to be leading the resistance against Zionist oppression. All it really does, for most Lebanese, is lead to hardship."

"If it's not good for Lebanon, why doesn't the Lebanese

military prevent the attacks?"

"Should Lebanon launch into a civil war, another civil war, for the protection of Israel? And besides, it's a civil war Hezbollah is likely to win. The potential of Hezbollah running the entire country, presiding over Maronite and Sunni communities, is nothing short of frightening. Our lives here would go from sweet, yet severely troubled, to bitter and devastated. Here, in Lebanon, there is a fine line between culture and chaos, and after the civil war the country has learned about the dangers of chaos. Practically speaking, at the end of the civil war, Hezbollah was the only group not to disarm."

"How did they get away with that?"

"Leading the fight against Israel, or so they claim. With weaponry and fighters, Hezbollah is at an extreme advantage compared to the Marionite, Sunni, and Druze. As much as we might prefer to get along with our Israeli neighbors, Hezbollah ensures that isn't a possibility."

"Okay, I understand their impact on Lebanese foreign affairs and domestic politics, but then, why are there so many checkpoints here in south Beirut? Is this Hezbollah turf? What are they afraid of?"

"The checkpoints are what make it Hezbollah's turf. It was the same in the civil war for all militias. They also can do silly things like enforce dress codes or keep out riffraff."

"Like who?"

"*Like us,* Remy."

"Are we in danger here, Zeina?"

"They might be drawn to wonder about you, since spending time in Northern Europe has you looking like one of those ogres who leaves his cave once every ten years. Does the sun ever shine?"

"I thought you said I looked tan! There are plenty of nice days, not enough of course. But an ogre?"

"A very cute ogre."

"I hope we can pass through the checkpoints without

problems."

"This is the building. Mohamad texted to tell me that he's got some friends over to watch the match."

•

Remy and Zeina stepped into the room. The match was already twenty-seven minutes in. Mohamad rose to greet the newly arrived pair, leaving his three friends huddled around the television.

"Nice to meet you, Remy. I've heard a lot of good things about you." Mohamad was tall, dark, and handsome.

"Not as many good things as I've heard about you." Remy nodded toward Zeina.

"Well, thank you, and, if you don't mind, I'd like to have a word with my girl here, so please have a seat with my friends. Guys, take care of him. He is an American."

"Hi, American," said the first man to Remy in an amused voice. "I am Jarir, and these two are Ali and Talib. Sit here, and tell us who is your favorite Premier League team. I've got Manchester United; Ali loves Chelsea, and Talib adores Arsenal."

"Tottenham represents the greatest diversity of fans."

"*You can't be serious.* You can like Liverpool, or Man City, even Aston Villa because they have cool uniforms. That, and nobody knows what city Aston Villa are from. Which city supports them?"

"I'm not sure. Birmingham maybe?"

"Ham? That is haram, forbidden. Aston Villa is not an acceptable club to love. And for the same reason you should also change from liking Tottenham."

"Okay, I'll support Newcastle. Great fans."

"You can't support a building! But you are American, so what do you know about football? Do you like American football?"

"Sure, I like most American sports."

"So Mohamad was right. You really *are* American?"

"Yes, but I've also lived—"

"Hey, Talib. You know that guy's number, what's his name?"

"You talking about Aybak?"

"Yeah. Isn't he Hezbollah?"

"For sure."

"Think he would want to meet an American in southern Beirut?"

"Definitely."

"How much you think he'd pay us?"

"I don't know. Want me to call him and find out?"

"Why not? At least we'd know."

"Aybak? Hey this is Talib. Look, what would you pay for an American?…He says he is a student, but who knows? You can say he was making mental notes of everything he saw…. I want cash, US dollars, not that counterfeiting crap you guys use on the streets…. Okay, call me back…. Yes this number is best."

"Mushin is going to call us back."

"Nice work Talib. Ali, why don't you go to the kitchen and see if you can find something sociable for our American friend here."

Ali jumped up and slipped into the kitchen. There was still no sign of Mohamad and Zeina. Talib now stood in front of the door holding his phone. Jarir loomed over Remy, standing a foot taller. Tension washed over the room as Remy still tried to smile, tried to convince himself they were only joking. Ali was in the kitchen making noises that sounded like metal, or was it glass, clanging, grinding, popping. Talib glanced toward the kitchen, but Jarir did not take his eyes off of Remy, whose heart began to race. Ali burst through the door, and Remy jumped out of his seat, looking for a way out.

"Beers! Who wants one? Ha! Look at Remy! He thought we were in with Hezbollah! No way, man. Those dudes are the worst. What do you think Jarir?"

"Stone Age thinking going on over there. If you are going to grow a long beard can't you at least trim and oil it? Please sit my American friend. Talib? Who'd you call? Do you really have the number of a Hezbollah guy?"

"I did phone a Hezbollah guy. Not just now, but before. Sorry, Jarir, I meant to tell you."

"What do you mean, Talib? *What have you done*?"

"I phoned for the hashish. You told me to find some for Affan's birthday party. At least for the after-party. I should have gotten some sooner, in case Remy wanted some."

"That's cool Talib," Remy said, trying to sound like everything was indeed cool. "I'm good with the beers. But really, you call Hezbollah for drugs?"

"They run everything. Drugs and counterfeiting. It's how they make their money to buy components for missiles and shit. Hashish is for the local tastes. They really make their money on the opium. Always pushing it. *The Feed* they call it. Ali, thanks for bringing the beers."

"Of course. This brand is Mohamad's favorite." He dropped in the chair next to Remy, handed him an open beer, and slapped him on the back. "Sorry to scare you man. Drink up, and let's watch the game."

•

"Wake up, Remy! Wake up!"

"Zeina? What happened? Are you okay? Where is Mohamad?"

"Remy, he drove us back to my house and went home. You know he can't stay here."

"So what's going on?"

"Have you forgotten everything? The bus is leaving soon."

"What bus?"

"The tour bus, silly."

"Where am I going? Sidon and Tyre? It would be great to explore Phoenician cities, but I prefer Bekaa."

"I bought you a ticket for the Sidon and Tyre bus. We can get you on a bus to the Bekaa in a couple days. Both buses leave at the same time from the same place, so if you want you can try to see if they will swap. Waqas will drive you to the bus, and he can try to arrange the switch if you'd like. Now, get up, get dressed, and get going!"

•

"I'm sorry, Remy, but the bus to the Bekaa valley is full. It's a private party you see; they've booked the whole bus. The company is willing to refund your ticket or book you on the next bus to the Bekaa, which leaves in three days."

"Thanks for trying, Waqas. I guess I'll be going south to Sidon and Tyre."

"Listen, I have the rest of the day off, but my family is busy. I was just going to watch TV. So why don't you get a refund? For the same money plus petrol, I'll give you a tour of the Bekaa."

"Waqas, you offer too much."

"It's nothing. It is in both of our interests. I'll have more fun and excitement with you than sitting at home. Please take the seat next to me. We have a lot to see. The first thing we do is drive over Mount Lebanon toward Zahle."

"That sounds great, Waqas; thank you. I'll get the refund, and we can head out."

CHAPTER 24

"George," Hadi said, adjusting the rearview mirror to better see behind them.

"Yes, Hadi?"

"It's those two again."

"How could they know we were going back across the mountains to the Bekaa? Where are they?"

"Six cars back."

"Are you sure?"

"I'd bet my life on it."

"Pull into this church; let's try getting behind them."

•

"Look over there, Remy, see that church? Doesn't it seem like it is guarding that bridge?"

"I see it."

"Before that building was a church it was a Crusader fortress. But before there was a fortress there was a church."

"So it was a church, that became a fortress, that became a church? Pray tell."

"There was an eastern church there that the Crusaders repurposed as a fortress. When the Crusader invaders were expelled, the fortress was reconverted into a church."

"And before it was an eastern church perhaps it was a

Roman temple, Greek temple, or Phoenician temple?"

"Yes, and there are many types of pagans to this day. But now it is a church. Would you like to take a closer look? There are many Crusader fortresses in Lebanon, but I think this is one of the more interesting examples."

"Waqas, you are already proving your worth as a tour guide. I would be glad to examine this church in detail."

•

"George, they turned into the church. They are following us for sure."

"Keep an eye on them Hadi; I've just received a message."

"They're leaving their car; they seem to be interested in the church. Do they think we are such incompetents? This is such an insult to our professionalism!"

"Quiet Hadi! It seems as though Hezbollah has made another move against Israel."

"Damn them. The radicals in that organization are going to bankrupt us, unless we get killed first."

"Speaking of professionalism, Hadi, this is no time for hysterics. Hezbollah appears to have conducted a raid. They've slipped over the border, killed police, and kidnapped civilians. The military is being called up, and the jets are already on their way."

"Surely they will stay to the south, right George?"

"This won't be a small thing Hadi. There's an election coming up, and after that thing in Gaza—"

"There's always an election coming up and a thing in Gaza."

"It is a bit more serious in Gaza. Israel has been planning for this. They have a deterrence policy, which Hezbollah has just challenged, and this is happening at a time of tension with the Palestinians. The Israelis have an immense target list that they are just itching to cross off."

"How do you know this George?"

"Don't insult *my* professionalism."

"So what are you directed to do George?"

"When I'm out of the house, Hadi, I make my own directions. But given the circumstances, we will need to move quickly to reach the border before it is sealed."

"George, apologies, but now it's *my time* to share information. All border crossings have been sealed. Our network is strong, as you know, but this type of crisis does not allow for our type of creativity. You're going to have to find another way out, or get comfortable. I have a sofa. And, if you don't mind smelling like chicken shit, Samir has a spare cottage and could work on getting a crossing organized."

"I think I prefer to stay near the coast, and not to venture further east or south. And that includes crossing this bridge. Besides, the time for us to have a little chat with those two *sightseers* has arrived."

•

"Remy, you can see some of the stone carvings from the time before the Crusaders arrived." Waqas pointed to several segments of the walls, built with stones that did not match the rest. "Those barbarians dismantled an 800-year-old church."

"A most regrettable time, those Crusades. Truly."

"Religion is a powerful thing. It provides an opportunity to do so much good, but also so much evil. And over here," Waqas felt a presence, turned, and yelled out, "Remy! Behind you! It's that man!"

"State your name and purpose," growled George.

"Who are you to demand names from us?" Waqas roared back.

Remy froze as he witnessed the speed of George's attack on Waqas: a low, lunging elbow to the groin that got Waqas to momentarily droop his head from the strike. George quickly whipped his head up, smashing into Waqas' jaw. George then powered into Waqas, right-temple, left-abdomen, elbow to right-temple, knee into left-abdomen. Waqas was down, and Remy had only a moment's awareness that Hadi had made a move. Remy steadied himself as Hadi charged. Remy leapt to the side and stuck out his back leg, tripping Hadi, who crashed to the stone pavement. Hadi rolled over, but then stayed on the ground, unconscious.

"Again I ask, what is your purpose?"

"Remy, journalism student."

"*For fucksake son*, I did *not* ask name and occupation. Obviously, you are an amateur. Who told you to follow me?"

"Nobody. I was just visiting, taking a tour with my friend."

"Must I break your 'friend's' arm? Perhaps I will start with the fingers. And when I run out of things to break on him, I'll move on to you. Now tell me, what is your directive?"

"I…I…I am researching."

George looked up before Remy realized the noise was the sonic boom of a jet passing through the sound barrier. Remy stared into the brilliant blue sky to see an Israeli modified F-16 streak past. George was already running. *To where?* Remy thought. Running away from the bridge, away from the church. Without understanding George's flight, he looked back up. A tiny speck drifted through the sky: as if a feather had fallen, or perhaps a leaf spinning its way down from the autumn trees. The moment was serene. Birds made their calls; Waqas began to stir; cars drove past. At length the object seemed to get bigger, but still it was just a dark dash in the wide blue above Remy. George shouted. Remy turned to see he had found a ditch between the church and the road. *Clever evil man, he found shelter, but from what?* Looking back up, Remy watched as the dash, ever so slowly, continued its approach. Life had never moved so slowly. Remy was mesmerized. *Why would someone run from such beauty?* A feeling of calmness, serenity even, pulsed in Remy's ears. Then, without warning, the object revealed itself: a missile, and the leisurely descent became the fastest thing Remy had ever seen. The impact sent a shockwave across the courtyard. The bridge was destroyed; the church collapsed. Thousands of fragments were propelled in every direction. The sound assaulted Remy's ears, and his head rang with tinnitus, the sound overwhelming. *Blinking now. Bright sun. The man. That man. Standing over. A hand?*

"You alright, son?"

"I don't know. I...I seem to be bleeding. And I can't hear you very well."

"Your hearing should return soon, hopefully. And those are just lots of small cuts, nothing to be concerned about. Here, let me help you stand, see if anything is broken."

"Thanks. I guess I'm good."

"Can't say the same for our associates."

"What? Where is Waqas?"

"Sorry about that. He's over there."

"Waqas! Waqas! I'm here!"

"He can't hear. The church partially collapsed. It's crushed him."

"You can't be serious."

"Dead serious, and that ain't even a joke. It's not just you: there's my guy Hadi. His car windows blew out, and he caught a jagged piece of glass in the chest. No safety glass on that jalopy. You'll see him just outside the church. Pretty close to your friend. Hadi is the one with the blood-stained glass; your man is crushed nearby. I don't recommend a look."

"What are you talking about? Waqas is dead?"

"So, you're a student?"

"Doctoral."

"American?" George reached down to Remy, and pulled him up by his hand. "I'll help you get back to your accommodation. My car, well, my guide's car, is as wrecked as my guide. We can use your friend's car."

"What car?"

"The one your friend Waqas drove. I already found the keys."

"Drove. Yes. Let's get back. I need to see if my other friends are okay."

"Back to Beirut then?"

"Please."

"Then get in; and the sooner the better."

•

"This car handles pretty well for a vehicle its size. I'll remember that." George was driving, and a stunned Remy was riding beside him. At length, Remy began to recover and looked over at George.

"Can I ask a question?"

"No."

"I think I deserve a question."

"That's a dumb way to demand something. Very American. Nobody deserves anything. Nothing."

"You'd rather sit here in silence?"

"Figured that out on your own did ya? I'll give you one question, for your friend that I…engaged with. Maybe that was a mistake."

"Who are you?"

"Next."

"What are you doing here?"

"Try again."

"Where were you going?"

"Cut the journalist bullshit. Who, what, where, when, how. Last try, my joviality is running out."

Remy thought, *Okay, he is helping me. Why? He could have killed me after the blast. I said I was American. He seems American. He must be some sort of government agent. Asking him about his identity and motives won't get me anywhere.*

"The Beak. Ever heard of it?"

"I'll answer your one question if you answer one of mine."

"You first."

"No."

"Okay."

"Where did you hear about The Beak?"

"On a box."

"Where did you come across this box?"

"With a friend."

"Where, not with whom."

"Now who's the journalist?"

"Tell me, or I stop, and you die."

"I found it in an Israeli settlement. It was odd to see a Lebanese address in an Israeli facility. I figured that if one day I came to visit Lebanon, I'd check up on it."

"They do feed."

"Feed?"

"Yes. For chickens."

"Israeli chickens?"

"Yes. There is a shortage of feed in Israel."

"That is supplied by Lebanese entities?"

"You saw the box."

"How do you know about The Beak? And Israeli feed flows? Are you in industry? Farming? An attaché? Economist?"

"I do logistics."

"What do you help move?"

"Enough questions. Here is the place. La Crêperie. Any good?"

"You tell me."

"Ah, so you did see me, and you remembered me?"

"I did."

"Perceptive. I'll remember that."

•

"Remy! There is a war on!" Zeina ran to him as he stepped inside the restaurant.

"Yes, I know Zeina. Waqas was killed."

"What?"

"Airstrike against a bridge. We were nearby at a church when the explosion collapsed the building on him. I'm very sorry."

"Waqas…but his family…." Zeina, as if in a trance, moved to the veranda. "We need to prepare."

"Prepare? For what?"

"The chaos. We must go and fill our car and all our canisters with petrol. Let's buy a solar panel. Bottled water. And flour. Lots of flour. With water, flour, salt, and heat, we can eat. With fuel we can cook, clean water, and move about to look for more fuel, food, and water."

"How long is this going to last?"

"*Who knows?* Already the airport is struck, the bridges, the boats. Look there, out the window, our navy is sunk. There are twenty sailors floating somewhere in the bay. I suggest you call your embassy. See if you can find a way out."

•

"Thank you for calling the US Embassy consular services. Akeem speaking. How may I assist?"

"Hi. I am a US citizen trapped in Lebanon. Can you help me leave?" Remy stood looking down from the veranda at the destroyed naval base.

"Are you injured?"

"Minor cuts, nothing serious."

"Then no, sorry."

"Have I called the wrong place? Do you assist in evacuations?"

"You have called the correct number."

"Then can you assist me in leaving Lebanon?"

"There is currently no program to evacuate."

"When will there be a program?"

"It is being worked on now."

"Can you tell me anything about it?"

"Certainly. There are many Americans in Lebanon. A large boat will need to be organized. We estimate a boat for 3,000 people. This takes time."

"How much time?"

"Three weeks."

"That long?!"

"Also, there is the issue of cost."

"What is the issue?"

"The cost for the evacuation. It is part of what is being planned."

"The cost?"

"Yes. The US Department of State warns citizens of the dangers of traveling to Lebanon."

"There are warnings for most of the world."

"Correct. And in this case, like many others, there is a cost to ignoring safety advice."

"Cost? What are you talking about?"

"It will cost roughly $10,000 per person for a place on the boat."

"You're going to collect thirty million dollars to rescue your citizens from a warzone?"

"It would not be fair to ask the taxpayer to fund your adventure."

"That's a bit unfair."

"Nevertheless, part of the program of evacuation will include a loan option."

"Loan?"

"We cannot assume everyone that wants to be evacuated will have $10,000 available at the time of embarkation. So, we will make loans available, even for those with poor credit, though their interest rates might be higher. It is all being discussed. I suggest you leave me your contact details, and we will contact you when more information becomes available. How do you spell you name?"

•

"Good morning, this is the US Embassy Consular Services calling for a Remy—"

"Speaking." Remy sat up. He was sitting on the veranda, again, gazing into nothingness, again.

"Please hold."

"Certainly."

"Hi, Remy."

"Oh, it's *you*. Hello. Never thought I'd hear from you again after the drive back from the church."

"And why not?" George pretended to ignore the fact that Remy had so quickly recognized his voice, though he was impressed. "We might meet again if you agree to a proposal I have for you."

"I'm listening."

"We've got a problem, and I am hoping that you are our solution. There are six unaccompanied minors that need evacuating. These are kids with citizenship who are visiting non-citizen family members. That sort of thing."

"Which makes them eligible for an emergency evacuation?"

"You've got it. I've got a place for you on a helicopter this evening if you can round 'em up and bring them to the embassy."

"Round up the children?"

"Yeah, there are six, but there are two sets of siblings,

so only four addresses to visit."

"Are they near me?"

"If the greater Beirut area is near you, then yes. They are all over the city."

"You don't have anyone else to get them?"

"This is your way out, if you want it. And no, there is nobody else. Everyone is busy, evacuated, or not permitted to go into war zones. Asking you to do so is a bit of a loophole. Plus, we go way back right? I know you can handle the job."

"Send me their details."

"I knew I could count on you. Get a pen. You don't have access to the internet."

•

Beirut was in war, yet again. The jets, empty streets, hiding, seeking ways out. Moving from neighborhood to neighborhood was a slow process. Rides were halted due to rubble blocking roads, or a hesitation by the taxi driver to enter an area controlled by a rival faction. Remy had to change taxis, walk, and hitch rides from friendly faces, first alone, and then with an increasing number of children.

Remy arrived at the US Embassy with only four children. Getting to the embassy was difficult, as many roads were blocked by the Lebanese Army. The taxi driver told Remy and the kids they were lucky to be with such a good driver. "I am not worried about the war. War, always war. Now oil prices. Here is what matters." Remy used his last dollars to tip the driver who, at great risk, had found a way up the hill to the embassy that overlooked the sea.

"Is this Alfa gate?" Remy asked.

"Freeze! Do not move," one of the US Marines shouted before three of them trained their M16s onto the little group of five. "What are you doing here?"

"Remy Ripken here, as per my instructions, with four

unaccompanied minors to be evacuated."

"Don't move." One of the soldiers went to check the story.

Once confirmed, Remy and the children were told to walk to another gate. This gate had people pushing to get to the front of the line to ask for emergency evacuations. Those who were not among the people on the list were barred entry. After much effort, pushing and shoving, asking and pleading, Remy and his young entourage got to the front of the line for the gate, where Remy passed the five passports through the bars to an awaiting sergeant.

"The children are on the list. You are not on the list. I do not see your name. Please step aside, sir!"

"No. No, please check again!"

Remy peered through the bars straining to look at the names on the document. The document was typed but at the bottom there was one handwritten name.

"There! I think that's me at the bottom!"

"No, that is not you," the soldier answered, "that name is *Renni*, that is not you."

"Renni! That is definitely meant to be me."

"No, I am sorry, sir, it is not your name, and you must step aside."

"Is Renni even a real name? It is a simple spelling mistake!"

"I am sorry, sir; you might not like it, but this is someone else's name, and I will not let you take their place."

"I am not trying to take anyone's place but my own. Let's ask someone else if they think Renni and Remy are likely confused. *Please*."

The sergeant nodded in agreement and walked over to a marine lieutenant who recognized that there was a similarity in names, and decided it would be worth talking to the captain. The captain came, noted the similarities of the name and that the supplicant knew about the evening evacuation. "Plus he had the kids with him," the lieutenant added helpfully.

A minute later Remy was on the embassy grounds. "Welcome back to the US. Drop your stuff and prepare for a cavity search."

A convoy of black Chevy Suburbans came to take everyone to another room on the grounds to wait. And wait. And wait. Finally, someone came with an announcement. The waiting evacuees were told that because it was getting late they would only have time to do one helicopter run to Cyprus. Half of the people who had traveled from across this besieged country, many of them families or the elderly, were not getting out. The official explained there was but one fair way to determine who stayed and who could leave: Those who were on the list to board the first flight would get to go, children mostly, the rest had to leave the embassy. Names were read, pushing and yelling ensued. Some families were going to be split, and while they argued and pled for their family to come with them, the official made sure that they understood the only way to not split the family was to wait until another day. Remy realized that, even here, where they were so close to safety, families were being torn apart by war.

The unaccompanied minors had nowhere else to go; they had to be evacuated, and, as their temporary chaperone, that meant Remy would also be evacuated. The hours crept on until darkness came. Then there was an Israeli bombing run, and all in the embassy waited until the skies were clear.

During the wait the lucky forty were taught how to wear the helmets and put on life jackets that the soldiers indelicately confessed would do nothing except "help retrieve your bodies." Remy prepared his young charges. Everyone lined up single file. The order was given to run to another spot, and then crouch. A moment later a helicopter flew in so low that it appeared to rise from the sea. It landed comfortably on the embassy grounds.

Marines ran over to unload the choppers, then they loaded the passenger bags, only one bag per person not weighing more than fifteen kilos, stacking them in the middle of the chopper as if they were stacking wood for a large bonfire.

The passengers ran to the helicopter, boarded, and were directed to sit along the sides, on the floor, or on mobile stretchers an inch off the ground. Cargo straps served as seatbelts for the passengers, and their bags. Then, quickly, off! The helicopters took to the sky. Flying low over the sea, Remy watched as the soldiers kept the back loading door open while firing a few rounds, a warning, into the warm waters of the Mediterranean. A view opened up, as the helicopter ascended, of a smoldering Beirut getting ever smaller. Remy wondered if Zeina would survive. *She will, of course*, Remy decided, knowing that he was merely comforting himself. The helicopter flew off into the distance, leaving Lebanon behind.

CHAPTER 25

Ronit, standing outside one of her warehouses, was trying to concentrate despite the heat. She always had everything planned out, yet the constant shifting of plans and strategies was starting to grate. Ronit pointed to two of the new goons resting under a nearby tree. "Dan, what the hell are the new guys talking about?"

"I don't know, Ronit."

"Go and listen. I don't trust them."

"I picked Kohav and Yair myself, did a lot of research."

"I'm sure you did; and now I am telling you to go check them again."

"Yes, Ronit."

•

"Kohav, what do you think of the boss?" Yair said as he tilted his plastic chair backwards to rest against the tree. "Scares the shit out of me. The pay is good, but if you ever crossed her?"

"I never would," said Yair as he brought the chair back down, "but I shudder to think what she would do if she got paranoid and started to suspect us."

"I hope that never happens. I'm into loyalty you know."

"Loyalty, Kohav?"

"Yeah, I am loyal to whoever pays me. I love money,

you see."

"Is there anything else you love in this world?"

"Yeah of course, you my man, and hummus."

"Hummus. Now you are talking my language. Abu Ghosh is the best no?"

"Ha! Yair you are too funny. That tourist trap on a hill? Turned against their own people in '48. Allied to us Jews over their Arab brethren."

"Still, many people think they serve the best hummus."

"Yes, but all of those people are tourists."

"Fine then Yair, where would you go for the best hummus?"

"Falafel Kaduri for falafel."

"That's a memory from childhood."

"Okay, so Hertzl Sabich for sabich."

"Odeh's Sabich is better, and you know it. But what about hummus?"

"Hummus…Abu Hassan."

"Yair, that is a serious answer. I might grant you that Abu Hassan is the best in Tel Aviv."

"And Jerusalem, and the south and the north."

"Most of the north, but not all."

"Who is better than Abu Hassan?"

"Hummus Said in Acre."

"Kohav, you have just noted the second-best place to buy hummus."

"I think not."

"Abu Hassan has better beans, better *fūl*."

"Granted, but Hummus Said has better bread."

"Can't disagree. But Abu Hassan has a grit that keeps the hummus together, to make it a meal."

"Grit? Who wants that? Said makes hummus that is smooth to the touch, like a woman you've never even dreamed of."

"I sleep very well. Especially when I am full on Abu Hassan."

"The *msabaha* is much better at Hummus Said's. That's hummus upgraded."

"You know what Kohav, the *msabaha*…it *is* better at Said's, and so I will change my vote. The best in the land is Hummus Said and the second best is Abu Hassan."

"Blessed are people who dine at Said's or Abu Hassan's."

•

Rabbi Avraham gazed into the hills as if he could see all the way to Jordan. "Shachar, what did you learn about Osama's Table? Where is your student friend Remy?"

"Remy has left, gone back to Europe. He flew to Brussels; I have a photo of his ticket, here, look. I think he was glad to get away."

"I'm sure he is. This is no region for the weak. And Osama's Table?"

"It's a bar. It serves alcohol and has mediocre bands that use naughty words. It's pretty risqué for the West Bank, which is why it probably gets mentioned, but every third apartment in Tel Aviv is probably coarser. I don't think it's worth going again, and now that Remy is gone it would be unnecessarily dangerous to do so."

"Fine work then Shachar. Upon reflection, it might have made things more complicated had we killed him. Will you stay with us a little longer?"

"I would be glad to. There are still nearby sights I wish to see, though this time from the safety of the settlement."

"A wise choice. There will be a meteor shower overnight. I'm not sure I will get up for it, but I highly suggest you do, and if not this time then soon, before you get like me."

"And what is that Rabbi?"

"Tired and maybe a bit cynical. God made the world perfect, and in that perfection everything we are given is also taken away. Time steals all. I prefer to keep my sights on reclaiming our birthright, not for myself, but for our future generations. For that I need rest."

•

At midnight Shachar rose from his bed. He wasn't sleeping well. The dreams were happening again. Shachar shut his eyes tighter, but the darkness only made it worse. Shachar muttered to himself, "I should have never come out here, gotten involved in this. I was balanced in Tel Aviv. Had my shit in order. Mostly. Successfully self-medicated at least."

Annoyed, Shachar decided to take the rabbi's advice and look at the night's sky. The air was freezing, and Shachar went to pull his comforter off the bed. Coming back out Shachar stopped as a wall of light appeared.

He slipped into his sandals noting the stiffness in his feet from the cold. He saw a truck leaving Har Kesem, its headlights bright in the moonless night. *At this hour?* Shachar grabbed his binoculars, and raced toward the gate of the settlement. The truck was to pass on the road below. There was a bus stop there with a streetlight. That would be Shachar's only chance to read the license plate. Breathless, Shachar got into position. Before the truck sped past into the deep dark night, he decided to change plans and not focus on the license plate, instead noting part of the registration number of the container the truck was carrying.

•

Planning on returning to The Sahara Lounge in the evening, Marwan decided to first pay a visit to Raffy. Major Rafiq al-Khana was the name on the nameplate that Marwan read as he pushed open the door, and noticed that his friend appeared deep in thought, *or was it deep in paperwork* Marwan wondered idly as he stepped into the office unannounced. "Raffy. I must apologize."

"Marwan! One should always knock, it is true, but to

delay your visit would be unforgivable."

"Thank you, my friend. I came here to tell you that I met Remy the journalism student. I must concur with your intuition in the matter: he is not a spy, and is unaware if he is being watched."

"And? *Is* someone watching Remy?"

"I lingered when he departed, wondering if there would be any sign of surveillance. I saw nothing, but of course most of Israel's spy work is at the office."

"I gave him a dummy phone."

"Only dummies think they are foolproof."

"A harsh truth. Where did you meet him?"

"Through a mutual friend."

"Who was?"

"A friend that was mutual."

"And you met him where?"

"The friend or Remy?"

"Either, or both. Marwan, you can tell me."

"I first met…"

The phone rang. "Hold on, Marwan." Major al-Khana listened, nodding into the phone, "Be there in ten minutes, no seven minutes. Keep him away from everyone…. That most certainly includes police…. How will you do it? Figure it out, or you can figure out how you became unemployed!" In one motion he replaced the phone, rose from his chair, and swung on his coat.

"What is happening, Raffy?"

"We've caught a Palestinian truck driver who thought he could sneak through Area A. Unless the Israelis launch an operation, the driver is ours to question. Come, let's find out if there is anything he can tell us."

•

Major al-Khana spoke to the truck driver handcuffed to a metal chair in the basement of the Customs Police building.

Like most, the driver had heard about the rumors of what happened in the basements of Palestinian security services. Knowing the rumors were true, he trembled with fear. Calmly, Rafiq asked, "What's in the truck?"

The driver tried to speak bravely, frightened not only of the police, but of his employers, "You've already checked."

"Yes, I have seen it, but I'd like you to explain it."

"Woodchips."

"Of what type?"

"I am not a dendrophile."

"You don't need to love trees to know your cargo. And besides, who doesn't love trees?"

"Even still."

"Even still, I would like to know where the woodchips came from."

"I picked them up at a warehouse."

"And which warehouse was that?"

"I forget."

"If you continue to forget we have ways of helping you remember, or you could cooperate and go home in a few hours."

"I need to keep the truck. It is my livelihood."

"Perhaps you should not be risking so much on illegal deliveries."

"There is nothing illegal about moving woodchips."

"Are you certain of that? I ask again, from which warehouse did you pick up the woodchips?"

"Do I get to keep the cargo as well?"

"Depends on how much you tell me before I lose my patience. I'll be honest with you: my commanding officer was killed. I am less interested in upholding the law than in exacting revenge. I will pursue. I will not stop. None of us will. Tell me or lose a limb."

"Raffy—"

"Marwan, if you don't have the stomach for real police work—"

"I will tell all I know," the driver whispered.

"See, Marwan?"

"Fine, but why don't you gloat less and question more?"

"Driver, what type of woodchips are you carrying?"

"As you know, they are olive woodchips."

"And where did you pick up these olive woodchips?"

"Bethlehem."

"And where were you taking them?"

"Will you release my truck?"

"Depends if I find your answer interesting."

"A farm."

"Which one?"

"The Poultry People."

"A chicken farm? Are you certain?"

"Yes, I have done this route before."

"What does a chicken farm do with olive woodchips?"

"I think they burn them."

"Why would they do that?" Rafiq asked, before shouting "*Why would they do that*?"

"I swear, I don't know. I'm just a driver."

"And who hired you?"

"My cargo, I must keep my cargo."

"Tell me who hired you."

"A courier service in Bethlehem."

"Name?"

"Assisi Associates."

"Take your truck, and your cargo, and get out of my sight. Consider finding a new line of work, or we might meet again when you can offer me less." Major al-Khana leaned over the prisoner, removed the handcuffs, then pushed the chair with so much force that the chair and driver were sent sprawling on the floor. As the driver looked up, petrified, he saw the door open and a young policeman ready to escort him out of the building.

•

"Raffy, were you really going to dismember that driver?"

"Would that trouble you Marwan?"

"Yes."

"I was not. Good cop, bad cop, that's all. We make a good team."

"Sure."

"Good. Now what would a farm do with olive woodchips? Did the driver's story about burning make sense to you?"

"It's possible. Olive woodchips burn for a long time, and give off a lot of heat. It would make some sense to use it for energy generation, especially if a factory did not want to rely on the electrical grid."

"Would the electrical needs of a chicken farm require such large amounts of power?" Rafiq asked.

"Or are there other activities that need to be supported?"

"As I said, we make a good team. Would you be interested in visiting a chicken farm?"

"I hear they smell for miles around, so no thank you. I have a reputation to uphold."

"To whom?"

"My own nose. I once worked for a courier service."

"And."

"And I smelled of cardboard box for days. It was like I was selling fish or meat at the market: the smell would just linger, and I could never shower it off."

"What did you do?"

"Two things. I quit the job, and I bathed in coffee."

"Coffee?"

"Yes. Not normal coffee, but instant. An expensive bath I know, but it worked and was worth every agorot."

"Qirsh. We use Jordanian Dinars here, officially at least."

"Officially I, and everyone I know including you, use Israeli Shekels."

"I also have US dollars."

"Which you use to change into shekels."

"Who will go to the farm? Not me."

"And why not?"

"I am allergic to feathers."

"You are not."

"How would you know?"

"Because when I slept over you had feather pillows."

"What a memory you have, Marwan! And I appreciate that you thought so highly of my station in life that you assumed I could provide such luxuries. No, sadly it was polyester. Soft, but not feathers. If only I wasn't cursed with such a malady as allergies. But, of course, you also have the problem of being able to smell too well."

"I'm not going. We'll have to find another way. Did you have that driver followed?"

"Of course."

"Let's see where else that truck goes. Perhaps we will be able to see what's going on through old-fashioned police work. Catch, release, follow, watch, and wait."

•

"Haydée, it was horrible." Remy was on the verge of tears, put on a brave face, and continued. "Lebanon was so beautiful, but the violence *so present*. It really is a tragedy."

"One of many tragedies in our world, Remy." A man entered the hotel bar and walked quickly toward Remy and Haydée. She saw him first. "Hello, can we help you?"

"The name is Giovanni Mancini, and you are Haydée?"

"What do you want?"

"Can we speak privately?"

"I'd prefer to remain here. Anything you say can be shared by my trusted friend."

"Then be quiet and listen carefully. I am an agent for UNESCO."

"The United Nations—"

"Yes."

"The one that guards cultural sites?"

"Yes. But we are much more you see. We protect against the smuggling of antiquities. As such, we have developed a capacity for tracking smuggling operations: artifacts or otherwise."

"I get it. You need me."

"We need you both, but you need me as well."

"And why is that?"

"You are wanted. There is a price on your head."

"Me? What do you mean?"

"There is a credible threat to your person."

"By whom?"

"A group of camorra out of Naples."

"Get real. Why would they care about me?"

"You are exposing smuggling networks, and someone powerful has tasked them with the job of cleaning up the mess."

"The mess being Haydée?" Remy said as he struggled to absorb the information.

"Unfortunately, yes." Giovanni turned his eyes to Remy, "And as for you, Remy, well, I can't trust my colleagues, and Haydée is in danger, and now, maybe, you are likewise, so until we can figure this out I'm going to need your help."

"What can I do?"

"You can help Haydée survive, and help me to catch the criminal behind the bounty."

"I don't need you two to survive this," Haydée cut in, "I've been through worse."

Remy agreed. "I have little experience in the matter. Further, I am quite busy at the moment you see—"

"Haydée's life is in danger! I know you have contacts in Israel—"

"How do you know that?"

"You are on the passenger list as arriving from Israel."

"That means I was at the beach, not making contacts."

"If you haven't made any then, perhaps you could."

"For what purpose?"

"There is a shipping container, and I need to know which boat it's in."

"How in the world could I find that out? How would I even know which container is the correct one?"

"Remy is just a student," Haydée protested. "Leave him out of this."

"We need all the help we can get." Giovanni looked at Haydée, who seemed to accept the point, then he turned back to Remy. "I know when the container leaves, and I know the destination is the southern Italian port of Taranto. On the heel, in Apulia, Taranto concentrates on transshipments: a useful specialty in the middle of the Mediterranean. From there the container will be transferred, but by then I'll be able to know the ship, and we'll be at the port to see where it'll go next."

"What does that have to do with us?" Remy asked.

"Because the tip I got that brought me here also said the way to find those that pursue Haydée is by following this container."

"Three questions," Remy asked.

"Of course."

"How do you expect us to trust you, what is in the container, and—"

"And I suppose I'll just wait for you boys," Haydée scoffed, "to keep me safe."

"Haydée, I will get to you. We'll need a way to keep you out of harm's way until I can get a handle on this case."

"You want me to disappear? That sounds a lot what you are supposedly protecting me from."

"Both of you are going to need to trust me." Giovanni looked past Haydée. "Shit," Giovanni hunched forward hoping he wasn't seen, "those two are camorra."

"Which two?"

From across the lobby two men whipped out pistols from inside their jacket holsters. Giovanni pushed Haydée to the floor as the smaller of the two fired his weapon into the overturned table. The gunmen continued to shoot, keeping Giovanni and Haydée glued to the ground. As the gunman approached, Remy tossed a chair and slid behind the bar. When the chair landed near the gunman, who glanced at it, Giovanni was back on his feet, service pistol drawn. "Drop the gun, Lucca."

Meanwhile the bigger gunman rushed in and tackled Giovanni, driving the wind from his lungs. The agent's gun fell to the thin beige carpeting with barely a noise.

"Looks like you've dropped your gun." The large man stood over Giovanni with a grin. "Is that the girl, Giovanni? You found her for us."

Haydée darted up and slammed her right knee into the big man's groin. Remy, armed with a napkin dispenser, hit Lucca in the back of his head, sending him to the ground, blood oozing. With one camorra down and the other dazed, Giovanni reached for his gun and rose.

"Don't, Giovanni."

"Dino, it's time for a nap." With that Giovanni hit the big man with the pistol, dropping him next to Lucca. Giovanni saw that Lucca was still down, but beginning to stir.

"Haydée, Remy, as I said, you'll need to trust me. Let's go."

CHAPTER 26

The flight to Rome was delayed. Once onboard Giovanni and Remy were quiet while Haydée seemed nonchalant, reading the inflight magazine and ordering a beer. Remy experienced waves of guilt for having left his friends in the Middle East. *Would I be here if I hadn't gone for a coffee with Haydée?* Giovanni tried to focus on the mission, about the next moves; but also marveled at how lucky he had been to reach Haydée and Remy in time.

Haydée continued to mask her utter confusion about the identities of her new traveling companions, and why she was in danger and on the run. *Wasn't Belgium safer than Italy? Aren't I in danger from camorra, who live in Italy?* Haydée shook her head as doubt bubbled up that Remy and Giovanni were not her rescuers, but her captors. Even while she feigned confidence, mentioning the new direct flight from Brussels to Marrakesh, she barely touched her beer.

Giovanni breathed a deep sigh of relief after touching down in Rome. Remy and Haydée could barely breathe. It was one of those perfectly clear Roman days, comfortable as long as you weren't getting beaten down by the sun.

"Where to now?" Haydée assumed she was in danger as soon as they'd exited the plane.

"To the first pizza I see. I'm starving," Giovanni answered, nonplussed.

Remy thought of the unsatisfying sandwich he had forced himself to eat on the flight. "I enjoyed the food in Belgium."

"But they lacked flavor, and refinement."

"The portions were large."

"Not everything should be supersized."

Haydée grasped at the opportunity for normalcy and joined the conversation. "Our Belgian cuisine is far more refined than tossing cheese onto bread and shoving it in an oven. Further, we are in the airport, how can you credibly suggest that there is gourmet food to be found here?" Haydée was feeling fed-up with the two of them. *At least Remy looks exhausted, but Giovanni seems to have forgotten that he wasn't home for the holidays,* Haydée thought, annoyed.

"Gourmet? This is Italy, everything is gourmet. Have you ever tried pesto from Genoa or balsamic from Modena? And the wine, oh the wine! The Piccione in Perugia, fish in Bari, arancini in Sicily, and did I mention the wine? And beyond all sits Naples."

"Naples? What about Rome?" Remy realized he was still starving, and the thought of good food, instead of the threat against them, was appealing.

"Rome is next. Rome takes from all Italian regions, mixes it together, and creates dishes that are concocted by master chefs. But each ingredient is better elsewhere."

"Are we going to sit in Rome," Haydée demanded, "sampling imitations of Italian regional cuisine?" *I should have eaten a sandwich, not ordered beer,* Haydée reflected.

"No. If we are being pursued by camorra then we must go to Naples to clear our names."

"Is Naples safe?" Remy tried to lean against the wall, but missed. "I've always heard that it is not. And if that's where they're looking for us…."

The doubt Haydée had felt for her companions resurfaced.

"Sicily may have the mafia, but they cannot compare to the ferocity of the camorra, the gangs and gangsters of Naples. But we'll be okay. You're with me after all."

Haydée tried to master herself. "It doesn't sound like Naples is the place to go for people interested in avoiding crime, danger and most especially the camorra."

"They will never expect it. Besides, we'll need to figure out which boss is after us and why. It is the only way to end it. A happy side note, Naples houses the best cuisine in all of Italy, and therefore the entire world."

Remy's stomach rumbled. "I thought you said Rome was the best."

"No, no, no. I was explaining how Roman cuisine is good given the superiority of individual radiance found elsewhere. But nothing can compete with Naples and it's buffalo mozzarella, golden wheat, and San Marzano tomatoes. Carefully cultivated ingredients, lovingly kneaded and fired over wood…this is the gold standard of cuisine."

"Great," replied an exasperated Haydée, "you are taking us on a tour of Neapolitan pizzerias on a quest for my last supper."

"Haydée, it would be God's gift to have a pizza in Naples as your last supper. Yet our deaths are not my intention. I have a plan to unravel the threat; and I promise that until then I won't order a pizza."

At least we know one of your motivations, thought Haydée and Remy at the same time.

•

"Hello?"

"Hi Marwan, this is Shachar."

"Hello, my friend."

"Any progress?"

"I've found, or we, I should say, have found a truck that is of interest."

"Us? Is Remy with you? I thought he had left."

"He has, I believe. I am with my good friend Rafiq al-Khana, a major in the Palestinian Customs Police. He is one of my oldest friends, and, as it happens, has already been working on cases involving Har Kesem."

"How can you trust an officer in the Palestinian police force? You know how corrupt they are?"

"I am police! And as I said, he is my oldest friend. Rafiq's mentor was recently killed in an operation near Har Kesem. And he spent the night on the run with our Remy. My friend Rafiq is already deeply enmeshed in our project."

"What did you find?"

"The customs police caught a truck with driver. Raffy, that's what I call Major al-Khana—"

"Is that what I should call him? I used to listen to children's music by Raffi. I love the song *Baby Beluga*."

"If you call him Raffi he will shoot you. Besides, the best Raffi song is *Bananaphone*."

"What happened with the bust?"

"The truck had olive woodchips—"

"Woodchips?"

"Are you capable of letting me speak? The driver gave us good information, and then we did a catch and release. We followed him. The driver delivered the cargo, and then drove into a heavily guarded compound near Bethlehem. We watched the compound and waited for the truck to come back out. Finally, a container truck with Israeli plates drove out."

"Marwan, what was the number on that container?"

"Let me finish. There was an escort."

"What do you mean?"

"It had a car that drove in front. It had three men.

There was another car with two people behind. The first car turned back before entering an Israeli controlled area, while the last car went with the container truck to Har Kesem."

"Is that so?"

"Yes. We waited again. And then late that night we were rewarded when the container truck re-emerged and then sped off. We tried to follow but it went deeper into Area C and eventually we lost track of it. It looked like the truck was headed toward the port."

"I caught a glimpse of a truck speeding through the night. Also seemed to be headed toward the port. Not much else down that direction."

"That's what we thought. We only got the first half of the container number."

"Fabulous! I got only the latter part of the container."

"Nothing else? No other details? What kind of cop are you?"

"I am not a cop. I am trained to notice other…details."

"Is that so?"

"Not saying I am happy about all the choices I've made in my life, just saying what I have been trained to do."

"Sorry I said anything. Any ideas how to track the container? Unless I get a better idea, Rafiq and I can return to our surveillance, see if we can get another chance."

"I've got a friend at the ports."

"Will he help?"

"I'm sure of it."

"Can we trust him?"

"One of my oldest friends."

•

"Menashe."

"Shachar?"

"I'm sorry about Ephraim."

"Shot in the middle of Tel Aviv. On the boulevard!"

"I know all about it."

"You do?"

"I was there."

"What else do you know?"

"That I need a favor."

"Does this involve my brother's killer?"

"It's important, that's all I can say."

"I am your servant Shachar."

"Do you still work at Israel Port Authority?"

"Yes."

"I need you to find me a container. I would like to know the ship, destination, and details of the shipping company."

"What is the registration?"

"Well, it came in two parts, mostly complete. Also, some other details of the truck."

"I'm sure I can find it, and maybe some of the other details you request, but then all debts are paid. Unless, of course, you catch Ephraim's murderer."

"Agreed."

•

"Remy?"

"Shachar. Nice to hear your voice."

"I have news."

"What news?"

"I've been working with Marwan. And apparently a major in the Palestinian Customs Police each of you know."

"Raffy al-Khana."

"They followed a truck that took a container, in the dead of night, from Har Kesem to the port."

"What's in the container?"

"Something important. We aren't sure."

"Then how do you know it is important?"

"We know."

"How?"

"Because we are all trained to know."

"Okay, so what in your training tells you that this container is important?"

"Remy. It is intuition. You wouldn't understand."

"I also have intuition. And mine includes asking questions in response to vague answers."

"Fine. Marwan and this al-Khana stopped and questioned a driver. That led them to a heavily guarded warehouse, which led them to a container on a truck, that itself was guarded. It went to Har Kesem, which is where I saw it speed past in the middle of the night. Look, Remy. There is something suspicious going on, and this container is our chance to see what all the fuss is about."

"So go look."

"I can't."

"Why?"

"It is already in the port. I cannot access it. Though I want to look, I also want to know who wants it."

"It being the container filled with—"

"With its contents!"

"Okay, okay. How can I help?"

"I was able to find out the information on the container, its number, ship, shipping company and destination. Remy, it is coming to Europe."

"Where is it headed?"

"Italy. Port of Taranto, in the south."

"Italy? I am in Italy! And I've been asked to look for a container at Taranto."

"Why?"

"Long story. Do you know where it is heading after it lands in port?"

"No. We were hoping you might be able to—"

"I'm a bit busy at the moment. You see, a gunman nearly killed us—"

"Who is us? Who else is there?"

"Haydée, who I met at a conference. She researches smuggling, diamonds most particularly. And Giovanni, an agent from UNESCO."

"Those anti-Semites!"

"The diamond industry?"

"What? You must know that UNESCO has given Israel some very unfair treatment."

"Nevertheless, UNESCO has developed an expertise in smuggling. Both of these people seem to know their stuff. I think they could be useful, and besides, I am already much attached."

"To Haydée? Or Giovanni?"

"Neither, or both, it's the situation. Complicated. A bit of three's company. We were shot at! We're in Italy to find out why we were targeted."

"How many of these investigations are you running?"

"I am losing track, Shachar. I've got Har Kesem, whatever I am doing in Italy, and my doctorate. It won't write itself you know."

"Forget the doctorate. You've got a murder investigation, and an attempted murder investigation. Isn't that enough?"

"Maybe I can ask for an extension."

"With what reason?"

"You just said yourself, murder investigations."

"I already tried that Remy, it didn't work."

"Tried what?"

"Using murder as an extenuating circumstance to re-sit for an exam."

"That was denied?"

"Hey, it's Israel. Death is life, and everything must always move forward. But seriously, good luck telling your panels and professional armchair sitters that you are involved in murder investigations and that you are being hunted. Would you have imagined this before you began your research?"

"They will think I am a lunatic."

"Let's get back to work to solve this, while not being killed…and then you can get back to philosophizing on the merits of dips versus schmears, or whatever the fuck desk jockeys do."

"What are the details of the container? I'll break the news to Haydée and Giovanni. They can either come with me or deal with their shit without me."

"Now you are talking like a lecturer Remy!"

"Get off it, Shachar. Giovanni is already interested in going down there. I'll be in touch."

•

"There it is. The container is getting loaded up on that truck there, can you see it?"

"Yes, Gio, I got eyes on it too."

"What about you Haydée? You ready at the wheel?"

"Gassed up and ready to go."

"The car is diesel."

"Did I say petrolled up or gassed up?"

"Just checking." Remy shrugged. "It happened to me once, and I destroyed the engine. Luckily it was a company car, and the mechanic kept it between us. People will do surprising things for a little bit of cash."

"Like living underground looking for diamonds, or trekking across the desert looking to sell them?"

"Remy, the truck is moving. I am going to lose contact soon. Want me to bust them through my badge? We can see what they are carrying, and then decide our next move. Driver wouldn't say anything to his employers, I am sure. He'd be dead in minutes."

"I see the truck. And I can see the container. Let's get back to Haydée and track it."

"Should we stop it?"

"You can always do that later."

"Not always," Giovanni warned, "once the container is amongst friends it will be much harder."

"Aren't we trying to see what is inside?"

"At this point knowing the contents is less important than seeing where it goes. We are relatively sure it is something interesting, or else we'd not be going to such lengths to track it."

"Relatively sure it is something interesting, are you serious? We are taking a pause in finding out why there are prices on our heads for something that might be interesting?"

"Come-on. I was just saying—"

"No, you were hedging."

"I'll own that. I cannot know for sure, but here we are, and there it goes, so let's just see this through; shall we?"

Remy was incensed. "Or shall we just not. We might be tracking t-shirts while we're getting tracked by killers."

"Guys, let's get going." Haydée cut them off. "Remy, wasn't it your friends who gave us this information? The truck is getting waived through customs. It'll be on the road in a couple minutes, and it also might be our best chance to find out who wants us dead."

CHAPTER 27

The truck sped through the night. By dawn Haydée was ready to wake Giovanni. The deep snore had helped her keep awake, but now, finally, it was beginning to grate. The headache that had been gathering from too much coffee and too little sleep had finally begun to overwhelm her.

"Giovanni. Get up."

"Are we there?"

"There? Where? Elysium? We are on local roads, but I am going to drive us off the next bridge if I hear another minute of your snoring."

"Well, I am up now. What's that noise?"

"Another snore-fest. Wake Remy up."

"Where are we?" Remy rubbed his eyes and yawned.

"A better question," quipped Haydée, "Who is going to drive now?"

Remy yawned. "Is there more coffee?"

"We are getting close," said Giovanni. "I can feel it."

"You're right; the truck is stopping. Seriously, where are we Haydée?"

The truck stopped outside a church. The driver got out.

"Salerno. Near the Amalfi Coast."

In the early morning light, they could see that an artist was painting the church.

"That's only an hour from Naples."

Another person emerged from the church. He climbed into the truck and began to drive.

"What's this all about then?"

Ten minutes later the truck pulled into a warehouse with a sign posted outside:

PROPERTY OF THE HOLY SEE

•

"Arlen, have you seen the reports out of Lebanon?"

"We have moved on that front, Gloria. All British citizens have been evacuated, at least those with enough brains to do so."

"Have you been to Lebanon, Arlen? It's magnificent."

"No, but I've lost plenty of agents there. A real hornet's nest; the honey can't be worth it."

"Then there is the Battle of the Trees in—"

"Reports indicate an ambush by Hamas."

"Don't those reports stem from Israeli diplomatic cables?"

"Sure, but just as the explanation works for them, it works for us. In any case, it's more than plausible."

"Agreed. Even though settlers should not have been there in the first place."

"I know, Gloria. And so do our politicians."

"That's a very anti-establishment thing to say Arlen; are we getting influenced by TV again?"

"I'm all about the internet now."

"No TVs in the office anymore?"

"Who needs them when we can get alerts on our watches. Good job of executing my directive to arrange those topical alert systems," Arlen said.

"Goes straight to agents who need the information, without bothering the rest."

"I really should congratulate myself for thinking of it."

"You only thought of it because you read an article on it. Probably printed on vellum."

"Far better than that papyrus rag Roy reads. I hear Egyptology is back in vogue."

"Nice one, Arlen."

"Thanks, Gloria."

"Now that we have decided to ignore the crises in Lebanon and Israel...."

"Just file those in the Near East folder, and let's move on."

"Okay then Arlen; why else am I here?"

"Belgium. Wasn't your husband going to attend a conference there? You submitted Form 1711-3012-1917 reporting that Roy might attend."

"He didn't go after all. Remy, his doctoral student, went instead."

"There was an incident. Everyone is fine. But there seems to have been an attempt to capture and kill the student."

"Remy?"

"Him or members of his party. As you can imagine, details are sketchy."

"What do we know?"

"Two gunmen were in Brussels and took a shot at Remy and a colleague named Haydée."

"But didn't get them?"

"No. An agent from the UNESCO Intelligence Unit saved the day."

"That Intelligence Unit is maybe the best thing the UN has ever accomplished."

"Those idiots?"

"Come on, Arlen."

"They find success by accident."

"Many important advances happened by accident."

"I suppose that's true. Can you imagine if some poor shepherd in Ethiopia hadn't tossed coffee berries into a fire and inhaled? Obviously an ignoramus, *who inhales smoke from a fire?* I guess he was trying to get high. I mean being a shepherd has got to be boring but—"

"About boring. The history of coffee is a bit off topic."

"Coffee is never off topic. I'm going to make some while we chat. Care for a cup?"

"Of course. Why was Remy considered a threat and to whom?"

"We have no idea."

"Then why did UNESCO send this agent to protect them?"

"You've got me, Gloria."

"Then why did you bring me here if you have no information?"

"Because your husband might have been the target, because his student is now involved, and because we don't know what's going on. And I hate that. And I'd like you to fix that. Immediately."

•

"Haydée, can we trust this Giovanni? Does UNESCO really have agents?"

"I've heard a rumor from friends working in Mali after Timbuktu was sacked by desert tribes. But I've not come across them yet."

"It's at least plausible then."

"If they exist, then it is possible they follow my work."

"And if they follow your work then maybe so do other less upstanding organizations."

"That's my thinking, Remy. But that doesn't explain two things. First, why would UNESCO know about a threat to me? Second, why would anyone know about you? No offense."

"None taken. Perhaps they confused me with my professor. I was standing in for him."

"I don't know if your professor's work would interest a

criminal syndicate."

"Just unlucky then?"

"Well, you met me."

"I did, and then it led me to flee for my life. I had a lead for my doctoral research in Israel until that led to a murder in the West Bank. I went to Lebanon to find something, but that almost led to my death in several other ways."

"Remy, you never told me what you were looking for in Lebanon; in fact, you never told me you were looking for anything."

"Haydée, I—"

"Remy, this is no time for secrets."

"I went to find more information about a company there, a company that might be involved in smuggling from Lebanon to Israel."

"I see why you are so fascinated by my work on smuggling then."

"One of the reasons."

"What is another reason?"

"Actually, it was just for that reason."

"Got it," Haydée frowned, "so do you think that investigation is linked to this?"

"I haven't a clue," Haydée nodded in agreement, "here comes Giovanni, back from the warehouse. Maybe he has the answers. Gio, what'd you find out?"

"That people in this country are far too easy to bribe. I never go over budget. Oh, and also the container is getting opened."

"Did you see what was inside?"

"I meant divided, not opened. It is in two sealed crates. One van going to Naples, the other to Rome."

•

"General Cohen, sir?"

"Yes, Captain Levy."

"I liaised with that double-faced fixer, Dan."

"Let's be kinder to our catch, eh?"

"Yes, sir, sorry, sir."

"What was said?"

"Dan told me about a container that went from Har Kesem to the southern West Bank, between Bethlehem and Hebron, and then on to the port."

"How can we find this container?"

"Dan said he didn't have any more information on the registration or destination."

"What about origin? Was it Bethlehem or Hebron or—"

"Didn't know or didn't say."

"Captain Levy, please tell me you at least asked what was in the container?"

"Dan told me he was positive it was valuable cargo. He didn't know the specifics, but he gave me this."

"A stone?"

"A white stone, sir."

"I can see that. Levy, I am not particularly happy about the level of detail you've brought me. I need more from my officers."

"Yes, sir, sorry, sir."

"Do you have clammy hands Levy?"

"General?"

"Do you have clammy hands?"

"At the moment I do, yes."

"The stone, it seems, is being washed of its white color by your pathetically nervous hands."

"And the stone is turning a yellow hue. Why is that?"

"The question is: do I care about the stone, the white powder, both, or are neither significant?"

"Well, sir, my apartment building is built from stone this color. Do you think it is a threat against me?"

"Ha! Don't make me laugh. Ha! That's a good one Captain. Care about you…Ha!"

"Sorry, General Cohen."

"That's alright. I always enjoy a laugh."

"Yes, sir."

"Good. Now if the stone is building material, and it is from the southern West Bank, then perhaps it is a type of marble."

"If I may, sir, it is the same color as my university building."

"You went to university?"

"Yes."

"And what did you study?"

"Geology."

"Geology! Damn-it man. Is that not relevant here? What is this rock?"

"Marble, sir."

"Then why are we guessing if you already know?"

"I don't know, sir. I didn't want to postulate."

Cohen slapped Levy on his left cheek, causing Levy to freeze, in shock, and then fear. "Now, Captain Levy, I am going to ask once, and you will think before you speak. If one was to drill into this variety and color of marble, is this white residue what would result?"

"It is possible General. However, the particles would normally be much larger, rougher. And it would be chalkier on my hand."

"Lick your hand."

"Sir?"

"Does it taste like rock?"

"I suppose…it has a bitter taste."

"How does your mouth feel? Is it dry like you would want to wash chalk out?"

"Not really. It's like the powder melted away. Actually, my mouth feels numb."

"I thought it might."

"What do you mean? Is it poison? Have I been poisoned? Am I going to survive?"

"Ha! You've done it again Captain Levy! Ha! Ha! You are too much sometimes. I'm glad I didn't order you demoted the other day."

"You were considering doing that?"

"And why not? Do you have a problem with that?"

"No, sir."

"Good."

"Were you happy you didn't demote me so that you could have me taste this poison?"

"Ha! Wonderful Levy. You should do stand-up. No, you will not be harmed. The powder is most likely cocaine."

"Cocaine? Will I overdose?"

"The question is not are you an idiot Captain Levy, because that is obvious, but rather does the stone have anything do with the cocaine?"

CHAPTER 28

"Your eminence."

"Monsignor Jerome."

"The crosses have arrived safely into your possession, in Salerno."

"Thanks to our Lord."

"They are expertly made. The pilgrims and tourists coming to visit Rome will be overjoyed with their wooden crosses carved in the Holy Land."

"How quaint. As for the rest?"

"The other batch of crosses are on their way to Naples, and then, minus the agreed tithe, will go to Antwerp."

"Larger tithes in this world lead to larger rewards in the next. Care to increase your donation?"

"Cardinal, I wish I could, but at this time there are so many other commitments…."

"Just be sure to send mine first."

"Of course, Cardinal."

"When will the next batch arrive?"

"We've had a brief delay due to a shortage of olive wood. This has been rectified, however, and we are up and running again."

"I'll expect a report on your progress. As for now I will look forward to my delivery. You have done well. Please may the Lord continue to bless our work."

•

"Which one should we follow, the one to Rome, or the one to Naples?"

"You'll both stay put," Giovanni answered, "I'm going to give my friend Baptiste a call. He's an Italian cop based in Naples, good guy, we go way back. He knows the camorra and can protect you in Naples better than I can."

"What are you going to do Gio?"

"I'll follow the one to Rome, and you'll follow the one to Naples, with the help of Baptiste."

•

"Thanks for coming at such short notice Baptiste. These two really are in the shit."

"Happy to help Giovanni, and they must be since I've heard all about them from my camorra friends, and that's no small thing."

"Then you know the stakes. Bap, I need you to follow the second van that leaves here. I will assume the first is going to Rome."

"Why would you think the first is going to Rome?"

"Because it is farther. They'll want to get that one on the road."

"It seems that you are trying to put more certainty into a fifty-fifty proposition."

"Not so, Baptiste. Life is full of surprises, yet the most likely scenario is…the most likely."

"All right, I'll take the kids, and you'll commute to work."

"You will follow the second van to Naples. If you know the recipient let me know quickly."

"Depends who it is, Giovanni."

"Bap, this is serious stuff, or I wouldn't have called you."

"And here I thought you just wanted to get a drink."

"After this case is over I'll buy you more than a drink."

"And if I tell you who owns a warehouse I'll be in the drink, know what I mean?"

"I hear you."

"Do you, Giovanni? Because this is my life and livelihood you are asking me to betray."

"I'm not asking for your life. The owner of whoever receives this van may also be the boss who has put the contract out on Remy and Haydée. You'll be able to bring those two into the boss, after you call me, and that will make-up for any small slips of information."

"I am taking them to offer them up? What are your terms?"

"What do you mean?"

"I bring them in and get the reward. What percent do you want for bringing them this far? Fifty-fifty proposition was it?"

"That's not what I had in mind Bap, at least not right away. I need them longer than that, so please, when you find out who is receiving the van, call me. Do not give up Remy and Haydée."

"Don't worry; I'll have your cut here when you return. You can trust me."

"That's why I called you. As I said, *not yet*. Follow the van, find the recipient, and keep Remy and Haydée safe. Get it?"

"I got it."

"Good."

•

"Naples."

"Yes, it is my home."

"Beautiful."

"It is."

"Baptiste, thank for you agreeing to help us."

"It was nothing, Remy."

"No, really. Giving us a ride while tailing the van from Salerno to Naples. You've done plenty."

"I am happy to help my friend, and people in need. It is my job, you know."

"How do you know Giovanni anyway?"

"We go way back to the police academy here in Italy. He was in my graduating class. Giovanni finished first, and I was last, but we supported each other all the same. Well, really, he supported me. Then we were excited to find we had been assigned to the same department. It was amazing, and we became even closer. When Giovanni took a position at UNESCO I decided to stay with the Polizia."

"Did you consider joining UNESCO?"

"No."

"Why not?"

"They didn't offer me a place, and so there was nothing to consider."

"Makes sense."

"Giovanni started to bust big time traffickers, and I the local ones. We would give tips to each other, and so while I owe him for helping me at the academy, he has benefited from the information I can give to him, maybe even more than he helped me. We are good partners, fighting crime, even if we don't see each other as often as we would want."

"Giovanni takes on international smuggling—"

"And I take on local smuggling. As a result, I know Naples and, more importantly for you it seems, the camorra. So, you see, we should not split up. While Giovanni chases the van to Rome, I'll escort you here."

"We could do more than be guarded, Baptiste."

"Is that so, Remy?"

Haydée tensed and looked for something sharp. She found nothing.

"Yes. We are sitting ducks without getting the contract

on our heads rescinded. We need to find the boss who issued the contract."

"That is a dangerous game, Remy. Haydée, have you thought this through? Wouldn't it make more sense to wait for Giovanni; maybe the whole thing will blow over. I can make some calls, and perhaps the order has been rescinded. It happens all the time."

"I think Remy is right. We should not count on luck. And Giovanni is three hours away in Rome, doing what? None of us know."

•

The van rolled into Rome heading to the Caelian Hill, finally stopping at St. John's Square in Lateran, just four kilometers from Vatican City, and yet still Holy See property. The square is bound by St. John Lateran Basilica, the final resting place of six popes, and the Lateran Palace, which hosts a museum, offices, and the residence of the Cardinal Vicar of the Diocese of Rome.

The Vicar General is a powerful individual, and so Giovanni dismissed his initial shock with a shrug. *Glad I get to work crime elsewhere, at least sometimes,* Giovanni reflected. *But yes*, Giovanni recalled, *the basilica was damaged by a bomb planted by the mafia in 1993. Clearly this part of the Holy See is not beyond the reach of organized crime.* With that in mind Giovanni sent texts to Remy, Haydée, and Baptiste. He then got out and walked to the gate the van had used to access the underground parking.

The sentry was not quite a Swiss Guard, and certainly did not dress the part, but nevertheless cut an imposing figure. "*Buona sera.* I am new to visit Rome. Being a historian, I find this city endlessly fascinating. Can you tell me what this entrance is for?"

"The private entrance for the Lateran Palace."

"Is it historic inside? Who uses this entrance?"

"It is modern. Nothing interesting to look at. A mix of parking spaces and storage areas."

"Is it big?"

"Very big. It runs under the whole palace. There is plenty of parking, but also much storage. The museum needs storage, the offices, the gift shop and the Cardinale Vicario has his personal apartments, and all need storage."

"Oh, a Cardinal lives here?"

"As I said, the Cardinal Vicar. He is Vicar General of His Holiness, officially, but he also was promoted to the Cardinalate."

"Is he nice?"

"Who? The Cardinal Vicar?"

"Yes."

"He blessed my shoe with spittle once."

"I see."

"I don't interact with him much since the windows on the vans he uses are darkened."

"Ah, of course. Think he has any fun?"

"Who? The Cardinal Vicar?"

"Yes."

"I heard he has a villa in Puglia, to the south of Taranto. Otherwise, there are the usual rumors about Cardinals and the Church."

"Are those true?"

"I don't know but I think—oh it is time for a rotation. My supervisor is on the way. I must look straight, like I care. Otherwise, they will think I have gone on strike and dock my pay."

"Gone on strike?"

"Sure. When we need an unscheduled break we go on strike. Five or ten minutes later, after we've eaten, taken a shit and smoked, maybe called a wife or girlfriend, the strike is called off and we go back to work."

"Do you register the strike?"

"We are supposed to. But when it is time to register the strike, we go on strike against the requirement to register the strike."

"I love Italy. Oh, here is your supervisor."

"Then it is time to move along, *signore*. Move along."

•

"Hi there."

"Hello."

"Who owns this warehouse?"

"Who wants to know?"

"The name is Baptiste. Detective Baptiste."

"Sorry, detective, I don't know who owns the warehouse."

"Okay, so who pays you?"

"My salary?"

"Are you salaried? That is very nice for you. Now answer my question."

"Nobody."

"Nobody pays you? You are a salaried volunteer then, I take it?"

"Something like that."

"What are you volunteering for?"

"To guard this warehouse."

"And whose warehouse is it?"

"I don't know."

"Can we agree there is a warehouse?"

"Yes."

"Can we agree we are standing outside the warehouse?"

"Yes."

"Can we agree you are being paid to guard the warehouse?"

"No. Who said I was guarding the warehouse?"

"You did."

"Maybe I misspoke."

"If you are not guarding the warehouse, then I may proceed past you, or are you guarding the warehouse?"

"I am guarding it, you cannot pass."

"Are you telling me, a detective, that I cannot pass?"

"I don't think you can; do you have authorization?"

"I do."

"May I see?"

"It is here, in my fist."

Moving quietly Baptiste eased himself into the warehouse. There was work going on: things moving, heavy things, voices, hard voices. Baptiste saw paperwork, snatched at it, looked for an address. Nothing. Nobody's name. Nothing about the cargo. Only a logo, *La Gabbia*, The Cage. Baptiste knew the gang. He quickly texted Remy what he knew, and asked if that symbol looked familiar to Remy or Haydée. *Footsteps.* Baptiste crept backwards toward the open door. Fresh air filled his lungs. Mission accomplished. The door closed with a slam. Heavy hands pulled Baptiste's arm backwards and twisted it down. *Is this an arrest?* Baptiste began to wonder until everything went blank.

"Remy, did you hear that?"

"I most certainly did Haydée. Was that pop a puncture?"

"You know it wasn't. We need to get away from here."

"Take the car?"

"Not on these streets. Did you see how narrow they are?"

"I was surprised the car could fit, and it's a tiny car."

"Then let's slip away on foot. If they catch us we kiss: tourist lovers."

"You think that will work? Even though we are wanted?"

"Unlikely, but if not then we are doomed, and it can at least be a last kiss goodbye."

"Perhaps it is better if we don't get caught."

"That's a good idea too."

•

"Remy, let me see that picture again."

"La Gabbia?"

"Yes. Isn't The Cage a funny name?"

"Not if you are used to being in prison."

"Perhaps it is a commentary on the condition of inner-city youth."

"Haydée you are lovely. I was thinking less urban and more about farms, chickens in fact."

"Chickens?"

"Yes. They are everywhere in my research. I went to Lebanon to find out about The Beak."

"I think reflections on urban life is more likely."

"Maybe we'll get a chance to ask. I haven't heard back from Giovanni after sending in the logo, you?"

"Nothing. Wait. Here!"

"What does it say?"

"Go for Pizza. Try *Antica*."

"That's it? Write back."

"Sent."

"And?"

"Nothing. Wasn't received."

"Not received?"

"No. Maybe the phone is in use."

"Or off."

"What does *Antica* mean?"

"I don't know. Look it up."

"Seems to be a pizza place. Highly rated."

"Are we supposed to eat there?"

"I guess."

"Did Giovanni understand your message Remy?"

"I wrote, 'Bap KIA, *La Gabbia* logo found.' Is that not clear Haydée?"

"I thought it was. Maybe KIA wasn't clear?"

"He is a security agent, not an auto dealer."

"Fine, so you told him his dear friend Bap was killed in action, and then told him who might have done it, and then he writes a pizza recommendation before his phone shuts down?"

"He might have gone somewhere without a signal. I lose mine all the time in my house. Stone and brick make stable connections impossible."

"I lose my signal all the time in the grocery store. I think they don't want me to compare prices."

"Maybe he could be in a plane."

"Or a train."

"Maybe underwater."

"In a tunnel."

"Or a basement, something underground."

"We need to get pizza."

"Are you saying we are losing our minds?"

"Let's put aside discussions of our sanity, which, as academics, is already highly questionable. Instead, what I meant was that rather than guessing why Gio's phone went quiet…we did get a message."

"So, we are losing it then?"

"It must be because we are hungry."

"Or exhausted, and just led Bap to his death."

"Okay, then let's go out for pizza. It is important to eat after a funeral."

"Did we just attend a funeral?"

"Might as well have."

"Then let's go to *Antica*."

"And figure out how to contact The Cage."

CHAPTER 29

Giovanni waited outside the Lateran Palace and considered his next move. The goods, he now knew, were under a secured building that hosted a museum along with the offices and the residence of the Cardinal Vicar.

The Cardinal, out at a function in the Domus Sanctae Marthae, rushed back to the Lateran. The Cardinal sped through the square and around the back gate to where Giovanni lingered. The guard had been replaced by his superior, Bosco.

As the Cardinal's car sped in, Bosco admired the Maserati Levante. It was hard not to look at the odd, yet desirable, SUV made by the luxury firm. Bosco turned back to ensure the gate was secure and then moved to offer security support to the Cardinal, and, to get another look at the car.

Thanks to the spectacle of the Maserati, Giovanni was able to slip in behind Bosco, but also realized, just too late, that the gate would prevent him from leaving just as it had prevented him from entering.

The Cardinal practically leapt out of the car, narrowly avoiding getting entangled in his robe. *Damn this thing. I love the color, the power, and it's so cozy, but sometimes walking around wrapped in drapery is a real pain in the ass.* With a sigh, and assuming a more restrained manner, the Cardinal ordered his manservant Lorenzo to pull the boxes out of the van. The servant of the servant of God woke the driver who had taken it upon himself to nap while awaiting his next order. Money was pushed into his hands. Lorenzo then saw Bosco, who, he realized, could babysit the driver in the guard's office while the van was unloaded.

"Lorenzo, are they both gone?"

"Yes, your excellency."

"Let's take a look then. What do we have in these boxes of ours?"

"There are a lot of boxes."

"Are any of them labeled?"

"Nothing written, but there are two different types of boxes. One seems to have a stamp of a tree."

"And the other?"

"Let me see…a rooster?"

"Magnificent! Take the boxes marked with the tree to the gift shop. The ones with the rooster please put in my private apartment, the study, if you please."

"Your wish, excellency."

Giovanni watched Lorenzo unload the boxes, sorting them as he extracted them from the van. Footsteps warned Giovanni of the approach of Bosco, who had again ventured out of the guard's office. Bosco's subordinate was able to entertain the driver, or at least Bosco had reasoned. Giovanni slipped out of view from Bosco's heavy step. Bosco hailed Lorenzo, asking if the manservant could use some help. Even though each box was not particularly heavy for Lorenzo, there were a lot of them, so Lorenzo allowed Bosco to help him unload the boxes. Bosco helped Lorenzo take the boxes up to the Cardinal's residence, chatting all the way about Italian Series A football. Then they went back down, chatting this time about Premier League football. Finally, they dropped the rest of the boxes into the gift ship, while their discussion moved to Italian politics, and then they returned to the van where Lorenzo strangled Bosco to death, tossed him into the van, and went to find the driver.

Giovanni saw his opportunity and darted forward. The van door was secured, and heading up to the Cardinal Vicar's residence was out of the question, so Giovanni decided to try the museum gift shop. The boxes there were stacked, and Giovanni had to pull the top box down without making too much noise. Giovanni reached for his knife and cut into the shrink-wrapped box. A hard go made Giovanni realize his blade was dull, and he made a mental note to have it sharpened or replaced. The box lid came off as he'd heard the faint sound of the van starting. Giovanni reached into the box as the wheels screeched on the painted surface of the parking garage. The lid wouldn't fully open, and Giovanni lost his patience, shoving his hand into the box and was rewarded with a scratch on his finger. As Giovanni closed his hand on the object and pulled it out of the box he felt the presence of the Holy Spirit that brought a shiver to his body, a tear to his eye, and a simple olive wood cross in his hand.

The sound of a box being cut and ripped open, while relatively quiet under normal circumstances, was deafening in the silence of the parking garage. Giovanni heard someone approach, slipped the cross into his breast pocket, and sprang to his feet. Giovanni saw Lorenzo approaching with malice in his eyes. Giovanni decided to make the first move by swinging his quick right hand at Lorenzo. Lorenzo deftly sidestepped Giovanni, caught his arm and bashed in his elbow, breaking Giovanni's arm. Giovanni tried to throw a punch with his other arm, but was again caught by Lorenzo, who, this time, used Giovanni's forward momentum to toss him to the ground. Lorenzo jumped on Giovanni's back, pinning his one functional arm with a knee that kept Giovanni pressed to the floor. Lorenzo took a handful of Giovanni's hair and smashed the head down into the floor. Giovanni mumbled but didn't struggle.

"Who are you?" Lorenzo snarled.

"Just a thief, I meant no harm and haven't taken anything. A big misunderstanding."

"You think being a thief means you meant no harm?"

"I just need a bit of cash to get by this month, and I thought maybe there would be something of value here, but I'm new at this, and couldn't even open a box without being caught. Please *signore*, I'll never come here again. My arm is broken. I've learned a lesson."

"If you come here again you won't walk out alive. In fact, if I see you on the street I'll do you in."

"Yes, yes, I agree; I agree."

"Then I'll see you out."

Lorenzo pulled Giovanni to his feet and roughly dragged him to an exit. Lorenzo slammed Giovanni to the pavement and walked back inside. Giovanni lay there until the door was shut, noting the gush of blood pouring from his split lip and battered nose. He managed to drag himself back to the car while feelings of fear, anger, and excitement mingled with the excruciating pain of his broken elbow.

Finally seated in the car and taking stock of his injuries, another pain surfaced, this one in his chest. That's when Giovanni remembered the wooden cross. He reached into his jacket to take out the cross. It was smashed, but as he lifted it rocks tumbled out, bounced off the clutch and dropped to the carpet. Giovanni felt the pain surge as he stooped down to grab one of them. In the pale orange glow of a Roman streetlight he saw not a pebble, but a diamond.

•

"Lorenzo! Get up here," the Cardinal Vicar barked. "There is a box missing. Go and check the gift shop."

Lorenzo, seeing his master distraught, took the steps two at a time, making it to the gift shop in under a minute. As Lorenzo pushed open the door he noticed the box stamped with the rooster had been opened by the thief. *That idiot Bosco,* Lorenzo thought as a surge of shame and rage rose. Lorenzo smoothed the tape and gathered the box, savoring the memory of Bosco's forced expiration.

•

Before Remy and Haydée stepped into the pizza parlor Giovanni's text reached its destination.

"Hey, Gio messaged."

"What does it say?"

"'Crosses have diamonds inside. Rooster on the box.'"

"Diamonds?" Haydée echoed. "What is he saying? There are diamonds smuggled inside crosses? I wonder where they are from."

"Could you tell if you saw one?"

"Not me, no, but one of my father's experts."

"That you trust?"

"That I've known my whole life."

"Well then, let's get one."

"A cross?"

"With a diamond."

"How would we get one? They went into the warehouse, along with Baptiste…."

"We need to sit down with the boss."

"The same boss who has a contract on our heads?"

"Most likely."

"Let's get started."

"Great. I'm starving."

•

Giovanni looked down at the clutch and wished, not for the first time, he had paid more for the automatic. One-armed driving on Roman roads was not a happy prospect. Giovanni had begun to gather his thoughts when the driver's side window was shattered. Giovanni felt a cord wrapped around his neck. Lorenzo pulled Giovanni through the window, cutting off his airway. Two Italian police officers turned the corner. Upon seeing Lorenzo with a cord around Giovanni's neck, pulling the latter through the window, the two officers turned on their heels and walked stiffly away. Giovanni struggled with his one arm, trying to pull the cord away from his neck with his hand, but Lorenzo's grip only tightened. Within seconds Giovanni was unconscious. Lorenzo felt for a pulse to make sure he hadn't overdone it and killed the thief, then reached into the car to gather the cross and diamonds. The glass, however, was everywhere, making it hard to find those valuable little pebbles. Lorenzo did his best to gather the diamonds, taking them, along with pieces of glass, shoving them into his pockets to sort later. With that done, he turned back to look at Giovanni for a moment, and felt a touch of panic that the thief might have slipped away. But the man was still there in the street, and so Lorenzo hefted him up and carried Giovanni back into the palace.

•

"The pizza was superb."

"Of course. You are dining at *Antica*. Care to order anything else?"

"I wanted to ask the manager a question."

"Is there a problem? I may be best able to assist you. I am at your service."

"Everything is great. Just a quick word. Nothing you have done is wrong, I assure you. Far from it in fact. I will tell the manager about the wonderful service we have received here, in addition to compliments to the chef."

"I would be glad to take your compliments to the *pizzaiolo* myself."

"I prefer to speak to the manager directly."

"As you wish. I will return with the manager."

•

"How may I be of assistance, *signore*? Is everything to your satisfaction?"

"Everything was superb."

"Thank you. I will take your compliments to the staff."

"I would prefer to make these compliments to the owner."

"I will let him know, *signore*."

"I appreciate your offer, but I think I would rather speak to the owner myself."

"He is not here to manage the restaurant."

"But then he is here?"

"I did not say that. I *can* tell you that he is indisposed at the moment."

"How could you know?"

"Because *signore*, he is a very busy man."

"I believe he will see me. Please let him know that Remy, Haydée, and the ghost of Baptiste are here."

"Ghost?"

"The boss will understand."

"Very well, *signore*. I will report your words."

•

"Remy, Haydée, you are welcome at my table. My father would host parties here, but I only use it as my office. Please sit."

"Thank you."

"It is my pleasure. How may I be of service?"

"You could rescind the contract on our lives," Remy ventured.

"And why would I do that?"

"Because we are innocents," Haydée added.

"Apparently not."

"So, you *have* been hired to have us murdered?"

"Of course. I do not know you, nor care about you, personally, that is. There is a job that was offered, and, for payment, I will complete the task. It was kind of you to turn yourselves in; saves me and my men quite a lot of trouble."

"Like what happened in Belgium?"

"Things of that nature."

"We didn't come here to make your life easier."

"And yet you have! I do appreciate it, however, and you will die quickly and cleanly as a result. But before that let's have something to eat. Have you tried our pizza?"

"We just finished eating."

"And what did you think?"

"It was very good."

"It's the best. Where else have you tried?"

"Tried what?"

"Neapolitan pizza."

"Are you seriously asking?"

"In Naples discussions over pizza are very serious. *Starita* with their controversial toppings is still good. I hate *L'Antica Pizzeria Da Michele* as they have similar name, and because it is the place of Julia Roberts, from *Eat, Pray, Love*. Do you know it?"

"I know of Julia Roberts but have not seen the film."

"Have you tried the pizza from *Sorbillo*?"

"No."

"*Sorbillo* is very good."

"We really haven't had time to sightsee."

"If I were you, I would have gotten a coffee, *Caffe Mayra* perhaps, get some pizza, order another coffee, then go over to *A'picio Spritz* for a drink. Or maybe get the drink, then pizza, and after that coffee."

"Next life I guess. We came right here."

"I am at least gladdened to hear you've eaten the best. It's too bad, though, you can't try the others. Some of our competitors make nice-tasting pizza, and I think you would have enjoyed them. And only then would you understand why my *Antica* is the best."

"We would be happy to go and sample them."

"How can I allow you leave when there is a contract to fulfill?"

"Perhaps you could send us with an escort."

"To give you a chance to escape? Or maybe find one of the nine police who are not on a camorra payroll? No, I think you will stay here. Our desserts are very good. Do you like tiramisu? I face critique by serving a dish from the northeast of Italy, but I just love it!"

"I would like it better if you weren't planning on our deaths."

"Your deaths would not follow the tiramisu."

"Then you will cancel our unjust sentence?"

"I cannot. My employer is not a person to cross easily. They have connections to higher powers as you know."

"I do not."

"Truly? You do not know the one who seeks you?"

"No idea."

"Very interesting."

"Who is it then?"

"Perhaps it is a secret I should not reveal."

"We are the walking dead. If we are to be murdered after the tiramisu…."

"As I said you will not be killed at that time. We will have an espresso first. Good for digestion."

"And then you will murder us?"

"Maybe we can enjoy a light conversation. You two seem quite an interesting pair."

"Who wants us dead?"

"Cardinal Vicar."

"Of Rome?"

"The one and only."

"Why?"

"I don't know. But he has gone to great lengths, or at least costs, to have you removed. Oh, if only you were free! Our coffee here is merely acceptable for this city, but still nothing can compare to a Napoli style coffee house."

"What?"

"We have our own culture here, as I hope you understand. One orders when they come in, bring the slip to the barista, drink a fizzy water, watch the espresso being made by pulling those large levers. I prefer twenty-one seconds, drop in the sugar, and then you drink. It is all very civilized."

"Sounds lovely. Care to take us?"

"Again, with the feeble escape attempt? Surely you are beyond such thoughts by now. But it would be glorious, no? I would not take you to *Caffee del Professore* because, as the name suggests, it is pretentious and out of touch."

"You are out of touch."

"What did you say to *me*? Nobody speaks to me like that."

"I meant no offense. I merely meant in this situation."

"Explain."

"We have reason to believe that you are sitting on immense wealth. Will you let us go if we tell you about it?"

"Or I could torture you."

"Let's assume you are honorable."

"Granted. Now tell me, I am listening."

"The objects you have in your possession, in your warehouse, are more valuable than you know. We have reason to believe—"

"If your reasoning is wrong I will consider that dishonorable conduct on your behalf and will be free to respond in kind, my honor still intact."

"The crosses that come from the boxes marked with the rooster are filled with diamonds."

"The boxes?"

"The crosses themselves. Get one and break it open."

"If you are messing about—"

"I sincerely hope we are not."

•

"Remy, Haydée, it appears you were correct, and I must apologize for doubting you."

"Think nothing of it."

"Thank you, Remy. We had unloaded four of those boxes to be delivered to…well it does not matter. They will not be receiving the boxes."

"Are they so valuable that you would risk a break with the Cardinal?"

"Yes. A Cardinal flies high, but for how long? And there are more in the van that were destined for the diamond markets of Belgium, so it seemed. They will also be ours."

"Belgium?"

"Yes, Haydée, I know where you are from. As I am no longer seeking the favor of the Cardinal the contract on your heads is canceled."

"Thank you…I didn't catch your name?"

"I'll pretend you didn't ask that. But I do think I owe you restitution for your troubles. I have so many now; please take this cross as a token of my appreciation and apologies. I will pray that you are able to enjoy the fruits of Naples now that you are to, at least for now, remain alive."

Before the camorra who guarded the van got word of the new plan, the van, driver and valuable little pebble passengers sped off into the night, not stopping except for diesel and a pack of cigarettes, until they reached Antwerp seventeen hours later.

CHAPTER 30

"Who do you work for?" Lorenzo asked softly, malevolence in his eyes.

"Do you work for the Cardinal Vicar?" Giovanni retorted.

The Cardinal stepped into the ornate chamber adorned with golden crosses, priceless tapestries, and two pillowed armchairs wrapped in plastic. "He works for me, yes. Lorenzo, please leave us."

"Yes, my master."

"Now then, as my man was asking you, who do you work for? If I have to keep asking I will need to bring Lorenzo back, and he is not a man to annoy. Ah, I see your broken body has already learned about Lorenzo's capabilities."

"I am UNESCO."

"Wonderful. I am acquainted with your superior then. Unless they hate you…we might be able to find a way forward. But if they do, you will burn in hell sooner than I think you expected."

•

"Giovanni, you stupid fuck."

"Commandant, I was following smuggled goods, and

I found—"

"I don't care if you found Mother Teresa, the True Cross, and the *Starship Enterprise*. You cannot mess with the Church."

"Why?"

"Because I care about your mortal soul."

"Really?"

"Of course not, Giovanni. I despise you. If you weren't successful you'd be a docent at a museum in Uzbekistan."

"I *am* successful. And Central Asia has many amazing UNESCO Heritage—"

"Enough Giovanni. The Church is not to be bothered. Do you know how many sites, how much land they own? We could scarcely claim to even be an agency that looks out for cultural sites without their cooperation."

"And yet here I am."

"Yes, in exchange for a massive sum to rehabilitate some abbey that will never be seen."

"And might not even exist."

"Enough I said! In any case, the other side of the deal I very much agree with."

"Which is?"

"Excommunication."

"From the Church?"

"Perhaps expulsion would be more accurate. You are to leave Italy and not return for a decade."

"You cannot be serious. The Italian government sanctioned this?"

"The point is, Giovanni, that you must depart Italy. If you prefer to stay you are terminated as an agent of UNESCO. If you want to keep your job and career, you will take your reassignment and leave this matter behind."

"Where am I going then?"

"Cyprus."

"That pirates lair? It's not overly safe to—"

"I'm sure you can handle yourself Giovanni. You took

on the Church in its own seat of power, I'm sure you can handle a few parochial Greeks."

•

"Giovanni is headed to Cyprus, and we should leave Italy as well. I'm going to take this shard back to my father; as you recall he is in the diamond industry. His experts can tell me where a diamond like this may have been bought, cut, or mined. It can give us a starting point if we need it. Where will you go Remy?"

"Back to the Middle East. I'll take this wooden cross back to Bethlehem and find its maker."

"Good. If you need back-up call me, and I am on the next flight."

"Same here, Haydée. I wish you luck."

"And to you, adieu."

•

"Shachar, it's great to see you again!"

"Remy, my friend, come and give me a hug." They met in a strong embrace. "How was your trip, Remy?"

"Hectic as hell."

"Is that so? Did the presentation in Belgium not go well?"

"The presentation in Belgium? Oh yes, that went fine."

"And?"

"And what?"

"Did you meet anyone else?"

"Are you referring to Haydée?"

"Who is Haydée? I was talking about The Beak, Lebanon, the main reason you left us."

"Lebanon.... I was there."

"Did you make it there before—"

"I made it into Lebanon before the war. But just as I

was beginning my investigations, well, you know what's been happening."

"I know innocent Israelis in our most northern villages are being attacked by mortars, rockets, and infiltrators. It must've been dangerous being in that nest of vipers."

"It certainly was dangerous. At one point it appeared that I was going to be kidnapped by Hezbollah, and another time I was almost annihilated by an Israeli missile."

"Hey, man, I've been there."

"Where? In Lebanon? With Hezbollah? Almost killed by an Israeli missile?"

"Yes."

"Right. Okay, so you know what I mean by hectic."

"I do. But for me the most difficult part was not borders, or the presence of the enemy, or risk of friendly fire. It was, no, *it is,* the reality of friends disappearing. Please continue."

"I also faced another danger, a mysterious man. An American agent."

"And what is your relationship to this agent, Remy?"

"I kept seeing him, I thought he was tailing me, but it seems he thought I was tailing him. Eventually we had a conversation to clear up any miscommunications. A conversation I barely survived."

"And of The Beak? Any information on that?"

"I said 'barely survived.'"

"So have many. The Beak?"

"I was headed to the Bekaa Valley to find out when the war hit. My driver was killed, and I was stranded in Lebanon."

"Of course, airports, seaports, bridges, tunnels, they would be the first targets after border posts and anti-aircraft positions."

"I said my driver was *killed.*"

"You mentioned it was hectic. *I heard you.* How, then, are you here already? The American evacuations are only starting this morning, weeks after the others. Did you hitch a ride with the British?"

"I took a choppier route, Shachar. A helicopter evacuation."

"And what did you do to deserve such royal treatment?"

"I located and escorted children for evacuation."

"How noble."

"A noble way to run."

"Nevertheless, you are back. Safe and sound, but with little extra information for the trouble."

"What about you, Shachar, anything new?"

"The best thing I did was to get away from that nut of a rabbi in the settlement. A very persuasive individual that Rabbi Avraham. I almost began to consider leaving my life here in Tel Aviv and moving there."

"To the settlement?"

"It's not moving to a settlement Remy; it's moving into the service of God."

"And you believe that now?"

"No…but I did find the whole thing oddly comforting in that I wanted to embrace its simple message, its certainty, that just by living somewhere I could be working as an instrument of God."

"An instrument of God?"

"Don't worry, I have not fallen under the sway of that crusade, merely appreciating its power, ita beauty, and its attraction."

"And?"

"And what?"

"Did you find any information helpful to our investigation beyond your spiritual awakening?"

"Of course, working with Marwan, who is eager to see you, we found the container that went between Har Kesem and the port to Italy."

"To the Port of Taranto. I know."

"Then why are you asking what else I did?"

"That was a few days ago—"

"As I told you, living with the settlers was an intense experience. I needed a detox from that."

"What did you do?"

"I got toxed on something else. Beach. Beer. Babes. The usual."

"The usual?"

"Sure. Why? You think I would do something harder?"

"Drug based? Yeah Shachar, do you have a mirror?"

"My shower is broken. And I have bedbugs. Fuck, man. We sent you the details on the container. Did you pick it up?"

"Yes, we did."

"We?"

"Haydée, who I met at the conference, she is into smuggling."

"That's nice."

"Then there is this Italian cop, Baptiste, but he was killed."

"Uh huh."

"You are a hard man, Shachar."

"Bet on it. Anyone else?"

"Yes, a UNESCO agent named Giovanni. Apparently, UNESCO has developed an expertise in smuggling, and, well, that reminds me, I had a contract on my head, a bounty it seems, and this Giovanni saved us, or, I think he did."

"It is getting dangerous to be near you, Remy."

"I fear for you, Shachar."

"Don't worry about it. I can take care of myself."

"I believe you on that score."

"Where is this Haydée and Giovanni?"

"The container was split in Salerno. Giovanni tracked the one that went to Rome, and Haydée and I, along with Baptiste, went to Naples. That's where Baptiste was killed."

"To recap, this Giovanni went missing, Baptiste is dead,

you are here, and where is Haydée?"

"She went back to Belgium. It's a long story, but Haydée and I ended up with something that was in the container, and we are trying to figure out its origins."

"What is it?"

"It is two items actually. I've got an olive wood cross, and she has a diamond that was hidden inside the cross."

"Remy, dude, you took a broken stick, and Haydée got the diamond. Unless you are engaged, you got yourself swindled."

"I don't think so. Haydée is from a family in the diamond business."

"Even worse for you. She can fence the thing."

"Get real, Shachar. She is going to investigate it, to bring it to experts she trusts. Maybe we can learn more about the origin of the diamond."

"Does the origin matter? Isn't it about the buyer?"

"They both are important. But if we are looking at the export side, that is, the Har Kesem side, then we would want to know who was able to ship it there in the first place. If we can figure out where the diamond came from, perhaps we can trace its path to whoever is using Har Kesem."

"And this wondrous piece of religiously inspired paraphernalia?"

"Aren't you religiously inspired now, Shachar?"

"Not by that. I ain't a pagan."

"Maybe you and your settler friends aren't praying to an idol, but they are praying to land. Holy statue, holy land. Both inanimate objects said to be imbued with the spirit of God."

"It's not the same. You know it's not."

"Perhaps, Shachar, perhaps."

"No, I am right on this. Though I did misspeak."

"How so?"

"I might be a pagan."

"Then you won't be too upset that I'll need to take this cross to Marwan. I'll need his help figuring out how to find the factory that made this cross, a cross that holds diamonds in its center."

CHAPTER 31

Shachar let out a shallow sigh as he pushed open the door to his flat, happy to be back in Tel Aviv, feeling sticky with notes of warm rain mixed with dust and grime. A golden beach was nearby, begging him for a visit. What a joy it was to be away from it all. Investigations, cops and robbers, cloak-and-dagger, so much bullshit. And, just like that, the warmth began to crumble as Shachar thought about his neighbor down the hall, grieving, and the death of his friend just blocks away. *This country is hell* whispered Shachar to himself. *The beach, the air, the vitality, the myth of democracy, is any of it worth the price?* Thinking of the Rabbi and settlements, all the killing at the Battle of the Trees. *Setting off a panic that will never end. A panic whose guilt is everybody's. Panic that has no enemies, no victims, no perpetrators, only sadness.* Shachar shut his eyes and tried to squeeze away the tears. He kept his eyes closed, but instead of finding peace, he found nothing but despair. This murder investigation, if one could call it that, was a break from the past. But now there were new traumas, things in the present, things that just happened, were happening, would continue to happen. Shachar thought of his new friends: Remy and Marwan. *They are just using me. They don't care. Nobody cares. And for what? Some fool down the hall who wanted to flee the country after coupling with a...*

no, never mind. I'm not that. Just fucking around. Fucking up. The strain, it's too much, I'm losing myself.

Shachar took a deep breath, looked up at the ceiling and saw the cracked paint. *Those cracks make an interesting shape—what do they mean?* Shachar chuckled to himself, *Look at me, I'm reading tea leaves, administering my own Rorschach test, throwing bones. Throwing bones, there are plenty of those being strewn about.* Shachar stood and stretched his arms to the sky, to the cracked paint above. He realized the light was off even though he had switched it on. *Who had come to tamper with my apartment? Israelis? Palestinians? Someone from Europe, even America? And what did they want? Was it audio or visual surveillance? Maybe somebody placed a bomb?* Moving carefully Shachar fetched his rubber gloves and a dented painter's ladder he had found outside of a construction site. Perching precariously on the trembling aluminum ladder Shachar looked at the fixture. "If there's an explosive here, moving the light bulb may set it off. Fuck it. I hope it does," Shachar announced to nobody. And with that Shachar twisted his wrist seeking to seal his fate.

But there was no pop or flash; there were no extra wires. Only a light bulb ready to be replaced. An object devoid of energy. And then Shachar remembered the light bulb blowing when he flipped it on, seeing that brief flash that tells you the light bulb is kaput. *Death of people, death of a light bulb. What does it matter? Once it was, then no more.* Through the haze of his sorrow Shachar vaguely recalled the moment the light bulb went out. He had just visited Gabe, who sold him that top notch dope. *But do I want to return to that type of release?*

Shachar stumbled down the ladder, went over to his tool chest, gravely looking for another light bulb. Felt a screwdriver. Touched a hammer. Found nails. Nails from a different owner, from a different time. *What were they for? Why did I save them? They are an echo from the past, but nobody has ears to listen, no eyes to see.* Propped up next to the toolbox was a gift from a commander whose life Shachar had saved. It was a beautiful Japanese machete, a *nata*. The commander had marveled at his determination and bravery to save a fellow soldier, and Shachar had dutifully beamed at the compliment. Yet deep down Shachar felt only spite, not for the officer, but toward himself. The life of the soldier was meaningless to him after the loss of so many others. It was an act of madness, not bravery, that brought the man back to his loved ones. *Every unit needs a soldier without loved ones*, Shachar thought ruefully.

Looking down, Shachar realized he was holding the *nata*. He watched his hands as they undid the clasp and slid off the case revealing a gleam of sharpened steel. Shachar felt the weapon, turning it in his hands and seeing what he had not seen before: a way out. A way out of crushing depression and endless loss. A life where an investigation of a murder, which led to the witnessing of other murders, served as a welcome respite from the memories of so many others. Shachar rested the blade on his wrist, the coolness of which raised the flesh. Shachar thought the blade made his skin seem yellow. *Was it fear?* Shachar firmed his jaw. He would not take the coward's way out of this life, no he didn't deserve that, rather he should keep on, continuing to suffer. *But the pain of it all.* Shachar looked down again; he still held the *nata*, but it had fallen to his side. Instead, it was his legs that moved. They carried him across the room past the entryway, where Shachar's arms and hands replaced the *nata*. The legs continued on, taking Shachar to his bedroom, and then kneeling, the arms came back to life again, pulling out a box from under the bed. Shachar looked inside. *Today I am blessed, I've got a fuck ton of heroin, and maybe a better way to die.* Shachar walked back to the couch, prepared his arm and the needle, jabbed it into his arm, pressed, sat back, and closed his eyes once more. When he opened them the ceiling wasn't cracked but covered in flowers, flowers of spring, flowers of funerals; it no longer mattered, nothing mattered.

•

"Remy, my friend! Are you okay?"

"Yes, Marwan. Why do you ask?"

"Are you tired? You look—"

"Very perceptive. I've been almost killed in a war zone in Lebanon, at a conference in Belgium, and in Italy, but I am here now."

"Given that, you look quite well!"

"Thank you for your kind words, Marwan."

"And how is Shachar? Please sit, have something to eat, drink."

"I just saw him. Seemed great."

"Good. Did you learn anything about The Beak?"

"Possibly. I tracked the container you and Shachar told me about, and this is what resulted. You and I have a new focus, this piece of olive wood."

"A cross?"

"Exactly. But this one is not solid but filled with diamonds."

"Diamonds you say?"

"Lots of diamonds. Where do we look for its maker?"

"There is only one place to look for olive wood carvings, Bethlehem."

The two men flagged down a taxi and took it to the mini-bus station. The van filled quickly and they were off. They stayed quiet, to think, to rest, and not to give anything away regarding Remy's background, or their connection.

As they hopped off the mini-bus Remy looked around at the ancient stone. "Bethlehem, so famous. I know so many who visited Jerusalem, but so many fewer who have been to Bethlehem."

"And why do you suppose that is, Remy?"

"Because it is for fewer religions as compared to Jerusalem? What do you think it is Marwan?"

"I would say that Bethlehem is in the West Bank, under occupation, surrounded by settlements. And that makes it harder to visit. It is a more dangerous place to be than in the rest of Israel where many tourists stay."

"Dangerous?"

"Any time you have increased exposure to people with guns, and you do not have one, you are less secure."

"There are some that take this stance Marwan, that having a gun means you are safe. But I'm not sure it makes sense to reduce gun violence by having more guns."

"I agree with you, yet the gun does even things: it takes some of the physical differences away. A small person can pull a trigger just the same as a big person."

"This is true, Marwan, for the physical, but it is also for the psychological: the ones who need mental and emotional help, and aren't getting it, are also capable of squeezing a trigger. Or worse, someone who's been turned from the side of light to the side of dark."

"Good and evil Remy? You are sitting well in the holy land wherein there are good deeds and sinners, soldiers and occupiers, terrorists and freedom fighters. Everything is so serious, dramatic, biblical. Which is why there's so much attention on us. I know people who are suffering here through our poisoned chalice of life in the Holy Land. But I think most observers are, as your Seinfeld put it, cheering for laundry. The blue and white team versus the black, white, green and red team. *Kippot* versus *Kufiya*. But then there is the game between the red, white, and blue teams, and the green teams, where do they fit in? Are they having their own match, or are they substitutes waiting to play, or coaches seeking to orchestrate? Our land is fraught with grotesque levels of violence and impossible political problems, but the resultant destruction is nothing on the scale of our neighbors in Syria or Iraq. None of those wars, those atrocities, get the type of attention that Israel and Palestine get."

"Are you saying that paying attention to the suffering of others is driven by laundry?"

"I don't say it glibly, Remy. I say it with frustration and indignity. But this is our lot in life. Here, we have reached it, Manger Square, the center of Bethlehem. Would you like to crawl to the spot where Jesus was born?"

"I'd like to do many things. If we crack this case we will have plenty of time to sightsee."

"I agree. Since the families of those poor victims would receive no succor from our fun we will do it together the next time you visit Bethlehem. Besides, there are many woodcarving establishments in Bethlehem, so there is much work to do to track down the origin of this cross."

"Where do we start?"

"Behind the square is an old street: a back alley today, yet a major thoroughfare in ancient times. There we will find the shops of the wood carvers. Many of them have skills developed over generations. You'll do well to note the details of their craft. The people who make these hollow crosses are experts, just like the carvers in each of these shops. Let's walk there and look."

"Okay."

"We are lucky already, Remy. Here is one such establishment." Marwan paused.

"Are you coming in with me?"

"I think they're far more likely to tell their secrets to you, an outsider."

"And where will you be?"

"I'd like to see birthplace of Jesus! I've never seen it before."

"I thought we were going together."

"Perhaps I will never have another chance. I'll let you know if it is interesting. And after that, an orange juice on the square."

"I see, fun for some, but not for all. I'll meet you in the square when I'm done."

"I'll be the one reading the paper and sipping juice."

"Fabulous."

•

"Hello, welcome to my humble shop, are you looking for anything in particular?"

"Yes, a friend gave me this cross, and I was hoping to find a match, to be able to see more of them."

"Of course. Allow me to see it. Yes, the wood is from this region. It certainly looks like the work of a local artisan."

"Might this have been made in your shop?"

"I would be devastated."

"What do you mean?"

"The craftsmanship, while good, it's not quite as fine as one would expect. Made by an apprentice, perhaps, who has not yet developed the patience necessary to shape a living thing into a lasting thing."

"Are you saying it was rushed?"

"In not so many words, yes. It's not bad; the maker had a steady hand, and there is knowledge there, awareness of the craft. But it's as you say, rushed."

"How do you know?"

"How do I know? Because I know. I'm an expert."

"Please, I'd like to learn. It is not every day I can meet a master craftsman."

"Here, look at this slight indentation."

"I see it."

"This is made because not quite enough care was used when extracting the carving tool, making sure it does not touch any other parts of the work. The more I look at it, the more I wonder if any of my colleagues will admit to it. Most customers wouldn't perceive the difference between this and another, but, as you now know, we are masters."

"Is it an imitation then?"

"Do not get me wrong: it's a fantastic piece of craftsmanship, far better than you could get from an artisan in Italy or Spain, and even an untrained eye can learn to spot the difference between a mass-produced model from the Far East. No, this one was done here. Would you care to buy another cross? I have many to choose from, all of which are better than this one. If you buy multiples I can give you a better price."

"I can see that the pieces you make are quite beautiful. The detail in this manger scene is incredible."

"Thank you, and of course it is much more expensive due to my many hours of labor, but also the size of the piece of wood I worked from. It is not always easy to get such large blocks of wood."

"Just a couple more questions about my cross, if you don't mind."

"Certainly, but let's keep it at that. I have much work to do…unless you are planning to make a purchase?"

"Can you tell the age of the cross?"

"Good question. Materials and tools have not changed much over recent years, so the difference is not in their manufacture, but rather their use. Being out in the world means getting scratches and losing a gloss varnish or glue. The most obvious is the presence of human oils. People grip their crosses and hug them to their chest with both hands while they pray, and these crosses are witness to this moment of intimacy."

"What if the cross is old but hasn't been touched? For instance, one mounted on a wall?"

"It will have other wear and tear like from the sun or natural decomposition."

"Or how about an old cross that stays in a box, for instance in a shop or as a family heirloom."

"As I said, the tools and of manufacture have not changed much in recent years, but over the decades and centuries there have been some advancements. I believe those were your questions, are you quite satisfied?"

"I do appreciate your time, but I'm still at a loss. I see that the quality of your craftsmanship is superior, and I may be interested in some of your other productions, but for the cross I'd really like to find the person who made it. Please, just look one more time."

"I am sorry I could not be more helpful."

"Is there nothing else unique about it, no other signs about the manufacturer?"

"I am sorry; the only other thing I can tell you looking at this cross is the dominant hand of the artisan."

"That could be of use."

"It is the right hand. Now I really must get back to work. You are welcome to look around, to enjoy my creations and, if you feel moved, to buy one; I'll just be in the next room working in my studio."

•

"Marwan, I visited five little shops, each made their wooden crosses onsite in a studio in the back. All impressive operations, yet none of them took ownership of the cross, nor could they point me in any type of useful direction."

"We knew this was going to be difficult but—"

"Maybe this isn't the way to move the case forward."

"Think it through, Remy. Were any of them more interested than others?"

"The first shop gave me a lot of their time, and a basic education in the trade. Most of the other shops weren't quite as interested once they saw I wasn't a buyer. At the very last shop the artisan seemed to examine the cross for a very long time before expressing his disinterest."

"Maybe you should've bought a gift for me."

"And what would you have liked, Marwan?"

"It's not what I would have liked, but that I bought a gift for you. Here. Sorry it isn't wrapped."

"An olive wood cross? I already have one, unfortunately."

"Not just any cross Remy, an olive wood cross from Bethlehem's Manger Square. And not just from any seller, but the church gift shop itself."

"From the gift shop? It must've cost a fortune, at least compared to buying directly from the carvers."

"Possibly, but at least the extra portion is going to charitable purposes. Now let's get something to eat; I was told about a fabulous little place not far off the main shopping street."

●

"Greetings, Monsignor Jerome, what brings you to my humble workshop?"

"Humble? You've grown, my friend."

"It is all of those sweets from Hebron."

"Have you had any of *Hebroni halqoum* from Sider Delight in the old city? Surely they make the world's best Turkish delight."

"I will save you some next time. Still, it does pain me to hear them called Turkish delights. Why must other cultures continually steal our heritage?"

"Carver, mimicry is akin to flattery."

"Flattery is nice, but I prefer profit. And you certainly brought me that, Monsignor."

"Only with the grace of God, my friend. Now then, we've secured a large quantity of wood, and, just as importantly, a large number of orders."

"That is excellent! What is the request this time? A statue of Mother Mary provides a deeper and wider cavity."

"No, carver, we'll stick with the current plan of crosses. They are so plentiful on the market, and of course we wouldn't want people praying to an idol, even if it was buried in the bosom of a wooden Mary."

CHAPTER 32

"Does your family call you Dan or Daniel?"

"Please don't discuss my family." Dan's eyes narrowed, staring hard into those of Captain Levy.

"But why not? Your continued cooperation makes an important impact on your family, no?"

"Listen, captain—"

"Who says I am a captain?"

"You are not the only one who can do research, captain. I've already given you information. I don't know much more that I can give, and even to find more details I'd be risking my life."

"You risk it if you don't help us, Daniel. That is, unless you fancy life behind bars. Perhaps the Palestinians in Megiddo prison would enjoy your company."

"An idle threat, captain, as you know, with my background I would not be imprisoned there. And what do you really have on me at this point? Any evidence you think you may have collected is expired; you can't hold things over a man forever."

"And why not?"

"Because we are not animals, and we have breaking points."

"Okay Daniel, you are right, help me again, and you will be free. Assuming the information you provide is worthwhile."

"I'd like that in writing."

"My word is my bond."

"And what of your commander? General Cohen is—"

"General Cohen is an honorable warrior. Why you think he would be involved in this is beyond me. I seriously question your sanity, Daniel, if you think such a man would stoop to dealing with people such as yourself."

"As you wish, captain, but as I said there are times when the hunter becomes the hunted."

Captain Levy audibly scoffed.

"Do I have your commander's word that I will be let go, if it is as you say, and he truly is a man of honor?"

"General Cohen's word is iron."

"And are you authorized to distribute iron promises?"

"Tell me what you know, Daniel, and you'll find out the extent of his magnanimity. What type of drugs are you moving?"

"Cocaine."

"And how does it arrive into Israel?"

"I don't know."

"Come now, Dan, do you want me to believe that someone of your position doesn't know a basic detail like that?"

"Large operations are often compartmentalized, not unlike some military operations. These are dangerous things to know. And when there is information like that, I would prefer not to know them."

"Fair enough. How do you distribute the cocaine?"

"By car, as you know from my arrest."

"I think not, Daniel. Given the size of your operations: the guns stolen, the warehouses. You are shipping internationally, and I'd like to know how. This truth, Daniel, will set you free."

"You might regret it, but I'll tell you what I know."

•

"That's what he told me, General Cohen."

"Then look into it."

"Yes, sir. One question."

"Quickly."

"If this information turns out to be accurate, will we still use him as an informant?"

"No Levy, you gave him my word, and my word is iron. If his information is as important, as lucrative as we now suspect, we will not only release him from our service, but we will also need to release him from life. Levy, you are dismissed."

•

"My love Gloria, you little honey bunch of oats."

"Hi Roy, my love of loves.

"Are you thinking what I am thinking?"

"No.

"Oh, I could have sworn—"

"Swear all you want, but that's all you are going to get. I've got to pack."

"Where are you headed?"

"You know can't tell you."

"I know you went to Belgium. And then left Italy."

"How did you know that?"

"I looked through your bag."

"Roy! These are state secrets you are messing with."

"I'd rather mess with you, but seeing your secrets seems like a nice booby prize."

"What is wrong with you?"

"I have a surprise for you!"

"What is it, Roy?"

"A surprise is a surprise."

"I am waiting."

"Waiting isn't easy."

"Your life isn't going to be easy unless you tell me."

"You talk first."

"Talk about what?"

"Where are you going next?"

"You know I can't talk about that."

"And I respect that you can't talk. So whisper it."

"I think whispering is still talking."

"A linguist colleague of mine says they are different."

"Is that true?"

"Does it matter?"

"You can be so infuriating. I am off to Cyprus."

"Why?"

"Because that is my next assignment."

"Seriously though, Gloria, is Remy in danger?"

"He certainly was. Look. I'll tell you, but only because your student is involved—"

"And my wife."

"Aww Roy, I didn't know you cared so much about me that you would be willing to listen to a state secret."

"Go on."

"The reported two gunmen were actually three. Two shooters versus a third, plus the students. The Belgians know this but aren't going public."

"Why would they do that?"

"Because they don't know what to do with the information. They don't really care as long as nobody got hurt; they aren't involved and don't want to be."

"They aren't bothered that there was a shooting on their turf?"

"Oh, they care, just not enough to want to wade into whatever it was. That's why they are so willing to share information on this one. They are not always so forthcoming."

"So, what happened? Since the Belgians are willing to talk it shouldn't be a big secret."

"They are sharing it with intelligence agencies, not the public!"

"I am intelligent, at least according to countless published accolades and the etching on my door."

"Is that statue dedicated to your ego built yet? Or is it just in the planning stage?"

"Isn't that joke getting old?"

"Not as fast as you are."

"Hey, you married me."

"We all make mistakes."

"OK so people with guns…"

"Right, so there were three. All of them Italian."

"Ah, so that's why you were in Italy."

"I was there to find out what was going on. By time I got there though the situation seemed to have been settled."

"How is that?"

"The contract on Remy and another was canceled leaving the two hired guns to slip back into obscurity."

"And the third?"

"Was there to stop the gunmen."

"Did you speak with this mysterious hero?"

"Not yet. The agent seems to have been captured, held for ransom, and been exiled."

"What are you talking about? Captured by whom?"

"Elements of the Church."

"You are joking."

"I wish. The agent works for UNESCO and was released in exchange for a large payoff. Then this person was sent out of Italy to Cyprus. And seeking him out is the reason I am going."

"Makes sense."

"And your surprise?"

"I am coming with you my love."

"To Cyprus?"

"Where else?"

"And why would that be?"

"Because I am giving a lecture there. At Cyprus College in sunny Nicosia."

"What a coincidence."

"Let's get our work done quickly when we arrive. Then we can enjoy ourselves."

"Are you being serious? Sometimes I can't quite tell."

"You know there is a place named Aphrodite's Beach? I wouldn't be surprised if you were born there, and you were going to the ceremony to update the name to Gloria's Beach."

"Again Roy, your illusions of grandeur never cease to amaze me."

·

"Shachar, are you home? I thought I heard you."

Yamina glanced around the flat. It was Spartan. She strained to see a flicker of a home, a memento of warmth, but was disappointed.

"Yo, Yamina, my favorite neighbor. Door is open."

"Shachar…are you OK?"

"Chillaxing."

"Is that a needle?"

"It's something to do."

"I'm not sure about that."

"Nobody knows the shape I'm in."

"I am here, Shachar. Tell me."

"Naw. It's fine. What's good?"

"The media is hounding me relentlessly, and I am getting nothing from Yossi's family. Have you been able to find out anything about Yossi's killer?"

"Yeah, there is something going on. I don't know how or why he got to Har Kesem, but it was with some bad people."

"Your phone is ringing. +970, a Palestinian number."

"My new friend."

"Your dealer, no doubt."

"Hardly, far from it."

"Looks like you've missed a bunch of calls."

"How many is a bunch?"

"Twenty."

"Damn."

"Who is it?"

"A guy I am working with to learn about Yossi's…. I am so sorry, Yamina."

"You've been amazing, Shachar. I just hoped maybe you'd be able to find something, but you tried, and that's more than anyone else has."

"No, I am sorry. Fuck. Let me get some coffee and call back Marwan."

"Sit. I'll make it for you, and something to eat. You look like roadkill."

"Thanks, I am going to remember you said that."

"I hope you do, and that it leads you to a bath."

•

"Marwan, what's up?"

"Shachar! Are you okay?"

"All good."

"Really? I've been calling and…are you sure?"

"Yes. What's up?"

"Well Remy and I were in Bethlehem checking on the origin of the cross."

"Yeah I remember."

"Why wouldn't you?"

"Did you find anything?"

"Yes! That's why I've been phoning you!!"

"Okay, so here I am, what's up?"

"We found a copy of the cross. I bought it at a gift shop while Remy was spending the day looking at other workshops."

"Ha! He must of loved that."

"I gave it to him as a fun gift, and then we went to dinner and realized it was a perfect match."

"Which gift shop?"

"The one for the church."

"Really?"

"Yes."

"When was that?"

"A couple days ago…when I started phoning you. Honestly Shachar, we were reading the newspaper, looking for your name. You need to give Remy your address. He is going to be staying at my friend Raffy's house—"

"I'll do that. Thanks for thinking of me."

"The next day we went out to find where the church gets their products made. It was in a little industrial area just beyond the soda factory."

"Ah, so they get thirsty making little wooden crosses, and so they locate the factory near a place where they can get their workers an endless supply of caffeinated cola."

"You joke."

"And why not?"

"Because this is serious. You sure you are okay?"

"Tell me more."

"The interesting part about the soda factory is that it is in Area C, and so totally controlled by the Israeli military."

"Yeah, so?"

"So, there is effectively a strong barrier protecting the factory from the rest of the city. The city is Area A, then the soda factory in Area C, and then factory in Area B. The factory is insulated from interference by other Palestinians."

"Is that common?"

"Yes, certainty. But it is still worth noting. Choosing to put a factory in an industrial zone such as that is a deliberate decision."

"Cool, so you found it. Now what?"

"That was yesterday, when I phoned, to discuss the 'now what.' Where were you?"

"Not important."

"But where could you have gone? Are you an agent for

the state? You have to tell me when directly asked."

"I can tell you two things. I am not an agent for the state, and that even if I was I would most certainly not tell you."

"Are you telling me you are an agent?"

"No!"

"Then where were you?"

"You wouldn't understand."

"Try me."

"I was coping. That's all."

"Oh, but I do understand. This has been a lot…I'm glad you are back with us, Shachar."

"Thank you, Marwan, so what happened next?"

"We decided to watch the place."

"Ah, good old-fashioned police work."

"You bet! It's not easy to wait, but patience is a virtue."

"Find anything with all your virtuous patience?"

"We did."

"And? The carvers?"

"No, a logistics company who told us about a container sent from Hebron. Grab a pen, you're going to need to take down this container number, and then give your friend in the port another call."

CHAPTER 33

"Yes, that's right Menashe, I need you to look for the information for a second container with a similar number, brought by a truck with a similar plate. Why is that so difficult?"

"Because, Shachar, I have my own job to do. And I am exposing myself by doing this."

"Help me out."

"I don't owe you."

"For your brother, Ephraim, then."

"What are you talking about? He was killed because he was helping you."

"Yes, well there is a reason he was killed, and obviously the people I am chasing are the ones who did it. Help me and I can try to bring your brother's killers to justice."

"Justice? That won't bring him back."

"What else are you going to do?"

"I am going to think about that question."

"Good. But until you figure it out can you get me this info?"

"I'll see what I can do. Hold on. Yes, I found it here."

"It was that easy?"

"We use computers to track things at the port. Do you know about computers Shachar?"

"I built one before I was eight."

"Congratulations. The issue is not finding it, the issue is accessing it. I am being tracked always. If this really is sensitive information then I could lose my position. I'm not supposed to search these records without reason."

"Will you be asked about it?"

"Probably not, but you never know. It could be my turn to be inspected, and then what?"

"You'll think of something."

"Will what I think of be the right thing to have thought?"

"Menashe, that is a question I will not spend time considering. Now tell me, what's the deal with this second container?"

•

"General Cohen, we are in position outside the factory Dan told us about."

"Excellent Captain Levy. Let's just see what our little birdie has provided."

"Do we have permission to execute Operation Leah's Veil?"

"Granted."

•

"What is the meaning of this?"

"Monsignor Jerome, I am honored to make your acquaintance."

"I wish I could say the same, but being dragged before an Israeli general is not what I call honored."

"You were merely invited."

"By soldiers. Seeking my arrest."

"Goodness no. They were not there to arrest you, only to invite you."

"Then I will withdraw."

"Of course. However, I would like to know a couple of details."

"Please ask, perhaps I can provide answers. And then I can go."

"You understand the situation well. It is nice not dealing with blockheads."

"Yes, I met your captain."

"Touché. The information I require is quite simple really."

"Which is?"

"The serial numbers of the containers you are using to send your goods to the port."

"That is not a small matter."

"I understand. I am not here to stop you from doing what you are doing. Merely, I am seeking to understand, and perhaps to protect you, so we can both flourish."

"That is very thoughtful."

"Now tell me about the containers that are being sent from Hebron."

•

"Ronit?"

"Monsignor Jerome. How surprising it is to see you."

"We have a problem. Someone tipped off a general about our Hebron operation."

"Who?"

"Who knows about the operation enough to provide information about the marble factory?"

"People work there: people you hired."

"They don't know where it goes when it leaves the factory. This general knew too much."

"When it leaves?"

"That's right, when it enters Israel. They knew about shipping and wanted to be able to track the container."

"What did you give them?"

"I told them we were very small. Just starting really. I gave the details to the container we sent to Cyprus. It is already there, so nothing they can do about it. The general offered protection…from what I am not sure."

"Probably thinks he can replace me. Men always think they can do better. The egotistical twats. You know I haven't read a book written by a man in years?"

"I only read books by men."

"Yes, well your profession is somehow even more structurally unequal than most, and that is really saying something."

"It's my religion."

"Save it."

"When did I go on trial?"

"When you decided to be religious. And also, when you told a general about our operation."

"As I said Ronit, it was only a small amount information. I was requested to furnish details of future shipments."

"Fuck that."

"Yes, I thought you might respond in such a way. I'll start looking for alternative locations."

"And I'll get working on sending out a few decoys. Maybe that will frustrate them long enough to find something else to do, someone else to harass."

"Who do you think gave us up?"

"The list is short. You, Monsignor Jerome, me, George, and Dan. Anyone else?"

"Not that I am aware of. Everything is fully compart-mentalized."

"My thoughts exactly. So, George or Dan then. One I love, and the other I trust."

"Love?"

"Kisses fade, but memories linger."

"When I was a young man, before I joined the church, I—"

"Keep your memories to yourself Jerome. We've got

work to do. George would have been more likely, but he was away on his Lebanon adventure. I can't believe it, but I am going to need to pay Dan a visit."

•

"Dan."

"Ronit."

"Who just left?"

"Nobody was visiting me."

"Tell me so I can help you Dan. I fear you are in grave danger."

"Ronit…."

"Dan, our lives have been intertwined for so long, you can tell me."

"I've been compromised."

"By whom?"

"A general, an Israeli general."

"Who?"

"Cohen, served by a Levy: a captain."

"Do you meet with this General Cohen?"

"No. It is through Captain Levy."

"What have you given to this captain?"

"Mostly misdirection."

"But of course you had to give them some truths. I understand. It's okay Dan. Tell me and we can figure out what to do. Together, like always."

"I told them where to look in Hebron."

"The factory?"

"Yes."

"It's nothing."

"What do you mean?"

"We can set it up somewhere else. It is already being done."

"Please give me an opportunity to redeem myself."

"They have hurt our business Dan; they have hurt us.

I feel it personally."

"I do too, Ronit."

"We will make them suffer for this. You will provide them misinformation, and then when this Levy goes to tell his master, you will go to Levy's home and kill his family."

"What?"

"They cost us; we will respond."

"But surely that is beyond—"

"This Levy must pay. We've done this to other organizations have we not? Our corrupt police forces included."

"Ronit that was against fellow criminals—"

"Dan, he twisted your screws, and loosened them. We must reestablish our policy of deterrence."

"Shouldn't we kill Levy and Cohen instead?"

"The general could prove useful; I'll think on it. But he should know what we are capable of. It can only help him to choose correctly when we provide him with an opportunity to save himself, and his family."

"I don't know, Ronit."

"I'll be blunt. We need to rebuild trust between us. When you revealed our location, you risked our business and our lives. I think the family of a crook is a small price for me to ask of you."

"I can't. There must be another way."

"Dan. It's Levy's family or your own. I've already arranged for the latter, and it's a go unless I say otherwise."

"I knew in my heart that one day your ruthlessness would turn against me."

"You are the betrayer. Now go and redeem yourself, and we will not speak of this episode again."

CHAPTER 34

"George, welcome back to civilization."

"Lebanon is a beautiful country Ronit, too bad you can't explore it."

"I've explored it plenty, George. And my time there ended similarly to yours."

"Which brings me to a question."

"Yes?"

"With Lebanon so volatile, and the region as a whole, must you simply accept that at times trade will be disrupted? How can you plan for such an eventuality?"

"George, I thought you had more faith in me. Of course we plan for complications. In fact, one of our facilities was recently compromised."

"By whom?"

"That's not important. What matters is that we were ready to pack up our shop and move it to another location."

"And how do you know you weren't being watched in this packing and moving?"

"With Israel's experience in Gaza, and your country's experience in Vietnam, I thought that answer would be obvious."

"Tunnels?"

"Yes, though it is nothing compared to the latticework

of overly enthusiastic militants. Using tunnels to smuggle goods is an age-old practice."

"You move from one warehouse to an adjacent one?"

"Most of our tunnels are a bit longer than that George. But not endless. Remember, we aren't deranged killers, merely traders."

"Some might say traitors."

"So might the people of your republic, George. At least if they knew about your travels."

"Yes, well, do you use the same tactics to get across international boundaries?"

"Again, we aren't terrorists crossing from Egypt or Gaza to Israel, nor from Laos to Vietnam. But there are some overlaps, of course."

"Anything I should know about?"

"I prefer you didn't, George. Know that there were myriad ways to bring you from Lebanon to me, war or not."

"And I suppose it's the same moving between Egypt and then Israel?"

"Of course. You've seen what passes through that border."

"And the other borders?"

"Who, Syria? No, that is out of the question. In the Golan Heights tunnels are everywhere; however, most of these are property of the Israeli military."

"Most?"

"Others are not ours but rather UNESCO sites, tunnels from ancient times. We wouldn't want to spoil those."

"Your respect for history surprises me Ronit."

"And why not? These tunnels were used during conflicts for storing valuable goods. I appreciate those uses. In any case, moving goods directly from Syria to Israel is not an option. The Quneitra Crossing is too infrequently opened and the rest of the border too fortified. Instead, things pass more easily through Lebanon. And of course, moving from Syria to Lebanon is as simple as opening an unlocked door."

"And what of Jordan?"

"Our ruthless friends to the east. Allies to Israel and America. It might surprise you, but Jordan is the worst place for our people to be caught."

"So, you ignore that border as well?"

"*Good god no*! We've tried all sorts of strategies. My favorites were our amphibious attempts. For a time, we were able to reach the Sea of Galilee and liaise with our fleet of fishing boats that would haul in the drugs. It actually worked well for a time, that is until the border was shored up in the mid-2000s."

"Then what did you do?"

"Well, we had these great swimmers on our payroll, who I hated to lose, even if it was just because planning these routes was so fun. We tried to swim from resort to resort."

"You mean on the Dead Sea?"

"Most certainly."

"Did it work?"

"Sadly no."

"Security too tight?"

"No, it was lax."

"Then what was the problem?"

"The water, George. It was too buoyant! We couldn't keep our packages from floating too far to the top. That, and the fluctuation in the depth made planning routes unreliable."

"Alright, so if by water, that left you with swimming in the Red Sea from Aqaba to Eilat."

"That certainly would be easiest in a way, particularly because it is convenient to Saudi Arabia and with good links to Egypt and Sudan. But the area between those harbors are heavily mined, and I wouldn't put anything over or under those. No, the best thing to do in the Red Sea is to have boats liaise further out at sea, which we do from time to time."

"Then the border with Jordan is not an option."

"Not so."

"What else can you do? I am assuming by truck would endanger your goods?"

"Yes, the threat of seizure by the armies of Israel or Jordan are too high."

"I don't see how you can..., do you have tunnels there as well?"

"No."

"No land, no sea, no lake, no tunnels. What does that leave?"

"The air George, the air."

"Airplanes?"

"No, again that would leave our products a bit too exposed. And have you seen the price of jet fuel these days?"

"So how then?"

"Drones George, drones. Rest up. I'll tell you more when I get back."

•

As Captain Levy sped off to report to General Cohen, Dan let out a deep sigh that did nothing to relieve the tightness in his chest and shoulders. Dan turned in the opposite direction from the military base, heading for Levy's family home. Gilad, one of the new underlings, watched the home and confirmed that everyone, save Captain Levy, was in. After providing Dan with back-up, Gilad needed to be removed from the scene. *Loose ends just lead to confusion* Dan thought. Stopping around the block Dan jumped out of the pickup truck.

"Who is in the house?"

"The whole family."

"Details, Gilad."

"Wife, two daughters, and a son."

"Ages of the children?"

"The girls are teens, the boy significantly younger. Seven?"

"Who do you want?"

"What do you mean?"

"We are here for blood Gilad. You are here to help, so you will help and afterwards you will find yourself raised."

"I want a raise, that is for sure. Will I command?"

"Possibly. Let's see how you perform. Now who will you take? The wife and eldest daughter first. Then the two youngest children."

"Is this normal?"

"What do you mean?"

"Do we often kill families?"

"We do this...reluctantly. We are protecting ourselves, that is all."

"If you say so, Dan."

"I do. You can take the wife; it will be easier for you."

"By take do you mean take to bed?"

"Never Gilad. Kill them quickly."

Dan moved toward the door and did a quick knock that resulted in a teenaged girl asking who was at the door to which Dan answered, "Delivery." As the door cracked open Dan kicked hard and smashed it into the girl's young face. Dan stepped over her unconscious body and moved forward. Gilad followed and looked at the girl with wide eyes. A voice from upstairs revealed the position of Levy's wife, Naomi. Dan signaled to Gilad to go upstairs, and continued into the home. The kitchen was to the left, and there Dan found the boy eating a snack. As the muscled frame of Dan stepped into the kitchen, the boy froze and did not make a noise, even when Dan shot the child through the heart. Dan then exited the kitchen in the direction of the television, where he found what looked like the oldest daughter. She screamed and threw the remote at Dan which delayed her death by only a second. Dan returned to the foyer and found Gilad dragging the middle child, the girl who had opened the door. "What are you doing Gilad? Did you go upstairs and kill the wife?" At that moment Naomi appeared at the top of the steps, despair already in her eyes and an old Uzi in her hand. She opened fire pumping bullets into Gilad. When the clip finished, Dan moved to the bottom of the staircase, looked up, and shot Naomi in the stomach, chest, and head. He turned and saw Gilad injured. Gilad managed to raise a hand before Dan put one in his skull. The middle child, just barely a teen, began to stir. Dan changed clips and strode over to the girl. The weapon was lowered but then Dan choked up and began to run, leaving the child to a lifetime of nightmares.

Without closing the door to the house Dan recomposed himself and walked calmly back to his truck. He took no note of Gilad's car nearby. Dan drove home to where his wife Mara and baby son Davi lived. Davi had been having nightmares of his own, and his parents had taken turns calming him. Dan walked in and heard his wife in the kitchen and stepped in.

"Dan? You startled me! What is on you? Is that blood? Are you hurt?"

"Mara, I love you." And with that Dan shot his wife of five years in the eye. With tears so thick he could barely see he turned and waited for his toddler to come and investigate the noise. When little Davi skittered into the kitchen he stopped and gazed, first at this father, and then at the lifeless body of his mother. "Davi my prince, you will now sleep without fear." Dan shot his son, set the house alarm, closed the door behind him, and left. Getting back into the car, Dan drove to Ronit's house.

Dan knocked on the door but did not hear a reply. Knowing the code for the door Dan typed it in, fumbling twice on the keypad. Dan opened the door and found himself facing George.

"Dan?"

"George." Without another word Dan drew his knife and began to stab. George caught the knife in his left forearm. The blade lodged into the bone, and Dan paused to pull it out. In that heartbeat George bent his right arm and slammed his elbow into the side of Dan's head, doing it once, then twice, and then a third time before Dan released the still lodged knife and began to move his hands up to guard his head against George's blows. As Dan began to shift his body weight, George took hold of Dan's shoulder and pulled him across his body, slamming Dan into George's right knee and driving the breath from him.

"What the fuck is this about Dan? Get a hold of yourself."

Dan smiled. George swung his boot into Dan's jaw leaving a mouth full of blood. Before George could ask again footsteps outside caught his attention, and a second later Ronit strode forward, grabbed a hold of Dan's hair, yanked his head back and began to saw through his neck without stopping until Dan's gurgling spasms ceased. Ronit, never blinking, let Dan drop to the ground and looked at George. Their eyes met, and George felt something he hadn't experienced in many years, fear.

CHAPTER 35

"General Cohen?"

"What is it?"

"I'm not sure how to say this."

"Say it by moving your mouth."

"The family of Captain Levy has been murdered. We haven't been able to contact him yet and thought—"

"It was right of you to contact me. Consider your message delivered."

"Thank you, sir."

•

"Rabbi Avraham?"

"My good friend Imam Ibrahim."

"Who gave you this number?"

"Why, you did, of course."

"Yes, that's right. For some reason I thought you had a better connection to god—"

"Ha ha, and he took a message and gave me the number—"

"Ha ha, yes and before that he sent me converts to the cause—"

"Ha ha, and before that he sent me donations—"

"Ha ha, he sent those to me too! I got gold!!!"

"Wow Ibrahim you have prayed well. I merely received silver."

"Do not give up hope, Avraham. The lord listens to those who pray."

"Amen."

"I have missed your company Rabbi."

"As have I Imam. It has been too long."

"Shall we meet?"

"I think we should."

"The usual place."

"The usual time."

"In peace then."

"Until then, peace."

•

It was time to look in on little Mehmet, and so Marwan looked for him. The boy was not at his new home, so Marwan went down to the madrassa. Imam Ibrahim was there.

"Welcome in peace, my brother Marwan."

"And to you, peace. I came down to look in on Mehmet."

"Alas he is deep in his studies. Mehmet is our star student you know. His uncle would have been very proud at what he has accomplished, and even more so about what God has in store for Mehmet's future."

"For us Palestinians the best we can hope for is, as the Americans say, forty acres and a mule."

"But for Muslims the best is eighty virgins in heaven. I think that my offer is better."

"So, you see no hope for us Palestinians?"

"I see hope in God, which I am sure you do, at least deep in your heart. We all do."

"That is well Imam. Please let Mehmet know I came and that I wish him well."

"I will do that. Marwan, thank you for coming."

•

"Har Kesem has a magnificent view."

"From the river to the sea, Ibrahim."

"When my people possess this land again I think I shall build a house here."

"To the lord or for yourself?"

"If I can build here, then the lord will already be smiling on me."

"Of course. Just as the lord smiles upon me now."

"Tides change."

"But not the lord's blessing."

"I am starting to see why meeting less is a good idea."

"Imam Ibrahim, let's get to business before our good cheer follows the way of our politicians."

"The handful that are not corrupt?"

"Just because together we can count them on our fingers does not mean they do not exist."

"Or have influence."

"Too true."

"Rabbi Avraham, how can I help you?"

"There is this American, Rabbi Michael Goldenblatt, who thinks Jews and Muslims should coexist. And that we should start right here in Israel."

"I have a similar problem."

"How is that?"

"We have this British woman, Eleanor Barnes, an Anglican."

"I never understood, is that protestant or not?"

"I researched this too! The protest is against dominance of the Catholic Church instead of the bible, and so they are Protestant. But of course, they are a state religion, so their freedom from earthly dominance went only so far."

"I do not follow the Catholic leaders, and neither do

you. Does that make us Protestants?"

"Well Rabbi, do you follow Jesus and only Jesus?"

"Of course not, and neither do you."

"Then we are not Protestant because we are not Christians. What is wrong with you?"

"It is this American rabbi. When I talk about him I start to lose my grip on reality, just as he has. But I am sorry Ibrahim, tell me about this Barnes."

"She is very devout and believes in ethics, morality, sin—"

"But you don't mind sinning."

"I don't mind sinning because I know my true faith will see me through."

"That sounds Catholic."

"And the Catholics are very successful, are they not? We talk of their organization with awe."

"Jealousy more like."

"Fine. But this Eleanor Barnes. She is so moralizing about how we Palestinians should conduct ourselves. She preaches at me from the church in Sebastia, north of Nablus. It is so demeaning. This lady runs around meeting with people, and afterwards they are asking me tough questions that I don't want to answer."

"Sounds like we are having similar problems. I have information that this Rabbi Goldenblatt is trying to organize a protest march to my settlement. He—"

"You have information? Where do you get this information?"

"I always have information."

"Which is why I would like to know from where it originates. If you want my help based on this information, I want to know about the origin of the information. I will be basing operations on this information so I should be told who is providing it."

"A high government source that supports the settlement project. I cannot say more."

"Avraham, that is most of your government."

"I have a good source, trust me."

"Can I?"

"Why would I steer you wrong?"

"Are you serious? To redeem your Land of Israel."

"And how can I trust you, you who wants to throw me into the sea?"

"Fine, fine. Tell me about your American rabbi."

"There is not much to tell. He has crossed a line. I need to stop his leftwing ranting."

"And by having me use one of my faithful, it will not only silence a critic but enhance your position of intransigence."

"Exactly."

"I know just the boy for the job."

"Who may I ask?"

"Is your information so good that you know everyone who comes into my mosque? Who studies at my madrassa?"

"No. Therefore it does not matter if you tell me or don't tell me. I asked merely out of curiosity."

"Then why waste our time?"

"Because I am fascinated to know who would commit suicide for such reasons."

"You will never understand."

"Israelis sacrifice plenty. We send our children to the army."

"Where they can hide behind their weapons and armor."

"That is because they prefer not to die even while making their sacrifice."

"Was Isak not ready to make such as sacrifice?"

"Yitzchak did not want to die. It was Abraham's sacrifice."

"Our mutual forefather."

"Our mutual namesake."

"Rabbi Avraham, I will tell you that it is a boy who was recently radicalized. They make the best subjects. And, more, that this boy was radicalized not in small part because of you."

"Have I such powers?"

"Evil powers."

"As you wish Imam Ibrahim. As long as you rid me of this headache."

"What I wish is that you use your evil powers, or connections with the official, or the use of your gang of youngsters."

"Students. Yeshiva students."

"As you wish Avraham. Just help me with this Brit."

"I have an idea. It will be done."

"I will not ask how because you will not tell me."

"This time I will. It will be done quite simply. Her visa will not be renewed. In fact, her visa may have already expired."

"You certainly have good connections with the government. Can you not do the same for your American rabbi?"

"Sadly no. He has Israeli citizenship you see. Spends half his time in Ra'anana starting trouble here, and the rest in America gathering funds to start more trouble."

"Know it will be done."

"Excellent. It was so nice to see you again Avraham. I wish you luck in this project, though of course failure in most others."

"What a sweet wish Ibrahim. I have enjoyed our meeting as always. If we were born at different times perhaps we would have been the best of friends."

"Unfortunately, we will never know."

CHAPTER 36

"Captain Levy, report."

"General Cohen, sir, we've taken the warehouse apart."

"And what did you find?"

"Not much, a lot of dust."

"What kind of dust?"

"I'm not sure general."

"So go back in and check. Is the warehouse a chemical weapons laboratory covered in anthrax, is it a crack lab covered in cocaine? Is it dust from the mountains? Perhaps it was a school, and its chalk. I'll hold."

"General, sir, there appears to be two substances, one a powder, and the other thicker, particles of dust."

"How thick?"

"Pebbles really, and shards."

"Of what type?"

"If I'm not mistaken, there are marble fragments all over."

"And the powder?"

"Seems to be cocaine."

"How do you know?"

"Some of the soldiers here, er, recognized the substance in question. I cannot comment on how or why they came by this information, but they seem quite certain, and were willing to, er, inhale deeply. If it was anthrax we would know."

"Well done Captain."

"One more thing."

"Yes?"

"When we disassembled an old telephone left in the office, we found a phone number."

"Whose?"

"I don't know, but it is a +972, Israeli. I've just sent the number over to you."

"Good. I'll access the system and trace the owner; you break down the operation and get back to base."

"Should I leave any soldiers to watch the warehouse?"

"If there are a couple of soldiers that annoy you, then go for it. But the criminals won't be back there anytime soon. We've already got plenty of information from the raid."

"We have, sir?"

"We know about the marble and the cocaine; we have a phone number. Moreover, we now know that they knew we were coming. As I said, mission accomplished. Return to base."

•

"Shachar. I am so glad you came."

"I wasn't sure I was welcome to return rabbi, but then I got your call and thought it might do me some good."

"Of course you are welcome here, now and always. In fact, it is a fortuitous coincidence that you have come at this moment."

"How is that?"

"I have invited another rabbi to visit us here in the settlement."

"It is not rare for a rabbi to visit a settlement. What's the big deal about this one?"

"Two reasons. This rabbi Michael Goldenblatt is—"

"An American."

"You know him?"

"No, of course not. It was just the way your face moved into a revulsive posture, and the way you said the name."

"Goldenblatt?"

"Michael."

"Ah yes. Well can you guess the second reason then?"

"You hate him."

"Why would you think that?"

"You said he was an American. And you rabbis can be a competitive bunch can't you?"

"Some, perhaps."

"Then why do you hate this rabbi, beyond his nationality's proclivity to annoy."

"He is a leftist and seeks to trade the land that was given to us by God for peace with Philistines."

"Then why are you inviting him here?"

"To try and show him the gift God has given us, so he might understand that which he seeks to lose."

"I see. And when he doesn't come to his senses do you want me to bring the fire and brimstone?"

"Good heavens, no. Just show him around. I figure since you are, or at least were, a lefty peacenik you'd know how to talk to him. Just show this Rabbi Goldenblatt the beauty of our surroundings, just as you discovered them not so long ago."

"Where do you want me to take him?"

"I'll show him our settlement, where he is staying, all that. Then you take him on a walk in the countryside, let it all sink in for him. The view from Har Kesem is particularly nice."

"Wouldn't that take me past the site of the Battle of the Trees?"

"Do not worry, a repeat of that is impossible, as the trees are not there anymore. That was in the eastern part of the valley, you can go from the west."

"Nearer toward the road?"

"Exactly."

"The view from Har Kesem is incredible. I'd be glad to see it again."

·

"Greetings Marwan."

"Imam Ibrahim, it is nice to see you. Are you well?"

"Fine for the moment, thanks to God. And yourself?"

"Good. I was coming to see Mehmet."

"You've just missed him."

"Where has he gone?"

"He was picked up by Anan."

"Which Anan? Anan the militant?"

"He prefers freedom fighter."

"And I prefer terrorist, so let's keep it at militant."

"He was also elected Mayor; we could call him that."

"The election was before he revealed his lust for violence."

"I might agree with you Marwan, but in reference to Mehmet, I had no choice in the matter."

"Explain Ibrahim."

"Anan came to visit, as do many of the faithful. He found Mehmet studying, started a conversation, and before I knew it Mehmet was saying goodbye."

"How could you let that happen?"

"I am devastated! To have one of my prized pupils plucked at such a tender age."

"This isn't about you! What about Mehmet?"

"He can make his own decisions."

"No, he is a boy. Where has Anan taken him?"

"I think they said something about Har Kesem, you know the place where his uncle…."

"I know it well."

"I wanted to stop them Marwan, I did. But some things cannot be helped."

•

"There Mehmet. That is Har Kesem."

"Yes, I see it. Thank you for taking me here, Anan."

"And look at those two walking there."

"Yes, who are they?"

"They are the ones who planned Ahmad's murder."

"The settlement and the settlers. On this great day God has placed them in our path."

"Mehmet, they will not recognize you. Walk slowly as you reach them, do not take a quick step until it is the last."

"How do I activate it?"

"It is quite easy Mehmet, very user friendly. Allow me to show you."

•

"As you see, Rabbi Goldenblatt—"

"Shachar, please, it is Michael. We are all equal under God."

"Does that mean you don't care about your honorific title?"

"What are titles but words and designations bestowed upon people by other people?"

"And therefore, you don't use titles?"

"Titles are good for fundraising, and a few other things. I am not vacating them. Merely when with another individual it is best for us all to remember."

"Remember what?"

"That we are equals, as we are both seen under the one God, or one vote, if we are speaking about a democracy, for example."

"I think I am beginning to understand why Rabbi Avraham thought it best for me to take you around."

"To spend as little time with me as possible?"

"You might be onto something, Michael."

"Then why do you serve him?"

"Serve who? Avraham? I am here as his guest, like yourself."

"Apologies, I meant no disrespect. But then, may I ask, what is your connection?"

"We go way back. I did not join his band of dangerously merry men, but we are friends of a sort. Look how magnificent it is out here."

"Truly. Now what do you make of that?"

"Of what?"

"That boy walking over to us. Seems young to be alone in this area."

"Lots of boys move around these parts. The West Bank isn't always chaos like in the news; millions of people live here. It does seem too warm today for that jacket."

"I wonder if he is unwell. This area is so remote, far from his home and near to settlements. Isn't it dangerous for him?"

"Let's see if we can help him. I know Arabic."

"Perhaps he speaks Hebrew, or English."

"I'll try Arabic. Hello there. Can we help you?"

"Yes, uncle. I need some help on a most important matter."

"Then come, let's speak."

Marwan jumped out of his car.

"Mehmet! Don't!"

"Marwan?"

"I know it was Anan who dropped you off."

"I trust him, he is famous."

"*Infamous,* Mehmet. He is using you."

"I don't think so Marwan. He has delivered me to where God wanted me to go. To exact revenge upon those who hurt my family, and near to where their plot began."

Shachar takes Michael by the arm and steps carefully back.

"No, Mehmet. This is not where God brought you; this is only where Anan brought you."

"Imam Ibrahim also says it is God's will."

"Did he?"

"Yes. Is he not a wise man?"

"Mehmet. Take off your jacket. We have much to discuss. These are not the men you seek."

"How do you know?"

"I know these men, or one of them at least."

"Are you in on it with them?"

"No, boy. I have been investigating Ahmad's murder, and I know that this man is not our target."

"What if he has betrayed you?"

"Then I will kill him myself. You do not need to do this. You have a long life yet to live. And these people are not whom you seek."

"Marwan…."

•

No reason to tell him about his family. I need him to focus on the mission and besides, he only has his career now. "Captain Levy."

"Yes, general?"

"The phone number you recovered connects to an official at Israel Port Authority by the name of Menashe. I've paid this man a visit."

"You have?"

"The man in charge of customs is a good buddy of mine; we served in the same unit."

"What did he say, sir?"

"This Menashe fellow was kind enough to give me a list of recent exports of stone. My buddy told me that marble, they call it stone, is a big industry in the West Bank."

"Oh?"

"Would it surprise you that stone is estimated to represent *twenty percent* of the Palestinian exports, produced by 1650 companies?"

"I had no idea. Do the buyers know?"

"The brokers might. But I doubt the residents of

apartment buildings, workers in a government office, or supplicants in churches and synagogues, both at home and abroad, are aware of the origins of these Holy Land stones."

"What was on the list? Did anything stand out?"

"I didn't need to decipher the document to know its contents."

"How do you mean?"

"I've already found what we need to know," General Cohen said as he leaned back on his wobbly chair.

"How is that, sir?"

"Menashe told me."

"The port official?"

"Yes. Quite a nervous fellow. He told me about a specific shipment bound for Cyprus. He said a security official came and asked him about it."

"Did he say who that was?"

"No, claimed he didn't know."

"Do you believe him, sir?"

"More important is that we know there is someone else out there. We know that the warehouse was cleared out by time we got there, and someone else has checked in on this shipment. We should be ready for a professional presence in Cyprus, but of what type we can only guess. Captain Levy?"

"Yes, sir."

"Congratulations, you've won yourself a trip to Cyprus."

"I have?"

"This is your big break, captain. I need you to go to Cyprus, find the shipment, and track where it is headed. If you find anybody watching its movements, I want them neutralized."

"Shot, sir?"

"Shot to death, Levy. You perform this mission successfully, and I'll have you promoted."

"When do I leave?"

"In two hours."

"Am I cleared to take my gun?"

"A weapon will be waiting for you when you land. It's early yet; you'll have a coffee in the airport in Cyprus, and that is when you will receive your hand luggage. Do you understand?"

"Yes, sir, I will not fail you."

"Be sure that you don't, captain, your career, no, your future depends on it."

CHAPTER 37

"Intelligence has found something Roy."

"What's that, Gloria, my darling?"

"The shipment we are looking for."

"Does that mean beach or no beach?"

"Put on your holiday clothes."

"All I brought are my holiday clothes; have you seen my new straw hat? Do you like my hat?"

"I like your hat very much, Roy. Now there is another thing. I'll be working with another agent, so I am going to need you to hang back. Be a tourist."

"I *am* a tourist, Gloria. May I have a couple drinks whilst I wait?"

"Are you asking me? I would prefer not but—"

"Great! I vote yes, you vote no, so I'll just have the one drink, instead of two."

"You were really going to have two drinks? It's the middle of the day."

"And I am a tourist who loves the sun!"

•

"Giovanni? My name is Gloria."

"Your reputation precedes you, Gloria."

"Your work in Belgium and Italy has created quite a stir.

Are you recovered from your last assignment?"

"Not entirely, but nothing that impedes my wits."

"Here comes my husband. Roy?"

"Gloria! What a wonderful day it is!"

"I thought you were going to have a drink."

"I had a drink! Who is this fine fellow?"

"Giovanni, perhaps you would give us a moment."

"Of course, nice to have met you, Roy."

"Likewise."

"Roy, this is serious business."

"Looks more like café business."

"Roy, I need to focus and work with this UNESCO agent. Please can you just find a seat and sit in it? Have a coffee, read the paper."

•

"General Cohen, sir. I have received your intelligence report about enemy agents. I see him and will take care of him."

"Immediately, and without delay, Captain Levy."

•

Captain Levy strode up to Gloria and Roy, thinking the latter was Giovanni. Seeing the movement, Giovanni moved to draw his weapon. The injured elbow seized up and Giovanni fumbled with the holster, then, moving awkwardly, slipped on the cobbled pavement. Levy shot Roy in the chest and turned to fire on Gloria, but Giovanni, lying on the ground, was finally ready, and shot Levy in the head. Giovanni wasn't sure, but it felt as though he'd twisted an ankle. Roy lay dead. Gloria, who had instinctively dropped to the ground, sat up in shock, and then felt a wave of anguish, followed quickly by anger. "Who the fuck was that?"

"I don't know," Giovanni stammered.

"Where did this shipment originate?"

"Israel."

"We are going there. Can you walk?"

"Not really. You'll need to go ahead of me. I can try to provide signals support from here. I'm sorry I couldn't do more, be faster."

"I understand that bad things happen to good people… and now bad things are going to happen to bad people."

•

"Governor! I am here for answers, cash or blood. Which is it?"

"Ronit, it's good to see you again. Please, have a seat. I will call my assistant Amira."

"Answer me, who is poking about my operations?"

"I am not sure what you mean by—"

Ronit grabbed the governor of Nablus' left hand, slammed it down on the desk, and drove a knife through it, pinning the governor as he screamed in pain.

"I have two more. One for your other hand, and the third for your tongue. If you won't talk you won't need it."

Amira walked in and her eyes locked with Ronit's. The fan above fluttered, and in an instant Amira pulled her gun cleanly out of the holster. In a flash, Ronit flung her second knife at Amira, and slid for cover behind a sofa. Instead of shots, there was a thump. Amira was dead on the ground, a knife protruding from her eye.

"Now governor…" Ronit said as she rose, "I have used my second knife. As I said, this last one is for your tongue."

"There is a reporter, or a journalism student, I am not sure."

"Be sure."

"The name is Remy. He is American, I think, but says he is coming from London. Doing a doctorate in journalism."

"Doctorate in Journalism? Are you selling me a bridge? Because I'm not buying."

"No, I swear it! He is the cause of your troubles. Everything was going well before his arrival? Please let me live."

"I will destroy the person who has caused this trouble. If this Remy does not exist I will return and dismember you. Otherwise, he can stand in your place. Now, *tell me where I can find him.*"

"Yes, most assuredly. Amira can help as she," the governor paused and glanced toward the ever-widening pool of blood with what used to be Amira's face at its center, "was keeping tabs on it. The last thing she reported," the governor swallowed, "was that Remy is staying at the home of a Major Rafiq al-Khana. It is not too far. If you release me I can even go with you."

"You can't drive with a knife in your hand."

"No, but I have a driver."

"I heard that Sultan is dead."

"How did you? Yes, he is dead. But I've hired two more."

"Those two? I took the liberty of jabbing needles into their necks on the way in. It made me sad, really, to think about how Sultan wouldn't have died so easily. I would have enjoyed meeting him in battle, but maybe it would have been less than I imagined. After all, Amira lost her life in seconds."

"So she has. So did they both."

"As will you, governor, if I do not succeed in finding this Remy."

"Then I wish you happy hunting."

"Thank you, governor. That does cheer me up a little. Now don't go too far because I will be unhappy if I need to go looking for you." And with that Ronit retrieved her knife from Amira's eye, went to the desk to rip out the knife from the governor's hand, wiped the blood off on his jacket, and walked out past the rapidly cooling bodies she left in her wake.

•

Rafiq's father, Zubair, had been a professor at the local university. He became embroiled in politics and eventually found himself in jail, first an Israeli one and then a Palestinian. He was finally released in part due to the efforts of his son, Major al-Khana, but lived in fear of a return to the cells. To protect himself, old Zubair had cultivated long fingernails that he trimmed into sharp points. Though it was hard to pick up most things, Zubair was able to spear grapes and did not need a toothpick.

Ronit drove up into the hills overlooking Nablus to a village with houses surrounded by large gardens. The home of Major al-Khana was dug partially out of hillock giving it protection from the afternoon heat. Ronit walked to the door and began to bang.

Ronit continued to knock until she heard a noise. A TV had been switched off, and she heard shoed footsteps echo through the stone house, into the stone courtyard, and off the stone outcroppings that typified the village.

Rafiq opened the door and, seeing a fit, smiling woman, began to relax and returned the smile.

As soon as the tension left his shoulders Ronit dropped her smile and raised her gun. "Hands up."

"What is this?"

"Get back into the house. I am looking for something, and you are going to tell me where to find it."

Rafiq raised his hands and began to back up. Ronit stepped inside and paused, waiting for her eyes to adjust. She began to move forward again, wordlessly moving Rafiq back. "Stop walking," she commanded, "Where is Remy? I know he stays with you."

"What do you want with him?"

Ronit pulled a knife out with her other hand.

Rafiq kept his eyes on the gun. "He isn't here."

Ronit slowly adjusted her hold on the knife.

Rafiq stared into the barrel. "I'm not even sure I know who that is."

Ronit moved forward; the gun moved with her. Her foot touched a carpet and she paused to take in the new information. In that moment Rafiq saw an opportunity and grabbed at the gun.

Ronit let Rafiq grab the barrel of the gun while she sliced into his spleen with the knife. She pulled the knife out and continued to stab Rafiq.

Rafiq held onto the gun and began to turn Ronit's wrist to point the gun toward her.

The knife went in again, and again.

The gun was nearly turned to point at Ronit. Rafiq leaned into it and pushed the gun into position, just as Ronit's knife penetrated his heart. Her smile, the one from the door, reappeared, and Rafiq, paused, no longer felt the knife. Confused by her beauty, confused by the wetness of his blood and the cutting of his heart, confused by something perfect, and yet not quite right, Rafiq crumpled to the floor.

Ronit felt pain too, and realized that the knife was falling from her grasp, that there was something stuck in her wrist. But before she knew what it was, she turned to see old Zubair extending a hand toward her neck. Ronit's quick reflexes allowed her to jump away. Zubair followed closely, ready to strike again, but Ronit raised her gun, and Zubair joined his son as a spirit in heaven, and as a body on the floor.

Ronit heard running behind her, and looked toward the front door as it was slammed shut. She didn't move, listening, trying to determine if there was a person inside with her or if they had left. Hearing and feeling nothing, Ronit dashed to the door, opened it and stepped out. Ronit again paused to allow her vision to adjust to the brilliancy of the day.

Her gun at the ready as she ran from the house, Ronit saw a foot around the corner and knew to expect a blow, countering it before Remy moved to deliver it. Ronit caught Remy's arm, wrenched the gardening spade from his grasp and hammered Remy in the nose with her free arm. Remy fell backward, hit the stone hard, and blacked out. A breeze woke Remy, who found himself tied to a chair in the rear garden. He felt his head pulse, the dried blood on his face, and the painful memory that Raffy and Zubair, friends and companions for many days, were gone. He felt the ropes around his wrists. They burned as the ropes dug into where his skin had not yet healed. Remy opened his eyes and saw Ronit, still holding a blade that dripped with blood.

CHAPTER 38

"General Cohen, this is Menashe calling. From Israel Ports."

"What do you want, Menashe?"

"Sir, a woman came here. She asked about you."

"And what did you tell her?"

"Sir, she came armed. I had no choice."

"You had many choices, Menashe."

"I am choosing to tell you about it."

"Should I be concerned with this woman? What is her name?"

"She said to tell you she is coming to collect a debt."

"What does that mean?"

"That's all she said."

•

General Cohen went outside and clambered into his jeep. *This wasn't a time to take chances.* Cohen drove to the Israel Ports Authority. He reviewed the video tapes. Saw the encounter of the woman with Menashe. Threatened Menashe. And prepared to drive away.

Gloria watched as Cohen got back into his jeep. She whispered a thanks to the intelligence she had received from Giovanni and her boss Arlen, who had called in

several favors to get the information, the weapons required, and the permissions granted. She was authorized
to carry weapons, but to use them only for self-defense.
The mission was to arrest Cohen, and Gloria relished the
opportunity to chase him down.

Cohen decided to take advantage of being out of the
base, realized he was famished and decided to stop for
lunch at one of his favorite shawarma stands. *I don't get here
enough.* The commander began to lose himself ruminating
over the decision to come: chicken or lamb. The chicken
was healthier but the lamb juicier from melted fat. And
then there was the decision between a pita and a *laffa*. The
pita was thicker, but smaller, whereas the *laffa* made a large
wrap. Cohen came to his decision: the smaller pita but
filled with lamb. The thickness of the pita *surely will help
with digestion*, Cohen reasoned incorrectly.

The prickly sabra went in and had his meal. Came out
again and went around the back to use the bathroom. He
washed, used the toilet, finished, washed again, came back
outside, and got into his jeep. Gloria watched. She was
determined, but human, and felt anger, wretchedness, and
fear mingled with hunger, thirst, boredom, and a need to
pee. Gloria decided to open her two car doors and squat.
When she'd finished she saw the general's car leaving the
lot, and she scrambled back into her car to continue her
slow and silent pursuit.

Cohen decided to stop for a coffee at the next rest stop.
Gloria became annoyed and decided to follow Cohen into
the shop. With her hand inside her jacket Gloria walked in
and saw the commander sitting down with another man. A
look from the new man revealed him to be a fellow agent,
she was sure. Gloria went back to her car and waited.

When General Cohen had finished his meeting the jeep
pulled away, and Gloria followed until the jeep reached
Cohen's neighborhood. Cohen turned onto his street but
found no parking near his house, but then located a spot

farther down the street. Gloria watched with increasing frustration as Cohen tried to parallel park again and again. *The spot was tight*, she reflected, *but either fucking park, or move the fuck somewhere else.*

The general finally, mercifully, parked the jeep, hopped out, and went into his house. He opened the door, stepped inside, and didn't even feel the butt of Gloria's gun as she swung down hard. The general fell to the floor, and Gloria stepped over him, noting the man was hurt but still conscious.

"Who do you *really* work for?" Gloria demanded.

Cohen looked up and saw Gloria. He spat. "Nobody."

"Tell me or I will shoot."

"Shoot, bitch."

Gloria shifted her weight, squaring to shoot.

Another voice spoke softly from the door.

"Gloria, don't do it."

Gloria took a step into the house to be able to see Cohen and the new speaker.

The new man stepped forward and she recognized him as the agent from the coffee shop.

"How do you know my name?"

"Allow me to introduce myself. The name is George."

"You are American?"

"Sure am."

"What are you doing here?"

"Same as you, sorta. This Cohen character is causing all kinds of trouble. I thought I'd have a sit-down with him and work some stuff out before things got out of control."

"In my mind they already have."

"I know about your husband. Terrible thing. I'm sure Cohen here didn't want that to happen. Now did ya?"

"No."

"I don't believe that for a second. Now, are you *the George*?"

"Is there more than one?"

"You tell me."

"I think I'm it."

"So, I have heard of you?"

"'fraid so."

"The legends are true?"

"Is what they say about you true?"

"Yes. And I've never lied, except once."

"When was that?"

"When I agreed to arrest the general."

"Well, we've caught him, where was the lie?"

Gloria shifted again, moved her gun from a position between the two men to one facing only Cohen.

"Gloria, don't do it."

"Why not George?"

"We are professionals."

"But we are also people, and *this one is personal*."

•

"Your eminence."

"Fabien, there is a problem."

"I heard."

"How is that?"

"If only I could tell you."

"You could."

"I wish."

"What else have you heard?"

"We need to replace Monsignor Jerome."

"Replace and remove, to be precise."

"Where do you want to do it?"

"Outside of his office."

"By whom? Do you need me to recommend someone?"

"I have people. Religious leaders are a rare breed. We are either in outright war or are the best of friends."

"And sometimes it is both."

"Correct Fabien. I am not asking for your help, only

mentioning there will be a few changes, and that you will be notified at the proper time; assuming you don't already know."

"I am always happy to hear from you, eminence."

"I assumed as much."

"Which religion then?"

"What do you mean?"

"Which type of churchman will you be using?"

"Islam. I used a rabbi last time; it is good to have options. Don't want to put all our eggs in one basket."

"I understand that very well."

"I know you do, Fabien. It is one of the reasons we do so much business. And we will continue to do so with the lord's blessing."

•

"George, where are we going now?"

"I've received a message, and we're going to follow up."

"Why am I coming?"

"Because I need backup, Gloria."

"Then you can tell me where we are going."

"To a village outside of Nablus."

"What's going on there?"

"An American is being held."

"Are we rescuing them?"

"I am not sure yet. We might be assisting."

"You would betray an American citizen?"

"Doesn't it depend what they are doing?"

"I suppose so. Who told you about this?"

"I couldn't say."

"You might as well tell me. Once we get there I am going to find out."

"I reckon you might, but I still ain't going to tell ya'."

•

325

"Ronit."

"George."

"Who have you brought?"

"Gloria."

"Who is she?"

"Works for British intelligence."

Gloria was surprised that George had revealed her identify so flippantly and was about to protest.

"Keep quiet, Gloria."

"Why did you bring her?"

"She was already with me."

"What were you two doing?"

"Gloria was shooting General Ram Cohen."

"Oh, that's good. Why did you not say that immediately? Wait, how much does she want?"

"I am not here for payoffs."

"Gloria, I said be quiet. I don't think she is here for money, Ronit. More for revenge."

"Then we are here for similar reasons. I too am seeking revenge. George, I wanted you here to help me."

"How can I be of assistance?"

"I was going to dismember him." Ronit pointed to Remy. "It's not the easiest task."

"Why in god's name would you do that?"

"Because he messed with my business. It must be known I am not to be messed with."

"But holy hell Ronit. You can't be serious."

"If you can't handle it, then you can just play lookout with your new friend."

"I'll stay."

"Good, you have quite a bit of expertise on the subject."

"I know how to ask questions, not this. Torture for information is still torture."

"The people being questioned deserved the treatment. Well, some of them at least."

"Nobody deserves torture!" exclaimed Gloria.

"Gloria, please wait outside."

"Gladly."

"This is for a purpose George. And it is to keep people safe."

"Who is being kept safe by mutilating Remy?"

"Me. The only person that matters; how do you know his name?"

"We've met, once or twice."

"Are you in on this George? Have you double crossed me?"

"No. I have never done you harm Ronit. Listen, I'm going to need you to release Remy. He has done nothing wrong to you, at least on purpose. You have a lot on your plate, so perhaps you should be putting your energy into rebuilding the enterprise. We need you out there. Not in here."

"No, George."

"Please Ronit. For us. For me."

"No."

"I won't let you do it."

"Are you saying you will stand against me?"

"Depends on the path you choose."

"George."

"Ronit."

"We've been together for so long."

"Always in our hearts, if not always together."

"Must it end like this?"

"It's your move to make, Ronit."

"I choose love."

Ronit dropped her gun and walked over to George. They embraced, cautiously at first, then with violent passion. As Ronit slid her tongue out of George's mouth she slipped her favorite knife into his abdomen.

"Ronit, but love…."

"I'm sorry, George. I love myself the most."

Gloria, through the doorway, saw the twitch George's

body made when it felt the knife enter. Ronit let George fall. As soon as George hit the floor, Gloria hit Ronit with an angry right fist. Ronit fell, rolled away, and hopped up. Ready.

"Come and get it, Gloria."

Gloria let out a scream and advanced. Ronit grabbed a chair and hurled it at Gloria, stopping the charge. Ronit took the initiative and began to slash at Gloria from odd angles. Gloria blocked and dodged until Ronit's attack was exhausted. The opponents took a moment to breathe and stare each other down, and Gloria noticed she was cut in several places while Ronit's wrist began to spasm.

Gloria moved in again, darting left then right, trying to find a way to get close to Ronit without feeling the searing pain of steel slicing through her skin. Ronit played a confident defense, using her weapon as a deterrent and waiting patiently for Gloria to abandon her attack. Gloria, aware that Ronit was waiting on a chance to counterattack, decided to play the game.

Gloria moved farther forward than she had meant to, and Ronit deftly cut Gloria across the thigh. Gloria dropped to one knee, and Ronit saw an opportunity and shifted the knife from one hand to the other. *What is needed is a good stab, point forward, ramming up into Gloria's groin* ….but this thought dissipated when she felt Gloria's hands close around her wrist.

Gloria had been quick, seizing on the opportunity to disarm Ronit.

The knife clattered, and Ronit lifted her boot to give Gloria's face a smash, but instead found herself on her back, Gloria's legs curled around her own, pushing up on the ankles, and down on the knee, pulling hair, pushing up, and pushing down. Finally, a crack, pop, and Ronit's knees were broken. Gloria sprang away in the event that Ronit had another knife, but Ronit lay there, gasping.

Gloria looked for George. He wasn't where he had

fallen. He was pressed against a wall, blood oozing. He straightened up as best he could, nodded to Gloria in appreciation, then stumbled toward Ronit.

"Well done, Gloria."

"Are you okay, George?"

"I'll take it from here."

"I can help you get her out of here; she can be arrested and put on trial wherever you prefer: US, UK, Israel, Europe."

"Gloria, this one isn't going to prison. Today she already stood trial, and lost."

"What are you saying, George? Are you going to be her executioner?"

"I am saying that it is my turn to tell you that *this one is personal.*"

With that, George emptied his entire clip into Ronit. Gloria watched, and then without speaking again, went out to the rear garden, untied Remy, rejoined George, who had yet to move, and the three of them staggered away.

•

"Mehmet, sit, tell me about your uncle Ahmad."

"Well, Marwan, he always talked about taking me to the sea, to the beach."

"I thought you might say that. Many have that dream."

"Can it be so? The beaches of Jaffa?"

"Are still a dream Mehmet. But Jordan has a lovely beach."

"Where?"

"Aqaba. Have you ever been snorkeling?"

"I am not a good swimmer…but I am a fast learner."

"Excellent. We will be meeting our new friend Shachar there."

"The one I almost killed?"

"The same. And he will be bringing a guest."

"Who is that?"

"The wife of Yossi, the Israeli who was slain near your uncle. Her name is Yamina. You each have been wronged, and so there is nobody better to share the grief of your loss."

"Share with an Israeli?"

"You will be sharing with a fellow *person*, Mehmet. Yamina's life was not so easy before her husband's murder."

"Does she have children?"

"No, Mehmet. But she is very loving."

"How do you know this?"

"Because Shachar introduced me to her."

"What does that matter?"

"Maybe when you are older you will understand. Let's get some *knafeh*, I'm starved, and we've got travel plans to discuss."

CHAPTER 39

"Cardinal."

"Anan."

"To confirm, you want one of your own people removed?"

"Yes."

"And this will be explained how? You alleged child abuse last time as I recall."

"This time he is corrupt. Stealing from the children's charity fund."

"I see you care much about children."

"They are the best objects for marketing and communication. I am sure you agree."

"I do, though I usually work with slightly older youths. Teens mostly."

"Ah, you should try them younger. My colleagues and I—"

"I am talking about teenagers on missions of divine inspiration. Helping them to develop a pathway to heaven."

"A pathway to heaven, my thoughts exactly."

"Cardinal, after this I propose that we cease our collaborations, at least for a time."

"But why? We have been so successful together."

"I'm aware."

"If that is how you feel Anan. I just hope you will not be in need of my support. Remember, if you no longer wish be an ally, I will not shield you."

"I'm aware."

"Fine. Remove this Monsignor Jerome, I'll let his bodyguard, Abdullah, know; take your payment, and we will consider ourselves mutually separated."

"I will have Jerome removed. We will both report on the corruption, but you especially."

"My office has already drawn up the news release."

•

"Father."

"Yes, Haydée, my dove."

"I've found something, and I'll be gone for a while to investigate it."

"What is it my dearest daughter?"

"Smuggling rings again. But this one isn't just about screwing the locals, it is much bigger, much deeper."

"That type of investigation does not sound wise. In our line of work some things are best unanswered."

"You've never said that to me before."

"Perhaps it is just my age talking. I fear for you. Can you expect less?"

"No, Father. But this is one I must do."

"Perhaps you've done enough; perhaps it is time to settle down?"

"I am still too young. Maybe after this—

"Yes?"

"Father, I will be going with someone."

"Who might this be?"

"When you meet him you'll love him."

"I'll know when I meet him."

"Then you will have to meet, but not until after our trip."

•

Remy paused to avoid the spray of a red double-decker bus, then continued walking down the street lost in thought. *Back in the rain again. I was here in grey grim London before this adventure that I had almost forgotten that the sky was blue, and now I remember why. The clouds sit low; is this what it feels like living in a rainforest? A deep, dark, damp, cold rainforest. But it is a civilized drudgery, life in the UK, where the only known cure for cold bones are baths and tea. So is being on time, which is impossible while moving across the city during a tube strike. At least I won't be early. I made that mistake once and had been duly chastised for making the other party feel bad that they weren't ready, and that therefore they would feel the embarrassment of having me wait. Now I wait outside of doors looking at my watch. The time changes, my knuckle knocks.*

I look ridiculous. Forgot how to dress here. I've still got my leather reporters jacket and a tan that screams I have not been in an archive. Why am I nervous? The doctoral examination board must see dozens, hundreds of dissertations.

How could I be worried about this? I've researched, wrote, investigated, wrote, edited. There are reams of new knowledge here. I was part of uncovering a criminal network! Is the standard of a doctorate higher than a Pulitzer?

"Hello, Remy. We are in here. Come and take a seat."

"Ah yes, thank you, and thank you for having me here, for reading my work."

"The three of us appreciate you coming in today. I am sure it's strange being back here after what happened to your supervisor, Roy Vandermere."

"It is. Thank you for saying so."

Why am I thanking them for everything? Whatever else they say next, do not say thank you.

"We feel you have written a marvelous piece of work."

"Thanks."

"But from our standpoint there is a problem."

"There is?"

"Rather. Look, Remy, we are sympathetic to your predicament, you've obviously done some good work, but without Professor Vandermere…you've lost your… direction."

"How do you mean?"

"We aren't happy with your submission. You were directed to do an investigative piece on food, namely hummus."

"That's right."

"But you've brought us stories of murder, diamonds, and drugs; some of which has been redacted. How are we to reconcile the variance between the assignment and the deliverable?"

"One led to the others, and the story became more interesting, more important."

"Yes, that is well, but you did not produce the article on hummus. If we were a news editor, would we be happy about that?"

"I think an editor might prefer what I found."

"They might, but they might also want to know what to do with a section on food they had assigned to you."

"I'm not really sure what you are asking."

"We want you to return to the field to write a report on a food, as you were assigned. It can be shorter if you wish, and it doesn't need to be hummus. It isn't as if we hadn't noticed what you did produce. But still, the boxes must be ticked."

"You want me to go back to the Middle East?"

"No, not after all we've all been through."

"We?"

"What with Roy and all. Very upsetting."

"Yes…then where?"

"What would Roy say?"

"What did you eat last."

"And the answer?"
"Chocolate…Belgian chocolate."

THE AUTHOR

Jonah Agus is a researcher with a talent for unearthing the stories buried beneath the headlines. Jonah's narratives draw on his vast international expertise, which includes exploring sixty countries, engaging in high-level negotiations, witnessing high-altitude airstrikes, and navigating [confidential content]. Alongside these intensive and immersive experiences, Jonah holds a PhD in Human Geography, an MBA in Conflict Management, and a BA in International Relations. When not writing or in the field, he enjoys biking, berry picking, and wild swimming with his wife and two children.